OF STEEL AND SCALE

New York Times Bestselling Author

Keri Arthur

Copyright © 2024 by Keri Arthur

Published by KA Publishing PTY LTD

All rights reserved.

No part of this book may be used, including but not limited to, the training of or use by artificial intelligence (AI, generative AI), or reproduced in any manner whatsoever without written permission, except in the case of brief quotations embodied in critical articles and reviews.

Cover Art by J Caleb Designs

Interior Art by Cat Cover Designs

All characters and events in this book are fictitious. Any resemblance to real people, alive or dead, is entirely coincidental.

Print ISBN: 978-1-923169-15-9

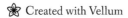 Created with Vellum

With thanks to:

The Lulus
Indigo Chick Designs
The lovely ladies at Hot Tree Editing
DP Plus
The ladies from Central Vic Writers
Cat Cover Designs of the lovely interior art
J Caleb Design for the gorgeous hardcover cover

1

I HEARD her well before I saw her.

She was a roar of wind, a caress of power, of wonder.

Excitement pulsed through me. I might have discovered the hunting places of the drakkons more than fifteen years ago, but being in their presence never grew old.

While drakkons weren't scarce here in Arleeon, they no longer soared over highly populated areas. That wasn't surprising, given the old ballistas still existed in both Esan and Zephrine—the two mighty fortresses that guarded the east and west gateways into Arleeon. It might have been well over a century since the large, crossbow-like devices had been deployed against the drakkons, but they'd nevertheless killed large numbers of the magnificent beasts. Drakkons weren't stupid, no matter what some thought, and they'd learned to remain in the wilder sections of our continent.

Which didn't mean they were any safer. I'd seen the evidence of that myself.

The Black Glass Mountains—the rugged sweep of mountains that lined the far reaches of East Arleeon, and whose foothills were a three-hour ride from Esan—was one of those sections.

I kept close to the shadows haunting the mountain's face and hurried along the narrow ledge. Up ahead, dawn had broken through the cover of night, and her golden fingers were bright against the starless sky. The stiffening breeze was icy and filled with the scent of the sea and the oncoming storm, though I was far enough away from the coast that I couldn't hear the crash of waves.

The path went sharply right. I slipped a hand into the hold I'd scored out of the black rock long ago and gripped tight as I edged around the corner. The wind hit hard, throwing me back a step as it snatched at my plaited hair and cloak and streamed both behind me. I caught my balance, then moved on, slipping my hand from one hold to the next. The ledge along this portion of the mountain was very narrow, and the drop to the grasslands far below sheer. If I slipped, I was dead.

Which might not be such a bad fate, given what I faced tomorrow. While I had nothing against marriage, I *did* object to the whole "marry a man who was basically a stranger" plan.

Unfortunately, my father was not only the Esan garrison's commander, but also the king of East Arleeon. I was his only child—and a woman at *that*—and while he was more liberal-minded than most, he would not—*could* not—ignore traditions and treaties. The confirmation of trading and military ties via a marriage that bonded Arleeon's two great houses every one hundred years was a necessity born out of a long-ago war that had almost torn our lands apart. "It's a ritual as necessary now as it was then" was my father's standard response every time I'd asked why.

Having finally met Zephrine's king and witnessed his arrogant "Zephrine does everything better" attitude, I understood the necessity of the treaty. *That* didn't make the fact I'd be living under that bastard's roof for the rest of my life any easier to accept, however.

The creak of leathery wings got stronger; she was close. So very close.

The path swept around to the left and then widened out, finally allowing more speed. A shadow swept past, and my pulse jumped. She'd swooped so low that the claw on her wing's tip scored the boulder half blocking the path ahead, sending a spray of black stone chips into the air. She flicked her long, barbed tail back and forth inches above my head, then her head snaked around to look at me. Her dark eyes were bright with intelligence and playfulness. I couldn't help but grin in delight. This wasn't the first time she'd acknowledged my presence, but it *was* the first time she'd flown so close that my sword could have sliced her wing or tail apart had I wanted to.

I didn't, and she was well aware of that.

She continued down into the valley, her burnished golden scales fiery in the rising glow of the day. It was such a glorious sight that my breath caught in my throat. She was at least eighty feet long, with a wingspan more than double that. The four main phalanges on each wing shimmered like flame, the leather membrane in-between glowing embers. Few drakkons ever got this big, but she wasn't any old drakkon. She was a queen. A mother.

She also wasn't one of *our* drakkons, but rather part of a grace that lived high atop the Red Ochre Mountains—the range that divided East and West Arleeon. Red Ochre graces—the name given to a community of at least twenty drakkons—tended to be this burnished color rather than the straight red of Esan's drakkons or the gold of Zephrine's drakkons.

The capras asleep in the grasslands far below showed little awareness of her approach—and wouldn't, I knew from past experience, until she was in their midst, scooping them up in her claws. The longhaired ruminants weren't the brightest of animals, and because the drakkons never consumed their kill in the valley, the capras had no lasting reminder of the predator that soared high above.

I slipped past the rock she'd scored, then swung my pack around, pulled out the rope, and quickly tied myself onto the heavy metal ring I'd rammed into the stone a few years back after a slip had almost cost my life.

Once secured, I moved onto the flat boulder that projected out over the valley and sat cross-legged near the edge to watch. She wasn't the only show; her drakklings would be here soon.

They appeared a few seconds later, and another happy smile escaped. The larger of the two—a female—was the same color as her mother, but the smaller male was red. They were less than a third of the queen's size and were obviously still learning flight skills, as they held none of her grace and were amusingly wobbly in the air.

I rested my chin on my hands and watched the three of them swoop toward the capras. The queen swung around near the valley's end, then dropped low and bugled. It was a deep, haunting sound in the stillness of the rising dawn.

The capras started to their feet and raced away from her—straight into the path of the drakklings. The female swept up several capras that were far too large for her to carry, and dropped one back to the ground. It didn't run off. It couldn't. One of her claws had pierced its body, ripping its insides apart. The smaller male missed his first grab, but not the second. Bugling in anticipation and hunger, the drakklings rose, their wings pumping hard to gain height while carrying the additional weight. As the rest of the herd fled for the forest at the far end of the valley, the queen swooped into their midst, scooping three into her murderously large claws before rising to follow her drakklings. They might have no enemy in these mountains beyond man, but they always retreated to the peaks to eat.

As the queen disappeared over the ice-capped mountaintop, I sighed and pushed to my feet. If I didn't get a move on, my father would send out the troops to retrieve me. While he'd long ago accepted my driving need to learn all I could about the drakkons, I was *supposed* to be spending the day getting ready for tomorrow's commitment ceremony. But I might never see these magnificent beasts again, and I simply had to come out one more time.

Zephrine—a fortress built deep into the volcanic rock of the Balkain Mountains—was the traditional range of the golden drakkons, but I had no idea where the aeries were in relation to that city. No idea whether they were within walking or even riding distance. No idea, in fact, how Zephrine or indeed my husband-to-be viewed drakkons.

For all I knew, an eradication order might remain in place. Just because I'd seen no mention of it in the missives we'd gotten from Zephrine's king and commander didn't mean it wasn't happening.

But I *hoped* it wasn't. I wasn't sure what I would do or how I would cope if it were.

I moved back to the scored boulder, undid the rope, and tucked it into my backpack.

It was then I noticed the smoke.

I straightened sharply. It wasn't just a thin stream, either, but a thick, black forest of the stuff. Something burned, and if the source location was anything to go by, that something was Eastmead.

But why would anyone want to burn that settlement? It was little more than an out-of-the-way fishing port on the very edge of my father's kingdom. It was also the only safe harbor between the treacherous but plentiful seas around the base of the Throat of Huskain—the nigh on impassable mountain that dominated the northeastern edge of Arleeon—and the larger market ports of Hopetown and Redding. Why would anyone want to attack it?

The only people who logically might have were the Mareritt—a warrior race who lived in the vast subarctic wilderness beyond the Blue Steel Mountains, the long range that unevenly divided our shared continent. Mareritten itself was a land so harsh that for nine months of the year its people lived in expansive underground cities that drew on volcanic heat to survive their long winters.

I had no idea what the majority of the Mareritt did during their three months of summer, but their warrior elite certainly used the time to attack either Esan or Zephrine. Or, at least, they had. So far this year there'd been only minor skirmishes, and that worryingly suggested they might be building up to something big. Of course, there were some who believed they'd finally accepted that neither Esan nor Zephrine could be broken. I personally thought the sky would bleed fire and fury before *that* ever happened.

Whatever the reason for the low number of assaults over recent months, that smoke couldn't be the first indication of a renewed strategy. The only way for them to have reached Eastmead from Mareritten was by sea, and if there was one truth about the Mareritt we were absolutely certain of, it was their all-abiding fear of the ocean.

I frowned and glanced uncertainly at the sky. Night still clung on hard, despite the ever-growing fingers of light. The smell of rain rode the air, and the clouds were heavy and ominous. If I were still on this mountain when that storm hit, I'd regret it.

But I'd regret not investigating that smoke more.

This was *my* land, even if I was leaving it. I might not be Esan's heir thanks to my sex, but I *was* a captain of the guard. I was honor-bound to investigate.

A somewhat ironic smile touched my lips. As excuses went, it wasn't one my mother would buy, even if she was the one who'd insisted on me being trained with sword and bow from a very young age.

I swung the pack over my shoulder and continued on. I'd taken this path down to the valley many times in the past, and it had been a time-consuming and somewhat treacherous journey. Hopefully, the recent foul weather and subsequent rockslides hadn't made it any worse.

Luck was with me on that account, but even so, by the time I reached the valley floor, I was hot, sweaty, and tired. There was a very good reason the agile capras were the only animal to roam the volcanic edges of the Black Glass Mountains—they were the only damn things that could easily traverse the mountain passes.

I grabbed the flask out of the backpack and took a long drink. It had to be close to midday now, and while Eastmead still burned, the dark stain of its smoke was almost indistinguishable against the ponderous clouds. The storm would hit well before I ever reached the fishing port.

Which meant I'd better send a message to my parents. If they wanted me back in time for the ceremony tomorrow, they had best send a boat—though in truth, I'd never been a fan of the sea, and the oncoming storm would make things even more unpleasant.

To which my mother would undoubtedly say, "Serves you right, Bryn."

Another smile tugged at my lips. I stoppered the flask and scanned the sky again, this time looking for a familiar speck. It took me a few minutes to spot her—she soared in wide circles above the capras, no doubt dreaming of eating prey she was far too small to ever capture.

I put two fingers to my lips and whistled her in. She spiraled down, her gray feathers silvered in the few gloomy rays of sunshine. Gray hawks were native to the continent, but they were far more prevalent here in this eastern portion of Esan. We'd used them for centuries to carry messages back and forth, and while the recent development of scribe quills—which used magic to pair one quill with another, meaning what one wrote the other copied—had made the hawks less of a necessity, they were still handy in situations involving much longer distances. They also made excellent pets, especially for someone like me. While earth and air witches were relatively scarce here in Arleeon—at least when compared to the lands of our trading partners—those with personal magic such as healing and spell casting were not, and both were revered to varying extents.

But I was the other kind—a strega, which was the rather derogative term for witches gifted with abilities of the mind, even if most *did* have an element of magic involved. It was a term that umbrellaed abilities such as the creation or manipulation of fire, the movement of objects, and mind reading. Oddly enough, when it came to the ability to mind touch, the term was only directed at those of us who could understand the thoughts of animals and control their actions. Human-to-human mind reading was considered a valuable asset.

While my mother also had the gift of animal control and, to a much smaller degree, seeress abilities, it was something of a puzzle as to how I'd inherited the ability to call forth fire. It was also an ability that had been the source of many whispers and much fear over the years, even if no one ever said anything directly to my parents or me. The latter *was* understandable, given our station, but the volatility of the skill during the early years of puberty had definitely fueled those whispers. It was a situation not helped by the red mote in my right eye—something all fire witches possessed—bleeding during those more explosive outbursts. It was a manifestation that scared some even today, even though my control over fire and the awareness of my own limitations meant it very rarely happened.

I raised an arm, and Veri landed lightly, her claws digging into the leather gauntlet but not cutting skin. She tilted her head to look at me, her golden eyes aglow and her mind awash with excitement. She knew a message meant food. I grinned and scratched her head, but she squawked impatiently and nipped at my fingers.

With a soft chuckle, I opened the small pouch at my waist and dug out a piece of meat. She accepted it daintily and swallowed it whole, then waited patiently as I undid the small message clasp on her right leg. Once free, she flew up to a branch and watched with interest as I unrolled the small, blank piece of specially treated paper. Kneeling on one knee and using the other as a makeshift writing surface, I grabbed the stylus out of my pack and carefully scratched out my message, not only telling my father about the attack but also asking for someone to be sent to retrieve Desta, my mount. Once the message was safely tucked back into the clasp, I called Veri down and reattached it.

"Straight home now." I handed her another piece of meat and impressed the order onto her mind. "No dillydallying above the poultry farms hoping to catch a juicy rodent."

She squawked—an offended sound if ever I'd heard one—then lifted off. Once she'd disappeared, I unwrapped the small parcel of dried meats and fruits I'd packed for breakfast and ate them as I continued on. It took me the better part of the day to traverse the valley and clamber up the ridge that divided it from the sweeping coastline on which Eastmead was situated.

What I saw from the top was not just a fire but utter destruction.

For several minutes, I simply stared, unable to believe what I was seeing.

There were no whole buildings, no pier, and certainly no boats anchored within the sheltered cove. All that remained were the blackened, broken remnants of boundary walls, homes, and workplaces that had once stood here. I had no idea what had happened to the hundred or so families who'd lived in this forsaken place—I couldn't see any bodies from where I was hunkered, but I couldn't see any sign of life, either. Maybe they'd evacuated, but where to? My gaze swept the wind-torn shoreline, but there was absolutely nowhere to hide. No caves or trees or any other kind of shelter. It was possible they'd managed to launch some boats and sail to safety, of course, but several mast tops sticking out of the water had doubts rising.

What had happened here? Who'd done this?

There was no immediate indication. No sign of foreign boats or any sort of invading force. It was as if the raiders had come out of nowhere, destroyed everything and everyone in their path, and then disappeared back into their nothingness.

Magic?

It was possible. The Mareritt were certainly capable of great magic. Maybe they'd gotten over their fear of the sea, or maybe they'd found another means into Arleeon—they surely couldn't have gone over the Blue Steel Mountains. Not only were they treacherous in the extreme, but both Esan and Zephrine had outposts dotted along their entire length. If they *had* attempted such an assault path, we would have been warned.

But if it wasn't the Mareritt, who could it have been? Arleeon had few other enemies, although I guess that didn't mean anything in the scheme of things. Sometimes it only took the replacement of a benevolent ruler on a neighboring continent for treaties and alliances to be torn apart.

History had certainly taught us *that.*

I frowned down at the smoking ruins for several more minutes, torn between the need to know what had happened and the knowledge that I might well be walking into trouble.

But it wasn't like I couldn't defend myself.

I flexed my fingers; sparks danced across their tips, and I couldn't help smiling. A sword and a knife were all well and good, but nothing beat flame when it came to attack or defense.

As a number of Mareritt patrols we'd come across over the years had discovered.

I scanned the ridge and found what looked to be a capra track heading down through the boulders and scrub. I followed it as fast as was practical while keeping half an eye on the settlement. Nothing changed.

Nothing except the weather.

The storm hit just as I reached the rocky shoreline. I wrapped my cloak around my body, then pulled on the hood, tugging at the strings to draw it around my face. The wind was fierce and icy, and every step forward became a battle. With the rain sheeting down so hard, it was almost impossible to see where I was going. I slowed, wary of walking into a trap in such conditions. Just because I hadn't seen any movement from above didn't mean there wasn't anything—or anyone —waiting here.

It seemed to take forever to reach the broken outskirts of the small settlement. I stopped behind what had once been a net repairer's to catch my breath, enjoying the speck of warmth radiating from the still-smoldering remnants of the partially collapsed building. While I could have easily used my inner fire to warm up, I preferred to save its force for any threat that might yet linger.

Despite the rain and the wind, the scent of smoke and ash hung heavily in the air. What I couldn't immediately smell was death, and that was puzzling. How could so many people utterly disappear? Even if most had managed to escape via their boats, surely some would have died. No attack, even those successfully repelled, went without casualties.

I drew my sword and moved on cautiously. In the waning light of late afternoon, the glass blade and intricately carved grip glowed like blue ice. This sword, like the knife strapped to my left leg, had come from the mages of Ithica, one of our major trading partners. Both blades had been fashioned in the arcane fires of Ithica's high temples and could only be destroyed in those fires.

While not all of Esan's soldiers had access to them, those of us whose task it was to scout Mareritten for any sign of activity or armed buildup certainly did.

But my father had personally commissioned this set and had given it to me when I'd finally made captain.

I suspected now it had been meant as a peace offering, because the pips had barely hit my shoulders when, on my thirtieth birthday, he'd informed me the commitment agreement had finally been signed.

I sucked in a deep breath and tried to concentrate on the destruction rather than the life-changing events of tomorrow.

Eastmead's layout was pretty basic, consisting of only three streets—one followed the cove's shoreline while another circled the central marketplace. The third shot off toward the south, eventually leading to the port of Hopetown. Not many folks used it—as roads went, it was long and hazardous, especially in bullock-drawn carts. Few here could have afforded a courser; aside from the fact fishermen had little use for swift mounts, the shoreline didn't provide much in the way of suitable grazing anyway. They could have held them in the valley to graze, of course, but that would have only made them targets for the larger drakkons who hunted there. Even stabling would have been difficult, as that would have meant importing feed. In fact, the few times I'd accompanied my father here on one of his inspection tours, the only stock I'd seen were poultry and a few domesticated capras—none of which were currently visible.

I cautiously padded on. This end of Eastmead had been devoted to all the different industries that a fishing village—large or small—needed. Aside from the net repairer, there'd been boat builders, blacksmiths, rope and barrel makers, fish scalers, and ice stores. While all the buildings here had been destroyed, there was little sign of the inventory or tools that each trade would have used. Even if much of it had burned, the fire wouldn't have been hot enough to destroy the blacksmith's tools and anvil. And yet, only the remnants of his forge remained.

It very much looked like the invaders had scooped up absolutely everything they could before they'd left... Which raised another possibility—had they also scooped up the people?

Slavery wasn't much of a problem these days. It was certainly banned here in Arleeon, and most of our trade partners had also either banned it outright or had never ventured there in the first place. But most wasn't all, and there'd been whispers of slave trading gaining traction on shores far distant from those of our trading partners. If that were true, we'd have to start stationing small garrisons around our outlying settlements. Or, at the very least, provide arms and training.

I paused again at the edge of the rutted and muddy ring road, looking left then right. Many of the buildings that had once lined both sides of this road still burned, though the flames were little more than flickers creeping along the edges of the blackened, broken walls. Despite the destruction, the central marketplace wasn't visible from where I stood. The beautiful old clock tower that had stood so proudly in the heart of the village for eons *was*, though it was now little more than a stark, skeletal structure—one whose still-smoldering support struts looked for all the world like blackened fingers reaching for the skies, pleading for help.

But there was no helping Eastmead. Not now.

I continued on warily. Tin rattled in the strengthening wind, briefly drawing my gaze left. Through a crack between one building wall and another, I spotted the smoldering mound that ringed the base of the tower. I had no idea what it was, but it certainly wasn't the collapsed remnants of the tower—the mound was simply too big. Too neat.

Intuition stirred, as did unease, but I didn't examine either too hard. Until I got closer, I really didn't want to speculate.

I kept following the road, my boots sticking in the mud, making every step that much harder. I checked each house I passed, but there remained no sign of life—or even death—in any of them. Nor was there any evidence of the usual household clutter; the fire that had consumed Eastmead had obviously burned white hot, so it was not surprising that all the furniture was ashed. But where was all the kitchenware? At the very least, there should have been clumps of metal that had once been eating utensils or pots. But there was nothing—not even broken remnants of plates and cups. The flickering sense of unease grew ever stronger.

I finally reached an entry point into the marketplace and paused to study the road ahead. It was tempting to continue down to the docks—or what was left of them, at any rate—rather than go left and confirm what suspicion and intuition were telling me about that mound.

But there was no guarantee I wouldn't find worse by the sea.

I drew in a deep breath and then resolutely turned left. The strong wind pushed at my back, as if eager to move me on, to make me see. My grip on my sword reflexively tightened as I moved from the mud of the road to the wide slabs of stone that marked the beginning of the central market area.

The closer I got to that mound, the more certain I became of what it was, and the angrier I grew.

Damn it, *why?* The refrain pounded through my brain, but the rain and the wind provided no answer.

I was ten feet away when my steps finally faltered. All I could do was stare at the horror that lay before me.

When I'd been standing on top of the ridge, I'd wondered where all the villagers were.

I now had my answer.

They were here. Butchered. Blackened. Broken.

Every damn one of them.

2

RAGE FILLED ME. Rage so deep and fierce that flames erupted from my hands, flowing like lava down the length of my sword to scorch the stones at my feet.

I clenched my free hand and fought for control. The last thing I wanted was to finish what the invaders and their flames had started. These people deserved better than that. They certainly deserved a more fitting burial than to have their bodies thrown around the old clock tower like so much rubbish and then set alight. Of course, affording each individual a sea burial—as was the custom in these parts—would be a task of monumental proportions, given everybody appeared to have been hacked into multiple pieces first.

Even the children.

May Vahree hunt these bastards down and torture their souls for all eternity.

And if the god of death didn't, I would.

I forced my feet on and walked around the ring of death and destruction, trying to see something—anything—that might point to who or what had done this. The scent downwind was horrendous, and my stomach churned. I tried breathing through my mouth rather than my nose, but that only coated my throat with the ash of death.

And no amount of swallowing could erase it.

Swords—or perhaps even axes—had been used to hack the bodies apart, but it was hard to tell if it had been done before or after death. I hoped it was the latter. I feared it was the former.

My gaze fell on a tiny hand that still clutched the remnants of a rag doll.

The distant stoicism I'd been trying so hard to maintain shattered. Tears filled my eyes and spilled down my cheeks. I raised my face to the sky and let the rain wash the grief away. It took a very long time, but the souls of these people deserved that, at the very least.

Eventually, I gathered the fragmented wisps of control and walked out of the marketplace, stepping back onto the road and following it down to the small harbor. The long pier jutting out into the cove's deeper waters had been destroyed; only a few stanchions and crossbeams remained. Where the rest of it was, I had no idea. Like the many boats that should have been here, it was simply gone. They might all be lying at the bottom of the sea, but surely if that were the case, there'd be more than a couple of masts sticking up out of the water, especially from those moored in the shallower waters.

Did that mean some of Eastmead's people had escaped, despite the evidence to the contrary in the marketplace?

I wanted to hope so—I really did—but my gut said otherwise. Whoever had done all this had wanted utter destruction. Had wanted to ensure this small outpost wouldn't easily be resurrected.

A flash of movement drew my gaze toward the neck of the cove; two longboats swept into view, riding high on the waves and the fierce wind, approaching at speed. Standing at the helm of the first was a monster of a man—he was tall, broad of shoulder, with a thick plait of silvery-gray hair that streamed behind him thanks to the force of the wind. Even though he was some distance away, I knew his brown features were weatherworn, and that his grin would be fierce and bright.

Knew because this was Rion Silva.

My father.

He might constantly berate my wanderlust, but in truth, he was little better. The need to get out, to see the world beyond the confines of Esan's glorious walls before duty closed in on us, was a fault we both shared. It also happened to be the reason I existed. Had his boat not sprung a leak all those years ago, he would never have ventured into Jakarra's harbor to seek repairs or met the island's fiercely independent bow master. According to my father, it had been love at first sight. For him. Apparently she hadn't been so convinced, and it had taken months of courting before she'd accepted his intentions were serious.

I envied their story, envied their love.

Wanted, with an ache that would now never be satisfied, someone to love me so fiercely, chase me so determinedly.

But their story would never be mine.

I drew a deep breath and forced the heartache, the anger, and even the brief stab of self-pity behind inner walls. I was a soldier—a captain. I had to act like it.

As the longboat drew closer, I spotted the man standing behind my father.

Damon Velez, firstborn son of Zephrine's king, and my future husband.

What in the wind's name was *he* doing here?

Wasn't it enough that we'd see each other when we married tomorrow? Did he really have to intrude on my last few hours of freedom?

I huffed out a breath and sheathed my sword. I didn't bother tugging my uniform into some semblance of presentability or run my fingers across my wet hair to smooth it down; both were well beyond that sort of quick fix. Besides, Damon might as well discover from the outset just what he was getting into when it came to our marriage. I was no royal wallflower—Mom had made damn sure of that—and the sooner he accepted it, the better.

The bow of the boat slid onto the sands, and several sailors leapt out to tie her off. My father didn't wait for the ramp. He simply braced a hand on the gunwale, jumped over the side, and then strode toward me. Damon followed. I couldn't help noticing he moved with the grace of a high-forest wildcat. My father was bullish in comparison.

I straightened and saluted. He might be my father, but he was also my commander, and I had no idea which I might be facing at this particular moment. "You got my message then, sir?"

"And sent a guard to retrieve Desta. Report, Captain."

His voice was curt, and relief swept me. Commander mode made it far easier to keep my emotions under control. "The village has been looted and razed, and all within murdered."

He stopped abruptly, his golden gaze darting to the burned remnants above us. "The destruction isn't the result of an out-of-control fire, as you'd initially theorized, then?"

"No. It's very definitely a raid."

My gaze found Damon's. His eyes were the rich, clear blue of the ice melt lakes and just as damn cold. He gave me a nod but little else in the way of greeting. Which was damn fine with me. The less I had to do with the man until tomorrow, the better.

My father glanced back to the longboat and snapped his fingers. His personal guard immediately leapt onto the sand and came toward us.

"Jarrod, immediate perimeter search."

As the tall captain saluted and started assigning his men locations, my father motioned me forward and then fell in step beside me. "Any indication as to who's responsible?"

"I haven't had the chance to search the southern end of the settlement as yet, but whoever did this has so far left nothing behind."

"The Mareritt are very rarely that careful," Damon commented. His voice was like good ale, so deep and smoky.

He'd fallen into step to my left. Despite the inner need to keep distance, I was nevertheless aware not only of his size, but also the barely restrained power in every movement. He'd certainly changed in the twelve years since I'd last seen him, and for the better. I wished the same could have been said about me, but I'd hit my teenage years tall and lanky, and had never really developed beyond that. According to the whisperers, my lack of "womanly" assets had been one of the reasons for the marriage agreement taking so long to finalize.

"Normally, no," my father agreed. "But neither has a summer passed without a major assault against either fortress before now."

"What happened here isn't their usual mode of operation," I commented. "Besides, they hate the sea."

"So do you," my father growled. "It's never stopped you boarding a boat when necessary."

"Yeah, but they live underground for nine months of the year," I snapped back, then sucked in a breath to regain control. *Commander, not father. Act appropriately.* "That's hardly conducive to boat building."

"Which doesn't negate the fact that it's entirely possible," he replied, "especially given the great magic their mages are capable of."

If magic *had* been used here, then it wasn't the type the Mareritt typically used. Why I was so certain of that, I couldn't say. It wasn't like I was in any way attuned to it. It was just instinct—a gut feeling.

But the only gut my father trusted was his own—and Mom's. Everyone else had best provide evidence to back intuition or remain silent.

I turned right and led the two men toward the marketplace, my gaze on the blackened fingers of wood rather than the stomach-churning destruction that lay underneath.

"It wouldn't be entirely surprising if this was the start of a new direction from them," Damon said. "Even the Mareritt aren't foolish enough to keep banging their blunt heads against the same impassable walls year in and year out."

"And yet they've done exactly that for centuries." My voice held an edge I couldn't quite conceal. "If they were capable of learning such a lesson, they surely would have done so before now."

He cast a somewhat scathing look my way. "It never pays to underestimate the enemy."

"Or indeed so-called friends," I bit back.

In the fading light of the day, I swear a glint of amusement briefly warmed his eyes. There was no alteration in his stony expression, however, so it was probably just a trick of the light.

"If not the Mareritt, then who else? Arleeon has few other enemies."

"That we know of," I said. "But we're a continent rich in pastoral and mineral wealth; that's always a lure to those who are less fortunate."

"If one of our allies were intent on making such a move," Damon said, "why start with a place as forsaken as this?"

"Perhaps they believed they could more easily traverse—" My father abruptly stopped, his expression dissolving into horror. "In Vahree's name, who would commit such an atrocity?"

"Someone who places no value on human life." Damon's voice was a low vibration of anger.

I could understand that anger. Could feel its echo deep within.

"There's no livestock within the mound that I could see." My gaze remained on the blackened fingers of wood rather than the bodies. "And none in the holding yards. Both the buildings in the industrial area and the houses surrounding the marketplace have been stripped of all usable items. Whoever did this came here, killed all its inhabitants, and then seized every single thing of value they could get their hands on."

"And burned the rest to hide anything they might have left behind that could identify them." My father swept a hand across his heavily plaited silver hair. "I wonder why they didn't simply leave the bodies to burn where they were? Why go to the trouble of stacking them here like this?"

"I don't think they were stacked. I think they were herded here alive, then killed and set alight." Damon's voice was flat and unemotional—at odds with the thick waves of his fury and disgust that rolled across my senses. "The way they have all fallen suggests they didn't put up a fight."

My gaze unwillingly swept the pile of bodies. Now that he'd mentioned it, there *was* something rather... planned... about the way the bodies lay. It was almost a crisscross pattern, as if those behind this atrocity had begun their killing spree at the back and methodically worked forward.

I rubbed my arms uneasily. "If they didn't fight, it would suggest they were either drugged or mentally prevented from doing so."

Damon's gaze met mine again. Something flickered through his eyes—something that vaguely resembled distaste. It was, of course, possible I was imprinting my own emotions about our impending pairing onto him.

"I doubt there's a telepath alive capable of controlling several hundred people at the same time—though you would, of course, know more about that than me."

The smile that briefly twisted my lips held little in the way of humor. "My talent lies with animals, not people, as I'm sure you're well aware."

"I've certainly heard you're more comfortable with the former than the latter." His gaze returned to the pile, leaving me wondering who'd told him that and whether those stories were another reason for the long delay in our inevitable binding. "It's possible they could have used magic. There *are* spells that can sap the will."

"But are those spells capable of entrancing a whole village?" my father asked.

"Yes, though it is not my area of expertise."

I'd heard rumors that at least one of the Zephrine king's many sons was a spell caster, though none had ever mentioned if it was either of his two legitimate sons or the dozen or so illegitimate ones. Nor had any rumor ever mentioned the type of magic Damon was gifted with. Which was decidedly odd given personal magic—aside from Strega—was usually celebrated rather than derided. "But you do know someone whose expertise it is?"

A cool smile touched his lips. "Indeed. I'll scribe her this evening."

Her. Maybe it wasn't my lack of womanly assets that had delayed our binding as much as another woman. Or two. Which was to be expected, given he was two years older than me and the king's heir, but it nevertheless annoyed me. I had by no means kept myself "pure" for our very delayed nuptials, but I'd also never really had a long-term relationship. I was a princess, even if not the heir, and there'd been more than one occasion where it was the supposed "prestige" that came with the title rather than the person that had attracted them. The last one had damn near broken my heart, and I'd basically sworn off attachments since.

Rion grunted, then turned to me. The sternness fell away, replaced by amused annoyance—an expression that was quite common when we weren't in any sort of official situation. "Your mother has threatened to place an embargo on our bedroom activities if I do not get you home this evening."

"But—"

"No," he said, obviously understanding what I'd been about to say. "Rutgar will take you home. I'll see you tomorrow, at the ceremony."

I ground my teeth in frustration, though my banishment was not unexpected. He might be the king, but my mother ruled the family. This was her order, not his.

I nodded in acceptance, then turned and strode away. I was more than a little surprised to find Damon falling in beside me.

"You're not staying here to help sort out the puzzle?" The question came out more terse than necessary.

"I am, but it would hardly be polite to allow my betrothed to wander a destroyed settlement alone."

I snorted. "We both know you didn't want said betrothal, Damon, so please feel free to be impolite. I don't really care."

"Oh, I think you care far more than you wish to admit."

I shot him a glance. "In part, I suppose you're right—I *do* care about a great many things. Sadly, you're not one of them."

He laughed, a short sharp sound that hung warmly on the cold evening air. "That may well be true, but we are, unfortunately, stuck with each other. We need to discuss a means of making this situation work for us both."

"Ah," I said, suddenly understanding. "You don't wish our commitment to hamper your womanizing."

He raised an eyebrow. "I'm not entirely sure what you've heard about me, but that's not what I meant."

"You deny the womanizing?"

"Of course not."

"Are we talking conjugal rights, then?" I have no idea what he saw in my expression, but his gaze narrowed. "Because I feel bound to warn you, Damon: If you touch me without invitation, I *will* gut you."

The glimmer briefly appeared in his glorious eyes again, though his expression showed little evidence of amusement. "Warning heeded, princess. But do remember that statement runs both ways."

I let my gaze drift lazily from the top of his smooth, clean-shaven head, down his well-muscled length, before pausing on his crotch. "Oh, I think it fair to say you're safe from me. My tastes run to men with a little more... hair."

He stared at me for several heartbeats and then laughed again. "Oh, if this is but a teaser of what is to come in our relationship, I am delighted."

"At least one of us is." I returned my gaze to the sea. The storm showed no sign of easing, and the waters in the cove looked dark and turbulent. It was going to be a hellish trip home.

I could feel the weight of his gaze on me. It had the inner fires flaring to life, heating my blood and making my pulse pound.

"It is a marriage, not an execution," he said softly. "You have nothing to fear from me."

But plenty to fear from Zephrine itself. He didn't say that, but it oddly seemed to hang in the air between us. "So says the man who gives up nothing. Not his friends, not his rank, not life as he knows it."

And certainly not his drakkons... and while they weren't "mine," per se, it was the cut that hurt the deepest. I'd see my parents several times a year, as there were regular councils between the two great cities, but I would never see the queen or her drakklings again. Zephrine was not where she hunted, even if her grace lay in the Red Ochre Mountains. Where, I had no idea. She'd never mentioned the location, and I'd never asked.

I took a deep breath and released it slowly, but it didn't do much to ease the inner churning.

"You are not alone in giving up your life or the things you love," Damon said, a bitter edge creeping into his tone. "Remember that."

My gaze unwillingly went to his. There was little emotion in either his expression or his eyes, and yet I felt the anger in him, the frustration. I couldn't help but wonder who he'd been forced to give up for this farce of a marriage.

If he'd given her up, that is. Zephrine's royal line did have a reputation for promiscuity, after all. I doubted being married to me would change that.

But then, this marriage was a tradition forced on us both; me because I was an only child, and he because his younger brother had secretly undergone a commitment ceremony, which he then presented as a fait accompli in order to negate any attempt to force the marriage onto him, as had been done in the past.

It was an action that threw another problem into the mix, at least where I was concerned. In marrying the heir, I would be under pressure to produce a son once we got back to Zephrine.

I really, *really* wished there was some way to put off going there anytime soon.

I continued silently down to the boat, all too aware of the man who strode at my side. Which I guess wasn't such a bad thing. Being physically attracted to the man I was about to spend the rest of my life with was a far better option than being repulsed.

Rutgar—a thickset man with a fierce red complexion and a matching plait of hair—waited at the end of the gangplank. His expression was anxious—no doubt he wanted to get a move on before the tide turned and night closed in. While there was an air witch on board—they were something of a necessity when navigating the treacherous seas around these parts—Rutgar was the old-fashioned type who preferred magic only as a last resort. Not that he'd be relying on his skills tonight—not in this storm and not with me on board. He no doubt had orders to get me back to Esan quickly and in one piece, and that meant putting the air witch's ability to manipulate the weather to full use.

When we reached the ramp, I stopped and turned to Damon. "I'll see you tomorrow."

"You will." He looked set to add something else but, in the end, simply bowed and strode away.

"Captain Silva?" Rutgar said. "We need to set sail, otherwise the seas will be against us."

"From the look of things, they already are."

"Close to, but we should make it out of the heads before things get too tricky."

I suspected the chance of escaping tricky seas had well and truly passed us by, but I held my tongue and stepped onto the gangway. After clambering over the gunwale, I moved to the stern of the boat and the small, covered area that lay underneath the vessel's ornately carved tail.

Oran—the air witch whose job it was to get us safely home—gave me a brief nod but his attention was already on the storm he'd soon be pushing us through. The air crackled with the force of his rising magic.

I sat on the opposite bench, dumped my backpack beside me, and tightly gripped the wooden hold above my head. The ramp was quickly drawn and, as the oarsmen assumed their positions, Oran's magic surged. Its force was so sharp that my skin crawled. I leaned back in an effort to put a little more distance between us, but it didn't really help.

The ship rocked from side to side as she eased off the sand ridge. I closed my eyes and tried to ignore the rising tide of fear. There was no logical reason for it, especially when we had an air witch on board. Controlling the weather was what they lived for, and Oran had long guided my father's ship to safety through storms far worse than this.

Once in deeper water, the ship surged forward, cutting easily against the wind and the waves as she headed for the heads and the open water.

I tried to relax, but my stomach felt as wild and stormy as the sea. The full force of the storm hit when we rounded the heads; waves crashed over the ship, washing her decks with their malevolence, drenching oarsmen even as they threatened to sweep away anything not tied down. The wind howled, and the ship pitched and rolled, the motion violent and unsettling.

Then Oran's magic sharpened, and we were abruptly wrapped in a bubble of calm. The ship settled and surged forward again, slicing through the seas at speed, the bubble preceding us while the storm's violence crashed into the foam of our wake. I sent a silent prayer to Túxn—the goddess of good luck—that Oran's strength outlasted the worst of the storm. I really didn't want to be sailing around the Throat of Huskain when it failed.

We were a little over two hours into the four-hour journey home when the vague feeling that something was wrong stirred.

At first I thought it was simply our nearness to the Throat; the seas that crashed against its fortress-like walls might provide rich pickings for fishermen, but the uncertain currents made it a dangerous area to traverse in calm seas, let alone storm-clad.

But the closer we got, the more certain I became the wrongness had nothing to do with the sea or the storm.

Then the vibration began along the mental lines.

I frowned and silently reached out, trying to find the source of whatever I was sensing. After a moment, I pinned it down—it was at the very far edges of my reach, and it was a mind unlike anything I'd ever come across before. It was fierce and cruel, a mind whose patterns of thought were both foreign and bizarre. In thirty years of existence, I'd not sensed anything like it.

But as I tried to forge a deeper connection, the link was severed, and so damn brutally that pain rebounded and made me gasp.

I blinked back tears and rubbed my head. Though I had no idea what I'd briefly connected to, I was certain of one thing. Someone *else* had severed the connection.

I rose, clipped myself onto the guide rail, and then stepped out of the shelter. Oran's bubble continued to protect us, but the seas around the Throat were so unpredictable the occasional wave got through. The unwary—or unsecured—could easily be washed overboard.

Rutgar hurried over. "Is there a problem, Captain?"

"Maybe."

I studied the white-capped seas uneasily. There was life underneath those waves—white-finned blackfish, sea devils, and deadly spear rays. None of them were the source of what I'd sensed.

My gaze rose. Light rolled across the darkness, a brief flash that lent the low clouds an ominous glow.

And hid whatever it was that now approached.

Rutgar's gaze followed mine. "You sensing a drakkon?"

"Drakkons have more sense than to come out in weather like this."

"Not so. We've lost ships to them before, and in storms far worse than this."

"Only because we were killing them en masse," I said. "There hasn't been an attack since the ballistas fell silent."

"Revenge is a trait both humans and drakkons share," he said.

And no matter what I said, I wasn't going to convince him otherwise. "Whatever is out there isn't a drakkon."

Something thumped heavily against the roof of the covered area.

I spun around, one hand instinctively gripping my sword. On the top of the wooden structure was what appeared to be a mound of dung. Dung that was melting *into* the wooden struts.

Before I could investigate further, a shout from the prow had me spinning around again. An oarsman was down. Rutgar swore and sprinted forward. I followed.

More thumps. More steaming piles of stinking dung. More men down.

Screams of shock and anger now filled the air, the noise almost masking another—a thick, ominous splintering.

My gaze jumped to the mast. A crack raced down its center, cleaving the thick beam in two. It crashed onto the deck, smashing into the gunwale and killing two oarsmen who didn't get out of the way fast enough.

"What in Vahree's name is happening?" Rutgar shouted.

"I don't know, but the sooner we get out of here, the better." I spun around. "Oran, we need—"

The rest of the sentence died in my throat. Oran was dead, slumped sideways on the bench, half his face sliced away. Something glittered in the bloody remnant of his left cheek—something that was gold and metallic.

I swore but before I could do anything, say anything, the bubble protecting us shattered, leaving us at the full mercy of the storm. The boat plunged steeply, sending me tumbling toward the broken part of the hull. A second before I would have plunged into the icy water, the safety rope snapped taut, cutting deep into my waist even as it stopped my fall.

"Ingrid, Tennent!" Rutgar was shouting. "Get the trysail and jib up!"

As they obeyed, I hauled myself up and away from the gunwale. More thumps on the deck. More blobs of brown. This time, they weren't just melting through the deck, but dropping into the bilge. Dark water welled up through the emerging holes.

I swore and ran for one of the hand pumps; it took a few minutes to ease the stiff lever into a constant rhythm, but even as it ejected water swiftly over the side, I knew it was useless. The pumps were too slow, and the hold filling too fast.

We were going to sink.

"Rutgar!" I shouted. "We need to get to the shore!"

"Can't," he replied. "We're in the middle of the Throat—the rocks will smash us to pieces."

And if we stayed out here, the seas would do the same...

The thought had barely crossed my mind when a massive wave broke across the bow and the boat began to roll.

Rutgar immediately shouted more orders, and the ship began to turn. For an instant, I thought we were safe.

But the incoming wave was too big, and the boat too small.

It swept us up, then smashed us down, breaking the ship into multiple pieces and pushing us deep under the malevolent sea.

3

FOR SEVERAL SECONDS, there was nothing but fear, cold, and turbulence. It tossed me, turned me, even as it dragged me down.

I fought not to breathe, not to panic, but both were hard in a world that was so black and violent. When the only thing I could hear was the rapid pounding of my own heart. When the weight at my waist dragged me ever deeper…

The safety rope.

It was still attached to some part of the ship.

I reached down and tried to release the catch, but the heaviness of whatever lay on the other end of the rope made it impossible to undo. I unclipped my knife and, holding it tight in the turbulent water, tried to cut myself free. It took several attempts before I succeeded. Relief surged, but I was far from safe. I kicked toward a surface I couldn't see, swimming desperately, hoping I was headed in the right direction, that I wasn't going sideways or, Vahree forbid, even down. In this world of dark madness, anything was possible.

It was a madness that seemed endless.

My lungs burned, and my heart pounded so fiercely it felt ready to tear out of my chest. My limbs were ice and my clothes heavy hampering progress. It didn't matter. Nothing did, except reaching the surface.

I kept kicking, kept fighting, desperate to survive, to breathe.

Then, abruptly, I could.

I sucked in air, treading water as I spun around, looking for Rutgar and the others. All I saw was darkness, bits of boat, and mountainous white-capped waves.

I had no idea where I was. No idea how far the shore and safety might be.

A wave hit, pushing me back down again. It ripped at my cloak, dragging it sideways, almost choking me in the process. I quickly released it, then sheathed my knife, making sure it was secure before I released it. Maybe it was stupid to care so much about a weapon when I was on the verge of drowning, but it was a gift from my father and one I wasn't about to relinquish—not unless there was absolutely no other choice. Not when I was about to lose everything else thanks to the damn marriage.

After tugging off my heavy gauntlets, I let them float away and kicked upward again. Another gasp for air; another useless turn. I shouted for Rutgar, but the words were torn away by the fierce winds. There was no response, no sign of anyone or anything. Nothing but dark violence all around me.

Túxn help me...

Given the goddess wasn't likely to hear such a plea, let alone answer it, I had no choice but to try a closer source of help—the white-fins. I sucked in another breath then held out a hand, my fingers splayed as I opened the mental gates and reached for the oft-hunted marine mammals that called these waters home. Direct mind-to-mind communication wasn't possible with all animals, only the larger ones whose intelligence was close to—or at the same level—as we humans.

For several minutes there was no response. The violent sea tossed me around, and it was becoming increasingly harder to keep my head above the water. I scanned the immediate area and pushed more force into my call. The "hearing" distance within water was far greater—and faster—than that of air, thanks to the density of it. If there was a school of white-fins anywhere close in these waters, they would hear me.

I only needed one to answer.

Just as hope began to fade, there was a brief, tantalizing brush of awareness. I pushed more force into my call and, a few seconds later, a large white dorsal fin briefly broke the surface a few yards ahead of me.

What need?

While the response wasn't actually in any language I would normally understand, the magic that allowed this sort of communication also translated for both of us.

Need help to shore.

Her large white fin broke the surface again as she swam around me. Studying me. Judging me.

Can't take all way. Shallows kill.

Close will be good.

She was silent for a moment. *Weapons carry?*

Will not hurt you.

Eat you if do.

I had no doubt about that. And, in truth, while my sword could easily slice through her flesh, there was no way known I could draw, let alone use, it in these seas. Not before the white-fin's sharp teeth sawed me in half, at any rate.

I promise no harm.

She had no reason to believe me. Not given how hunted her kind were by mine. And yet, I wasn't surprised when she assented. In my experience, animals of all kinds were far more trusting *and* trustworthy than humans.

Hold, she said, and broke the surface next to me.

I locked my hands around her dorsal fin and held on tight. She surged forward, undulating through the water, dragging me along easily despite the storm and the fact she preferred the depths to the surface.

What followed was a long and arduous nightmare. I lost my grip more than once, but she always circled around to collect me. My body became numb, and my teeth chattered so hard my jaw ached. I used just enough inner flame to keep frostbite from my extremities, but dared not do anything more. Aside from the fact it would scare my helper, the heat was better kept for when I reached dry land.

If I reached dry land.

I had no idea how much time had passed before the change of sound in the crashing of the waves intruded on my consciousness. I looked past her dorsal and saw a faint ribbon of white—sea foam washing up onto a shoreline.

No farther, she said. *Shallows ahead.*

I released her fin and slipped away from her sleek body. *Thank you for your assistance. Keep safe.*

Only safe if yours no hunt.

And with that, she turned and disappeared under the sea. I resolutely headed for the shore. I wasn't a great swimmer, and it turned out to be a whole lot farther than it first appeared. By the time the waves inelegantly tossed me onto the stony beach, I was shaking with exhaustion and so damn cold I could barely move.

Somehow, I crawled away from the reach of the waves, then drew my knees to my chest and hugged them close as I called to the inner fires. Though it was tempting to go full flame, I knew enough about frostbite to resist the urge. Instead, I pushed the heat out cautiously, warming my body so slowly that my teeth continued to chatter long into the night. The wind didn't help matters—it spun around me, stiffening my clothes and sheeting them with ice. Medical wisdom suggested stripping off, but I didn't have anything else to wrap myself in, and there wasn't anything along this forsaken shoreline to use.

Nothing except the occasional scrap of bleached wood that spoke of all the other ships that had found their death in these waters.

The inner heat eventually chased numbness from my limbs, and the shivering eased, even if it didn't completely stop. I pushed to my feet, my still-wet leathers clinging like a second skin. I eked out a little more heat in an effort to dry them, then resolutely walked up the beach. Yellowed razor grass lined the ridge above me, defining the end of the sand and the beginning of whatever lay beyond. I scrambled up the slope, my feet slipping on the uneven ground, my fingers brushing the stones as I fought for balance. By the time I reached the ridge, my breath was a harsh rasp and my legs burned. I was fit—as a soldier you had to be, even if skirmishes with the Mareritt were currently few and far between—but right now I felt weaker than a babe.

The land beyond the top of the ridge was flat and empty. The only signs of life were the thick patches of razor grass and the bones of old trees. There was absolutely nothing here that gave any clue as to where I was. I turned back to the sea. The shoreline stretched on endlessly to my left. To my right, distant and vague, were the jagged edges of a mountain range. It had to be the Black Glass Mountains, but the angle was very different to anything I'd seen previously. Which meant I was on the edge of—or, more likely, given how distant those mountains looked—deep within the boundaries of Mareritten.

I swore and thrust a hand through the tangled mess of my hair, my fingers tearing into multiple knots. I shook the dark strands free and watched the wind sweep them away. I couldn't help but wish it would grant me the same sort of lift—if nothing else, it would make getting home a little faster.

After another look at the surrounding desolation, I slid back down to the beach. Walking on soft sand might be more arduous than keeping to the flatter ground along the ridge, but I had no idea how well guarded these lands were. No idea what sort of traps the Mareritt might have set for the unwary. Of course, the beach might prove no safer in that regard, but I was betting their dislike of the sea made it less likely for traps to be set here.

Resolutely, I set off for the distant, shadowy mountains. Until I got closer, I wouldn't be able to call either Veri or Desta to me, and they were my only real hope of rescue. My mother would know something was wrong the minute the ship didn't dock on time, and she'd no doubt attempt to find me via the tracer stone I still wore.

But tracer stones, like the scribe pens, were a product of magic and notoriously unreliable range-wise, and if I *was* deep within Mareritten territory, well, there was no way any receiver, no matter how powerful, would find me.

The storm eased as the night wore on, though the chill remained. The wind remained blustery and uneven, one minute throwing me sideways, the next chasing my heels and hastening my steps along the sandy shore.

Dawn's pale pink fingers were seeping across the distant horizon when I made my first attempt to reach either Veri or Desta.

All I got was an odd sort of static; I remained beyond communication range.

I swore and lifted my face to the sky, blinking back tears of frustration and tiredness. All I wanted was to lie down and rest, but I couldn't; not here, not until I was sure help was on the way.

I stumbled on. Dawn came and went, but the day remained gloomy. Although there *was* one bright spot—I was at least missing my wedding.

Not that it actually mattered. The political and trade agreements had already been signed by both parties; the commitment ceremony was little more than a formality, even if one full of pomp and splendor. If I *did* happen to die in this forsaken place, it would have little true effect. Garran—the firstborn son of Mom's oldest sister—had long ago been made my father's heir, and it was highly unlikely Damon would mourn the loss of a wife he didn't want.

Even so, regret drifted through me. I might not have wanted the marriage, but I couldn't deny the wisp of attraction to the man. It would have been interesting to see if time together produced anything approaching a loving relationship.... I shut the thought down. I had no time for regret, because I had no intention of dying.

Not before I caught the bastards behind the deaths of all those in Eastmead and all those in the boat.

Morning moved into afternoon. My head throbbed, my throat was raw, and there wasn't a single part of my body that didn't ache. Every damn step was becoming an effort.

I *had* to find somewhere safe to stop and rest. Now. Before the decision was taken out of my hands and I utterly collapsed.

A sharp cry to my right had me reaching for my knife and spinning around—too quickly. The beach did a brief but crazy dance, and nausea surged up my throat. I swallowed heavily and studied the ridge, eventually spotting the source of the sound. It was a kayin—a large seabird known for its ability to soar for days on the wind's currents. They didn't often land in open, flat areas like this, as their size made it difficult for them to take off again. Their usual haunts were the peaks high above the sea, where they could easily launch from mountain ledges and catch the updrafts.

I warily moved closer, my gaze moving between the bird and the ridge, my aching muscles humming with readiness to move—to fight —should this be some sort of trap.

The bird made no effort to get away, and I soon saw why; it had been shot through the chest. The cry I'd heard had been its last.

But the arrow hadn't come from an Esan bow. We didn't use this type of wood, and we certainly didn't fletch them with blue feathers.

This arrow was Mareritten.

Túxn help me... Despite the long hours of walking, I remained in their lands.

I breathed deep, trying to control the instinctive rush of fear. I might be alone, I might be bone weary, but I wasn't without weapons. The bastards wouldn't take me down as easily as they had this kayin.

I moved past the fallen bird and cautiously scrambled up the slope. The lands beyond the razor grass remained desolate. There was nothing to suggest anything or anyone watched this place. And yet the hand that had fired the arrow had to be near; the kayin wouldn't have been able to fly far with the arrow in its chest.

I carefully retrieved its carcass and placed it beyond the razor grass, where it was easily visible. Then I stretched out on the ground, the grass brushing my face, leaving tiny cuts in its wake. I ignored them. Moving farther down the ridge meant I wouldn't be able to see the lay of the land or what might be moving across it.

Time ticked by. I remained absolutely still, though stones dug into my stomach and tiredness pulled at my eyelids.

Then I heard the soft crunch of stones.

I carefully looked left. A figure appeared over the slight rise in the land, and my pulse skipped several beats. He was pale of skin, with wide shoulders and a thickset body. There were six fingers on his hands rather than the usual five, and the tips of his short, spiky hair gleamed like blue ice against the cool grays of the sky.

Mareritt.

The instinct to rise, to fight, surged, but I ignored it. I had no idea if he was alone, and until I *did*, I couldn't react.

He stopped on the top of the small hill and scanned the area. His gaze swept across the ground between us and then paused. For too many seconds, he stared at the thick grass inches from my face, and my fingers itched with the need to unleash the flames burning against their tips.

I didn't, and after a moment, his gaze moved on to the kayin. A bright smile flashed across his rough features, and he strode forward. He wore leathers rather than armor, and the only weapon he had beyond the bow was the knife strapped to his left thigh. My gaze shot back to his face, for the first time seeing the telltale features of youth —the lack of scars on his cheeks, the absence of malice in his expression.

He must be in the midst of p'asazhis—a rite of passage that all Mareritten warriors apparently went through, which had them living unaided—aside from the knife and bow—off the land for the three months of summer.

I released my grip on my sword and reached for my knife instead. I had one shot, one chance. Youth or not, I couldn't let him get close. I simply didn't have the strength or speed for hand-to-hand combat.

He moved forward, his gaze on his prize rather than keeping watch for anything or anyone else. I waited until he was so close that his foul scent—a thick, unpleasant musk—stung my nostrils, then leapt to my feet and threw the knife. He was fast, I'd give him that. The blade that should have pierced his heart got his shoulder instead. He tore it from his flesh and, with a scream of rage, drew his own and charged. I raised my hand, called to the fire, and pierced him with heat. He was dead before he hit the ground.

I sucked in another breath in a vague effort to ease the red-hot needles now boring into my brain—a warning that I was skirting the edges of strength both psychically *and* physically—then warily moved forward, my hand on my sword and my gaze sweeping the area on the off chance he wasn't alone. The desolation stretched on, undisturbed by further movement. After retrieving my knife, I moved across to the Mareritt and knelt beside him. His stench filled my nostrils again, briefly making me gag. I switched to breathing through my mouth and quickly patted him down. There was nothing under his clothes or in his pockets. A small water bottle was strapped to his left hip and a carryall pouch on his right. I sliced away the latter and tipped its contents onto the ground. There was a flint stone, a striker, a basic first aid kit, and random bits and pieces such as coral, oddly colored rocks, and... my heart skipped several beats... a small golden feather.

The same sort of feather I'd briefly glimpsed sticking out of Oran's cheek before the boat had come under full attack.

I picked it up. It was heavy, cold to the touch, and definitely made of metal. Dried blood dotted the end of the hollow shaft, which in normal feathers meant they'd been shed from flesh. But what sort of bird had metal feathers? None, as far as I was aware. None that existed in either Arleeon or Mareritten, at any rate.

So, was this a new form of weapon from the Mareritt? Had their mages twisted life and created something bizarre and deadly? It would certainly explain the odd unnaturalness I'd felt before the connection had been so brutally severed.

If it were the Mareritt, though, why would they attack an out of the way settlement such as Eastmead? Why not Esan or Zephrine? Creatures capable of producing acidic dung would surely cause substantial damage to the thick walls protecting either city.

Then again, if the Mareritt *were* behind the attack on Eastmead and the boat, why would this youth have collected the feather as a trophy? From what I understood of p'asazhis, their "treasures" were meant to be unusual or unexplained items from which stories could be spun.

I'd always found it hard to reconcile the image of Mareritten storytellers with the brutal reality of their warriors.

I pocketed the feather and untied the small water bottle. The liquid inside was tepid and had a somewhat sour, metallic taste, but right then, nothing had ever tasted so sweet. I resisted the urge to gulp it down, drinking only enough to ease the fire in my throat, then capped it again. I had to make it last, because who knew how long I'd be out here.

I rose and made my way back to the kayin. I wasn't about to let its death go to waste—not when my hunger was so fierce it was a deep and never-ending ache. I moved back down to the beach, carefully burned away the feathers, then increased the heat of my flames to cook its flesh.

Dusk was settling in across the skies by the time I'd picked the last of its bones clean. I briefly thought about resting for the night, but the desire to get out of Mareritten lands was stronger.

I pushed to my feet and kept on walking. The moon was high overhead when I made yet another attempt at contacting either Veri or Desta. Static washed through my mind, and I closed my eyes, resisting the urge to give up. To collapse on the stony sand and just let the rising tide wash me away. Maybe it would have been better to have gone down with the boat than die by slow degrees from exhaustion and hunger....

Then, from out of the static, came a brief, very distant, *I hear.*

Desta, not Veri.

Tears spilled down my cheeks. Hope. There was yet hope of rescue.

Can you come?

Run free. Able.

Meaning Mom had let her loose in the vague hope that I was alive. *Then come.*

I had no idea if such an order would work. No idea if the magic that allowed this connection could also act as a type of locator beacon. It did with Veri, but she had the advantage of long sight and being able to fly over vast tracts of land to find me.

I turned and studied the ridgeline. The razor grass had finally given way to high sweeps of cliffs. I'd have to go up, because Desta would never get down.

I drank the last bit of metallic water but didn't toss the bottle aside. Who knew, there might be a spring of some kind atop the cliffs.

I resolutely headed up the foreshore, angling toward what looked to be the easiest path up the crumbling, dangerous-looking cliff. Climbing was a long, slow, and arduous journey involving scraped hands, a number of slips, and plenty of cursing. By the time I finally crawled over the ridge, my hands were bloody, my body was locked in pain, and my head spun. I gulped in air and looked around. The landscape was a sea of rock and wind-twisted paperbark trees; while it offered patrolling Mareritt plenty of cover, it also had relief surging. I knew these lands. Or, at least, had done patrols through them. While I was a long way north of where I needed to be, this wilderness swept down to the bogs designating the end of Mareritten land and the start of Esan's.

I was close, *so* close, to safety.

But I was also exhausted. I had to sleep. *Had* to.

I glanced around, looking for somewhere that was protected from both the weather and Mareritt gaze. I eventually settled on a tower of rock that had, via wind and eruption, formed a V-shaped cave. The wide, high entrance gave me a good view of the surrounding area while the deepness of the cave meant a casual glance by a passing Mareritt was unlikely to spot me.

I walked to the very back, stripped off my sword, and placed it across my knees once I sat down. While I was well aware that death too often preyed on the unwary, I could not deny exhaustion. Sleep caught me within minutes.

A velvety nose nudging my shoulder woke me who knew how many hours later.

Desta. Tears hit my eyes and spilled down my cheeks. I was safe. Or as safe as one could be when we were still in enemy territory.

I reached up and rubbed her nose. She snorted softly, her breathing hard and the scent of her sweat stinging the air. She'd run a long way to find me.

"You, my darling girl, can have carrots any time you damn well please from now on."

She snorted and pushed my shoulder. *Want now.*

I laughed. *Sorry, we have to get home first.*

Then we go.

No. Rest first.

No need. Am strong.

Yes, my darling girl, you are.

I nevertheless waited until her breathing had eased before pushing upright. Every muscle I possessed went into immediate spasm mode. I groaned, pressed my hands against my knees to keep them locked, and breathed deep in an effort to control—or at least ease—the wash of pain.

It seemed to take forever.

Eventually, I sheathed my sword, then grabbed a fistful of dark mane and dragged myself onto Desta's back. She immediately turned and left the cave. The minute we were in open ground, she broke into a gentle canter. I moved with her easily, gripping lightly with my thighs, not needing to guide her or even to hold her mane to keep on. She and I were long used to traveling without bridle or saddle; in fact,

I'd made a habit of it whenever I went out to see the drakkons. If something ever happened to me, I'd wanted her free and unhindered by any form of restraints to either return home or wander the lower grasslands as she pleased.

Dawn was once again creeping rose-colored fingers across the sky when I heard the shout. I pulled Desta up, my hand on my sword as my gaze swept the long shadows ahead.

Another shout. Desta snorted and, through my contact with her, I felt my mother's presence. A heartbeat later, four figures crested the horizon and galloped down the long path meandering through the portion of bog still dividing us.

Relief hit so hard it left me shaking. I did the whole deep breath thing again and fought the urge to send Desta flying toward them. This area was a dangerous place for the unwary and had to be navigated carefully.

My mother, it seemed, hadn't gotten that notice. Her mount—a huge gray stallion—flew across the land, leaving the other three in her wake. My father wasn't amongst them, but that wasn't surprising. He'd no doubt be involved in the search for survivors along our shorelines.

I kept Desta's pace even, but couldn't stop the smile that grew ever wider as we drew closer. Mom's gaze swept me critically and then rose, the sheen of tears bright in her blue eyes. She didn't normally show her emotions in public but, as we stopped our mounts side by side, she leaned across, wrapped her arms around my shoulders, and hugged me fiercely. "I feared you dead for the longest of times."

Tears fell, hers and mine, but for several minutes, I neither moved nor replied. I simply hugged her back, enjoying being in her safe arms once again.

Eventually, she pulled away, her gaze sweeping me again, this time a little more critically. Mom's home—Jakarra—was the largest of the five islands that lay to east of Hopetown, and like many of her island kin, she had thick, wiry hair that was the same brownish red as her skin. While I'd gotten my darker coloring from my father, I'd inherited her lean build and—according to my father—her fierce tenaciousness.

She gently thumbed the tears from my cheek, her touch so cool against my overheated skin. "I cannot see any injuries, but—"

"Other than exhaustion and a bit of sunburn, I'm fine." I hesitated. "Were there any other survivors?

"A few boat fragments and five bodies are all that has washed up on the beach so far."

Meaning she'd been down on the beaches alongside my father until she'd felt my presence in Desta's mind. "Rutgar?"

"Unknown."

I closed my eyes and sent a silent prayer to Vahree to care for all the souls lost in the attack.

"Your father," she continued, with just the lightest trace of amusement in her voice, "did warn Damon you were too damn ornery to die."

"I bet *that* ruined his day."

She laughed. "Probably. Let's get you home." Her gaze moved from mine. "Ren, take point. Deni and Cal, rear guard."

She nudged her mount on, then handed me a pouch containing trail rations. "What happened out there? Oran's never failed us before—"

"He didn't. We were attacked."

Her gaze snapped to mine. "By the same force that attacked Eastmead?"

"Unknown, but likely."

She swore colorfully, and a smile tugged my lips. The bow master was never far away, even though she'd been immersed in palace life for nigh on forty years now. "As much as I'd like a full report, it can wait. Let's get you home and rested first."

I nodded and undid the pouch; it was little more than nuts, hard cheese, and dried meats, but it went some way to stopping the terrible, gnawing ache in my gut.

It took another two hours before Esan came into sight. She was situated in a mountain pass known as the Eastern Slit—an angular break created by a long-ago eruption that sliced right through the mountain. Water tumbled from the edge of the upper slice to the lower, a leaping, silvery stream of water that plunged into the deep pool dominating the entrance of the Slit. The fortress's wall was barely visible through the wash of rainbow spray, but rose at an angle, a thick blot of darkness as smooth as the sides of the mountain pass it spanned. No Mareritt had ever breached that wall or gotten into Esan itself, though that was due in no small part to the earth mages who used their ability to manipulate earth to fortify her during an attack.

The clarion call of trumpets announced our arrival. By the time we'd crossed the lake's wooden drawbridge and were riding toward Esan, the vast metal gates were open and my father—aboard his brown mount—galloped toward us. I was a little surprised that Damon wasn't with him, and I absolutely hated the sliver of disappointment that stirred.

My father swung his stallion around to ride on the opposite side to my mother. "Glad to see you're safe and alive, daughter."

"Glad to be safe and alive, Father. It was touch and go for a while."

"We'll need a full report—"

"*Not* before she bathes and sleeps," my mother cut in curtly.

"One of these days, Marin, you'll let me finish a sentence."

"Miracles are not unknown," she replied, amusement evident.

He snorted. "As I was about to say, it can wait until tomorrow. Damon should be back—"

"Where's he gone?" I asked.

"Like mother, like daughter," Rion muttered. "Bless the gods for only giving us one—I'm sure I would have lost the capacity to speak had we any more."

"When you get perfection the first time, there is no need for others," I murmured.

Mom laughed. "A truth I have often stated."

"He is," my father said, the amusement in his eyes belying his severe tone, "still with the party searching the accessible shoreline for more survivors."

"They've found no more?" Mom asked.

"One, though he has lost a limb, and it is unknown whether he'll survive. But that is not unexpected."

Because the Throat rarely releases those she claims.

We rode through the gates and into the deep tunnel that ran under the walls. Portcullis slots were placed every twenty feet, and there were regular murder slits in the ceiling. If the Mareritt ever *did* get this far, they'd be greeted by boiling liquid.

Once out of the tunnel, we wound our way through the military section then on through the various public levels until we reached the main keep. It was a vast building built into the sheer rock face and made of the same black volcanic stone. The palace was a rather grim and unadorned structure that really didn't fit the name.

We rode underneath the secondary wall—another huge structure that hosted not only the war room, but also all the administrative facilities for both the military and the city—and came into the main courtyard from the tunnel.

I halted, dismounted, and rubbed Desta's ears as a stable boy approached. "I promised her plenty of carrots, Mik."

"More than her daily ration, then, Captain?"

"Double it. And add an apple. She deserves it."

He nodded and lightly grabbed her mane. "Come along then, my girl."

As the two of them disappeared, I turned and followed my parents up the steps to the palace's vast metal doors. The entrance hall was small but bright, thanks to the heavily fortified light wells cut into the ceiling, and the colorful tapestries and paintings adorning the walls. A grand black stone staircase dominated the central space and swept up to the accommodation quarters, both private and those for guests. To my right was the grand hall, and to the left, the kitchens, buttery, and stores. Tucked behind the staircase was our private chapel.

It was only when we reached my apartment and were totally alone that my father wrapped me in his big strong arms and held me tight.

He didn't say anything. He didn't need to. It was all there in his hug, and in the kiss he eventually brushed on the top of my head.

"Rest as long as you need to. The report can wait."

I wasn't so sure that it could. I pulled the metal feather from my pocket and handed it to him. "Ask the smiths if they know what this is made of and whether they've ever seen anything like it before."

He accepted it with a frown. "Why?"

"Because one of these things sliced Oran's face in half. I found this one in the pouch of a Mareritt."

His gaze shot to mine. "You think this is part of a new weapon they're developing?"

I hesitated. "I don't know, but we were a long way out to sea when the attack happened."

"No more questions," Mom cut in. "Let her bathe and rest, Rion."

He looked set to argue for a moment, then simply nodded and headed out. Mom cupped my elbow and lightly guided me across to the bathing area. "Shall I order you a meal before I leave you in peace?"

"That would be great." I quickly hugged her. "Thank you for coming to find me."

She laughed softly. "My darling girl, not even a full battalion of Mareritt could have stopped me once I'd felt you in Desta's mind. Rest up. We'll talk more in the morning."

She kissed my forehead, then left. I ran the bath, then stripped off and stepped in. By the time the hot water had soaked away the worst of the aches and I'd eaten a good portion of the mountain of food she'd ordered, I was all but dead on my feet. I walked across to the sleeping platform, crawled under the blankets, and was asleep before my head hit the pillows.

It was the awareness of being watched that eventually woke me. My hand slid instinctively under the pillow for the knife I habitually kept there, my fingers closing on the hilt a heartbeat before I recognized the warm, spicy scent teasing the air.

Damon.

"What in Túxn's name are you doing in my room?" I released the knife's hilt, then pushed the tangled strands of hair out of my face.

He'd pulled one of the lounging chairs up close to the sleeping platform, on which he rested his bare feet. His closely shaven head gleamed like newly oiled blackwood in the sunlight streaming through the light well above us, highlighting the sharp but very pleasing planes of his face. His linen gambeson was undone, and his undershirt open at the neck, providing teasing glimpses of his muscular chest and stomach, while his leathers hugged the rather impressive mound of his crotch and emphasized the lean and powerful length of his legs.

Desire stirred, as did amusement. At least physical attraction was never going to be a problem for me. Who knew what *he* actually felt.

"Technically, it's *our* room given that, for all intents and purposes, we're already married." His blue eyes shone with amusement, and I had a vague feeling he knew exactly where my gaze had been dwelling.

"Then I'm surprised you didn't decide to sleep on the platform rather than simply pulling up a chair." I pushed upright but didn't bother to tug the bed coverings back up. While I might have had my own quarters as a captain, I'd bunked in with six others in the years before that. Nudity was something you grew immune to.

His gaze swept me, brief and somewhat perfunctory. "I considered it, but given your earlier threat, I thought it likely you slept with a knife under your pillow."

I reached under and pulled it free. "And you would be right."

His laugh was warm and rich, and spun around me as sweetly as any caress. It was *very* annoying, this attraction thing, especially given there was very little indication it went both ways.

Unless, of course, the man had utter control over even the most instinctive of physical reactions.

"Your father has called a council for midday. He wishes your presence, if you're up to it."

Which didn't leave us all that much time, given it was close to eleven thirty now. "I bet 'wish' is not how he actually phrased that."

"Well, no." Damon lifted his feet off the platform and rose. "Do you want something to eat beforehand?"

"No, I'll grab something later. But thanks." I tossed the blankets off and climbed out of bed. His gaze scanned me, another of those non-caresses that had heat flaring. I silently cursed errant hormones and walked across to the bathing area, quickly washing and then dressing, all the while uncomfortably aware of the man who now stood near the air slit, staring out at the narrow view it provided of the courtyard.

Once I'd strapped on my weapons, I said, "Ready?"

He turned to face me. "Always."

The smile glimmering briefly in his eyes left me wondering if perhaps I'd been reading him all wrong, even if his ungiving expression suggested otherwise. He was of Zephrine royal stock, after all, and given their womanizing reputations, my lanky lack of womanly features might not be such a problem....

I pushed the thought away, spun, and walked out. He fell in step beside me, and we moved quickly through the palace and out into the courtyard. A multitude of men and women went about the daily business of palace life, filling it with color, noise, and a multitude of aromas, some good, some bad. I greeted those I knew and nodded to those I didn't, then clattered up the metal stairs on the far side and through the guarded doors beyond. We headed right, toward the military areas rather than the administrative, our footsteps echoing, announcing our presence long before we arrived.

The guards at the far end of the hall saluted and opened the heavy metal door as we neared. I returned the salute and stepped inside. The war room was a long but gently sweeping space that ran the full width of the wall. Windows dominated the two main walls; one side provided a view across the courtyard while the other looked over Esan's great outer wall. From this height, the soldiers manning her looked minute. Beyond that wall, Mareritten lay stretched out like a map, enabling us to see any attack long before they reached us. It was a huge advantage the Mareritt had yet to find a way around.

Of course, that might no longer be the case if they *were* the source of the attack on both Eastmead and our boat.

One long table dominated the center of the room, while multiple smaller ones holding strategic maps and troop placement boards lined the courtyard windows. Eight long-viewing scopes lined the sweeping curve of the front windows.

My father sat at the far end of the table. My mother was on his right, while our day- and night-shift generals—Vaya and Jarin—sat opposite her. Damon's father, Aric—a tall, ruggedly handsome man in his mid-years who possessed the same dark skin, blue eyes, and closely shaven head as his son—sat several seats down from my mother. Franklyn, the heavyset man who'd only recently taken over duties as chief smith, sat opposite him.

My father gave me a quick, warm smile before stating briskly, "Captain Silva, please make your report."

I stopped at the end of the table and stood at ease with my hands behind my back. Damon continued on and claimed the chair to my left. I quickly and without emotion detailed everything that had happened, from the moment I'd first sensed the presence to finding the metal feather in the Mareritt's pouch.

When I'd finished, my father scrubbed a hand across his chin and said, "And you never actually saw the things that attacked you?"

"No, sir. But as I've said, I've not encountered a mind like that anywhere within Arleeon."

"So, it *could* be of Mareritten origin?" Aric asked.

I hesitated. "It is within the realms of possibility."

A smile tugged the corner of my father's lips. "But you don't believe that's the case?"

"No. I've ridden through Mareritten multiple times and felt the presence of many of their animals. This didn't have their feel."

"Many isn't all," Aric noted.

"Indeed," Mom said quietly, "but all the creatures of this continent—be they from Arleeon or Mareritten—do have a similar resonance. If this felt foreign, then it most likely was."

"Is it possible what you sensed is a product of magic?" Damon asked. "It could explain why these creatures felt foreign."

I glanced at him. "It could."

He raised an eyebrow. "But you don't believe that's the case, either?"

"If it *is* magic, then I don't believe it is of *this* continent." I waved a hand. "To be honest, the only thing I'm sure of is the fact that we don't know enough at this point to be sure of anything."

"A true enough point," Rion said. "Franklyn? Have you and your team of smiths had a chance to fully examine the metal in that feather yet?"

"Yes," Franklyn replied. "And it's been the cause of many an argument over these last fifteen hours, let me tell you."

"Did you reach a conclusion?"

"Two, in fact." Franklyn's expression was grim. "That metal very definitely isn't of Arleeon origin."

"Have you seen its like before?"

"No."

"And the second?" Rion said.

"That feather was not made by human hand or magic. It is, by all reckoning, the actual plumage of an avian species."

4

"BIRDS MADE OF METAL?" Aric said. "How is that remotely possible?"

Franklyn glanced at Aric. "I don't believe they're made of metal. The blood at the end of the quill very much suggests a creature of flesh and blood."

"Could it be some sort of armor?" Rion asked. "Something along the lines of chainmail worn as protection?"

Franklyn hesitated. "It's certainly an option, but it doesn't explain the blood. *That* is reminiscent of a feather still in the growth phase being shed."

"I don't believe these were randomly shed. The only person I saw hit by a feather was Oran, and while I can't be certain, given the chaos that ensued, it felt like they were targeting him," I said. "It's the acidic dung, more than metal feathers, that's the bigger problem here."

"It *is* possible the dung won't affect stone in the manner it does wood," Rion said, "but I do agree we dare not take that chance. I'll talk to Yaris and see if she can work on some countermeasures."

Yaris was our head earth witch, and a woman of such a great age that she'd probably forgotten more about the workings of earth magic than our other four witches even knew. If anyone might have heard of acidic dung before or could figure out a means of protecting our walls against it, it would be her. As a general rule, water did counter the effects of acid, but how in Vahree's name did we pump it along the walls without sweeping defenders off their feet?

"You'll need to send a warning missive to the rest of your ports," Aric said. "If this *is* the opening foray of a planned attack, there're likely to be the first hit."

"Already done." There was just the slightest edge in my father's voice—he did *not* like being told what to do in his own house. "But what makes you think any assault would center on us here in the east and not the rest of Arleeon?"

"They had the advantage of surprise," Aric said. "Why wouldn't they use it to destroy the major ports both here and in Zephrine? It would have crippled our trading routes and hampered the efforts of any allies we might have called on for aid."

"Perhaps it was merely some sort of preemptive strike," Damon said. "A means of testing and perhaps disabling any sort of defenses they might encounter."

Aric glanced at his son, a hint of... perhaps not contempt, but something close to, in his eyes. Which was odd, given Damon was his heir. "Again, why Eastmead? We're alerted to their presence now, even if the disadvantage of not knowing who they are or where they come from remains. Why would they forsake such an advantage for a place such as Eastmead?"

"As Damon has already said, as a means to draw out and examine a response?" I replied.

"Very likely," Mom said, her gaze on Aric, not me. Though her voice was even, there was a spark of annoyance in her expressive eyes. While she'd always treated Aric with the respect due to him as Zephrine's king and commander, she'd never warmed to the man. Ever. "But until we know more about this situation and indeed what happened in Eastmead, those are not questions we can definitively answer."

OF STEEL & SCALE 53

Aric bowed his head in polite deference. Mom's eyes narrowed. I couldn't see Aric's expression from where I stood, but I doubted he'd be so foolish as to allow his well-known prejudice against women in any sort of authoritative position to show. Not when my father was in the room.

"Anything else, Captain?"

My attention snapped back to my father. "I don't believe so, no."

"Then you're dismissed," Rion said. "And I do believe you have a marriage to get ready for."

Unfortunately. I somehow managed to stop that escaping, but when my gaze met Damon's, the gleam in his eyes left me in no doubt he knew exactly what I'd almost said.

I saluted and left. Damon rose and followed me out of the war room.

"You're not staying?" I asked, surprised.

"There's nothing further I can contribute at this point in time, given how little any of us really know of the situation." He slanted me a sideways glance. "And you're not the only who has to get ready for our nuptials."

I couldn't help smiling. "Somehow, I'm not seeing you being bathed, pampered, and otherwise fussed over."

"I could return that statement twofold." He paused at the exit and motioned me to precede him. "I think it safe to say you're the least 'princessy' princess I have ever met."

I raised an eyebrow. "Given I'm an only child and your father mainly has sons, I think it safe to say you wouldn't have met all that many."

"In that, you'd be wrong. Our trading partners have daughters aplenty, and they certainly wouldn't mind an alliance with a kingdom as rich in mineral wealth as Zephrine."

"And were you forced to give up one of these daughters to marry me?"

"No, I was not." He paused. "What about you?"

I snorted. "It appears the only prince who'd have me had to be forced into it by treaty and tradition—and even then only because his younger sibling found a way around it."

"Yes, but that sibling is a fool now caught in his own deceit."

I swung around to face him. "And did you say that to him?"

While a smile teased one corner of his lips, there was something hard in his eyes. It would have been very easy to believe the two brothers did *not* get on, though there'd been no whispers of such a division between the two legitimate sons on the military grapevine. But then, it didn't have a whole lot of gossip about the illegitimate sons, either.

"No, I did not," he replied.

"Why not, if you truly do think that? And why then did it take ten years to haul *your* ass into treaty negotiations?"

His hesitation was brief, but nevertheless there. "I had a life—"

"Suggesting I haven't?"

"No—"

"Then tell me," I continued, "what was so damn important about *your* life that only a threat to halt trade between our two nations dragged you and your father back to the table?"

His expression hardened. This was not a subject he wanted to talk about. "I was studying offshore."

My eyebrows rose. "Why? Aren't Zephrine's academies said to be among the best?"

"That depends entirely on what you're studying." Bitterness—and perhaps more than a little anger—sparked briefly in his eyes. "In this particular case, my needs were best served amongst my mother's people."

I'd been under the impression his mother was Zephrine born, but obviously not. "Who are?"

"That is perhaps a tale for another time."

"In other words, ask no questions, be told no lies. A fine way to start a life together, Damon."

"It's not so much a matter of avoidance—"

"Then what is it?" I held up a hand to stop the reply. "You know what? Forget it. I'm not interested."

Amusement tugged at his luscious lips and briefly washed the chill from his eyes. "Oh, I think you are."

There was no denying that, as much as I wanted to. There was also no denying I was being utterly unreasonable when it came to my reactions around the man. I even knew exactly where it came from, and it *wasn't* the frustrating way my hormones had fixated on him. It stemmed from my inability to lash out at either of my parents for giving me tradition rather than choice. For denying me what the two of them had enjoyed for close to forty years now.

I strode away. He followed, his gaze burning into the back of my neck, a caress that wasn't, and one that had arrows of desire shooting through my body. I silently cursed them and increased my pace. The vague hope of losing him in the press of everyday life moving through the yard was quickly erased. The man had the advantage of longer strides.

I all but galloped up the steps and strode into the coolness of the foyer. The main hall was alive with sound and movement as everyone readied for this evening's celebratory feast. The thick scents of roasting meats jostled for prominence with the aroma of baking bread, and my stomach rumbled a rather loud reminder that I hadn't yet eaten.

I continued on up the main stairs, well aware of the big presence silently following. At the first landing, I hesitated and looked over my shoulder. "I'll see you in the chapel."

"I look forward to seeing the princess rather than the warrior."

"Then be prepared for disappointment."

His laugh followed me up the remaining stairs. I ignored it and quickly headed for my apartment. I didn't care if he thought I was running away, because in many respects, I was.

I slammed the door shut, then leaned back against it and closed my eyes, trying to control the churning in stomach and mind.

"Well, isn't this the picture of bridal anticipation," a dry and very familiar voice said.

"Dread is a more apt term."

I pushed away from the door and walked over to the seating area. Kele—a fierce-looking but slender woman with closely shaven blonde hair and a puckered scar that ran from temple to chin on the left side of her face—handed me a tankard. The thick richness of the honey mead inside teased my nostrils, and I took a long drink. If anything, it only made the churning worse.

"Why? From all accounts your man is well able to keep his women satisfied, both in the bedroom and out."

I held out the tankard for a refill. "I do *not* want to think about satisfaction. Or the bridal bed. Or anything else to do with the man, really."

Kele raised a pale eyebrow. She and I had been friends for over twenty years now, and she knew me better than anyone else— possibly even better than my parents. Like me, she was a Strega witch, but her ability to call forth and control fire was even stronger than mine. Duty and rotating shifts might have cut into our ability to socialize in recent years, but I couldn't think of anyone else I'd want by my side, be it in battle or as my second in this unwanted marriage ceremony.

"It's too late to fight this, Bryn." She picked up the jug of mead and refilled both our tankards. "You've been signed, sealed, and delivered, whether you want it or not."

"I know. I just—" I hesitated and dropped down beside her. "I just don't want to go to Zephrine. It's not home. It'll never be home. Which sounds utterly churlish, doesn't it?"

Her answering smile was lopsided, thanks to the tightness of the scar. The healers had offered to ease the puckering to make it less noticeable, but she'd refused. She'd gained the scar in a skirmish against more than a dozen Mareritten warriors while we'd been on patrol just over eight years ago now, and it was both her badge of honor and her reminder of those we'd lost.

"I daresay your mother thought the same when she left Jakarra to come here."

"The difference being she loved Dad."

"It's compatibility that's necessary for a happy marriage, not love."

"Says the woman who swore not so long ago she wasn't about to commit to either man or woman if they were too damn frightened to publicly or privately declare their love."

She chuckled softly. "And we both know why."

Indeed. Her two suitors—one man, one woman—were both dragging their heels when it came to full commitment; the declaration was her way of informing them she was getting tired of it. I actually suspected she'd end up with both, if only because Kele was too much woman for one mere person to keep satisfied. Or so she'd declared on numerous drunken occasions in the past.

"The point being—you have the choice."

She nudged me lightly. "It could be far worse, you know. At least he's extremely good-looking, and, from all accounts, not the ninny-hammer his younger brother is."

I laughed. While the whispers I'd heard about Tayte had suggested he was indeed somewhat bereft when it came to brain-power and conviction, he'd certainly been clever enough to get out of the marriage with me—although Damon's comment *did* make me wonder if he was now regretting his choice. I personally hoped that to be true. I might not have wanted to be bound to the man, but I couldn't help being annoyed at such a sneaky rejection.

I drank more mead. "What do you know about Tayte? Damon made a comment today that led me to believe they don't get along."

"Unfortunately, the military grapevine is remarkably ambiguous when it comes to the king's many sons—other than the fact that they all have rather healthy sexual appetites, of course."

A soft knock at the door had me looking around. "Enter."

A silver-haired woman in her mid-fifties appeared. Her gaze swept the room, and her expression became severe. "Your mother sent me here to hustle you along. Just as well, by the look of things."

I grinned and downed the rest of my mead. Patrice had been my handmaid up until I'd left to live full-time in the military section, and she'd always treated me as one of her own—and she had eight of them. How'd she'd found the time to run after me, I had no idea.

"And you, young Kele, need not be looking so amused. You'll not be entering our church smelling like old boot leather. Up, both of you, and get your asses into thermae."

Kele cursed under her breath but nevertheless followed me down to the hot bathing facilities usually reserved for guests. Mom had declared tradition *would* be followed, and that meant soaking away the grime—and sins, if you believed the myths about the heated mineral springs—followed by a full body massage with scented oil. My wedding attire also followed tradition—hair woven into an elaborate braid and a deep red dress made of the finest silk. It skimmed the full length of my body, revealing little skin and yet hiding absolutely nothing—including the fact that I was long and lean, with little in the way of curves. The long slit up the left side was designed to expose a thigh garter for the groom to tear off with his teeth before hauling his lady over his shoulder and carrying her into the bedroom chamber, but I'd let Vahree take my soul before I'd allow Damon to do either.

By the time the church bells tolled in signal for all to move inside, the combination of the massage and mead had at least curtailed most of my nerves.

I slipped on the ridiculously delicate red silk slippers, then picked up my knife and strapped it on where the garter should have been.

Kele chuckled. "Your mother's not going to be pleased."

"She's lucky I'm wearing a bridal dress rather than my sword and full armor. As a captain of the guard, I'm entitled to." And I'd certainly feel more secure in full armor rather than the dress of a princess. I took a deep breath and released it slowly. "You got the ring?"

Kele patted the hidden pocket in her dress. "Indeed, I do."

"Then let's get this over with."

"It's not the end of days," she said gently.

"No, but it *is* the end of life as I know it."

"Make a new one. Or simply just ride that lovely-looking man senseless at night and find new drakkons to play with during the day."

I wish it was that easy. But for me, it wasn't.

"I don't *want* to ride that man." At her raised and very disbelieving eyebrow, I grinned and added, "Well, okay, I do, but that isn't the point."

Kele caught my hands and squeezed them lightly. "You're strangers. You have to give it time—only then will you know if love can grow."

Nothing can grow in barren soil.... I drew in a deeply quivering breath and released it slowly. "I know. But I'd still rather face a horde of rampaging Mareritt than walk into that damn chapel right now."

She laughed and hooked her arm through mine. "Sadly, it appears not even the Mareritt can save you from this odious duty. Shall we go?"

I nodded. As one, we turned and headed out, making our way through the halls and then down the stairs. As was custom, Damon waited outside the chapel. Our witnesses and parents would already be inside.

Kele lightly squeezed my hand in a gesture of support, then moved past us and headed in. Damon's gaze skimmed me and, just for a moment, something stirred between us—something that could have been heat, or desire, or maybe even imagination on my part. *He* looked utterly divine. His rich golden tunic hugged his broad shoulders and the V of his torso, and his pants emphasized the muscular nature of his legs.

"So, it's the princess rather than the warrior who appears." Amusement creased the corners of his bright eyes. "I have to admit, I was expecting full battle armor, with a sword at your back and a knife at your side."

"I considered it, but in the end decided against annoying my mother." I shifted enough that the deep slit in the dress revealed the knife. "I am not without a stinger, however."

He laughed and offered me his arm. "Shall we get this over with?"

"I guess we'd better."

I slipped my arm through his and tried to ignore the heat of his body and my unfettered response. Heard his sharp intake of breath, though I couldn't say whether it was an echo of my awareness or simply a "girding of loins" against the irrevocable change we were about to undertake.

As one, we stepped through the vestibule and into the chapel. It was small but decorated with colorful tapestries depicting the might of the many gods and goddesses that blessed our nation. There were four pews on either side, but only the first two were filled—my parents and Kele to the left and, on the right, Aric and Gayl, an older woman who was apparently Damon's aunt and mentor. Of what, I had no idea, as she'd been keeping well out of my path. It was just one more mystery to solve.

Marshall—the friar who'd looked after the religious health of our family for over forty years now—waited for us at the altar. Kele and Gayl rose as we walked past their pews and moved to stand beside us. Marshall sent a quick wink my way before getting down to the serious business of the ceremony. It didn't take all that long and ended with Kele and Gayl handing us the simple rings made of black and gold stones. Once we'd placed them on each other's fingers, I stepped around the pulpit to sign the chapel's register then moved away to give Damon space. When that was done, Marshall declared our union official in the eyes of the gods. There was no invitation to kiss the bride—this was a business deal rather than a love match, and Marshall was well aware of that.

And yet there was a part of me that mourned the loss. A part that wanted nothing more than to press myself against him, to feel every inch of his warm, muscular length against every inch of mine. A part that longed to brush my lips against his, to taste and explore his mouth until the kiss became a heated, wanton prelude to the passion that waited for us deeper in the night.

Just not *this* night.

Capriciousness, thy name is Bryn.

As the bells rang a second time, announcing the finalization of our nuptials, I once again slipped my arm through Damon's, and we led the way out of the church.

Raucous cheers greeted us when we entered the great hall. By tradition, the ceremony was a private matter only attended by parents and the ring bearers, but the banquet feast was attended by not only the wider family circle, but also as many friends from both sides as could be easily seated within the hall. On our side that was close to fifty—Mom had a *lot* of relations here, and Dad many friends, as he was also an only child and nearly all of his cousins were either dead or too old to travel. By contrast, there were only a dozen or so here from Zephrine, and all of them, aside from Gayl and her partner Joseph, Damon's friends—though in truth, none of them were acting overly friendly. That there weren't more of his father's relatives here was also extremely unusual, and it just added fuel to my suspicions of a rift between the father and his heir.

We made our way slowly to the main table, greeting everyone on the way through. Thankfully, after a couple of quick speeches and a toast to the renewal of treaties and the linking of our two great families for another century, the feasting started.

It was a long night, made longer by the fact I was hyperaware of the man sitting by my side. Every move, every sound, every vague brush of his body against mine had a weird mix of anticipation, desire, and dread pulsing through me. While I was thankful for the attraction, he was still a stranger, and I had a long history of not being intimate with any man until I was comfortable in their presence. As Kele had noted on multiple occasions, I'd probably missed plenty of good sex because of it. But I was the only daughter of the king, and such decisions had always been a matter of self-preservation, then and now.

Of course, the inner tension might not have been such a problem if I simply drank my reluctance away, but I had no desire to give myself an excuse. No matter what happened in our bedchamber tonight—no matter what decision I made in regard to the start of our sexual relationship—it would be done with a clear head.

As the bells finally tolled the midnight hour—the traditional time for our departure—a cheer went up, and two lines were hastily formed between our table and the hall's main doors.

Damon rose and offered me his hand. "Shall we brave the gauntlet of well-wishers?"

"And grain. Don't forget the grain." I placed my hand in his and rose. Heat stirred where our fingers touched and, just for an instant, I saw its echo in his eyes.

"Ah, yes," he murmured. "Though I'm thinking neither of us are quite ready for the gift of fertility it supposedly represents."

"Oh, I think *that* is a really safe bet."

He laughed softly and led me from the podium. Our parents were first in line; I hugged mine fiercely, pretending a happiness I didn't really feel. Mom no doubt saw past it, but my father, at least, looked relieved. Of course, this wasn't our final goodbye—that would come in a few days' time, when all my possessions had been packed for the sea journey to Zephrine. I daresay there would be tears at that point—both his and mine.

Of course, the attack might well put a temporary halt to all that, but now wasn't the time to raise it. But if I knew my mother, she'd have already started discussions on the matter with Aric.

I made no move to greet Aric in a similar manner; his dour expression suggested it would not be appreciated. For whatever reason, the man didn't like me.

A feeling that was certainly returned.

It took a good half hour to make our way through the rest of the honor line; every guest, it seemed, had some vital word of advice they needed to impart about our wedding night or about marriage in general. I smiled and laughed until my cheeks were aching, and I was damnably glad to reach the door, where both Kele and Gayl waited.

I untwined my fingers from Damon's and stepped into Kele's arms. Her hug was fierce and strong. "I'm going to miss you. Badly."

And I her. But she knew that—I'd said it often enough in the last few weeks. "The offer of personal guard is always open, remember that."

"Maybe. One day."

"One day" would forever remain on the horizon, and we both knew it. Her life, her loves, and her mother were all here. She wouldn't—and couldn't, in the case of her mother, who'd been blinded in a Mareritten attack back in the day when she'd been a soldier—leave them.

I forced myself to pull back. "I'll keep in touch."

"Do, or I swear by Vahree, I'll send a flame bird to burn your ass."

I laughed, even as tears prickled. A flame bird was a rather beautiful piece of inner magic in which she crafted a bird out of her flames and sent it winging into the world—though to date, it had only lasted a little over a mile before fading. Zephrine remained well beyond her reach.

"Fail to answer, and I'll send a drakkon."

She grinned. "No, you wouldn't, because you wouldn't risk their safety that way."

That was certainly true, if only because the drakkons who once lived and hunted across the mighty Balkain Mountains were apparently few in numbers these days. I had no idea if that was because they'd been brought to the edge of extinction or if they'd simply left our continent to find safer hunting grounds.

I'd always hoped it was the latter. I'd always feared it was the former.

I hugged her one more time and then left before the self-pitying tears could escape. Damon caught up to me in a couple of strides. "My bride is eager to reach our chamber, I see."

"The bride still wears her knife and is not afraid to use it."

He laughed, but the slight edge in his tone had me glancing at him. His expression gave little away, and his gaze was cool. Reserved. It made me remember that he'd no more wanted this union than I did.

"Relax, Bryn," he said softly. "I have no intention of going where I'm not wanted."

"And I have no intention of bedding a stranger."

"I wish I could say the same, but like most of my sex, I'm sadly unopposed to seeking the pleasures of the flesh with someone I've only just met."

A smile tugged my lips. "I have heard that about you."

He opened the door to my chamber and ushered me through. "You seem to have heard a whole lot more about me than I have you."

"And I daresay what you did learn was derogatory, given it came from your father." I quickly undid the braiding and then ran my fingers through my long hair in an effort to shake loose the grain. The stuff was everywhere, and by Vahree, it *itched*.

"He said you were a soldier. In my father's eyes, there can be no greater sin for a woman, let alone one of royal lineage."

I glanced at him, eyebrows raised. He'd loosened the ties on his tunic and pulled his undershirt from the waist of his pants. A circle of golden grain lay around his feet, and more fell as he shook the loosened material vigorously. The urge to let my fingers play amongst the smattering of dark hair being revealed on his chiseled chest—to follow its lead down his stomach and beyond—was so damn strong I had to clench my hand against it. "Zephrine has plenty of women in their military ranks."

He dropped onto one of the well-padded sofas and kicked off his boots. "Indeed, but you'll never see one lead. They are seen as expendable, as fodder for the Mareritt, nothing more."

Bastard. No wonder my mother didn't like him.

"At least that explains the contempt he was barely concealing a few minutes ago." I picked up the insulated flask of shamoke—a bitter brown bean that was mixed with cane crystals to make a pleasant hot beverage—and glanced at him. "Would you like a drink?"

When he nodded, I poured two cups, then walked across the room, handing him one before sitting opposite. Tiredness unexpectedly washed through me, and I took a sip of shamoke, hoping to stave it off. "It does make me wonder why he didn't call my father's bluff in regard to this marriage, though."

"Remember, while Zephrine is high in mineral wealth, much of our lands are not so suitable for farming. In the end, it comes down to him valuing the trade treaties far more than me." Humor and old bitterness vied for prominence in his blue eyes. "I do, in fact, have suspicions that Tayte's so-called 'surprise' nuptials actually weren't."

"But Tayte's the second son and not the heir—why would he value him over you?"

"Tayte is far more like our father than I ever will be."

"I did get the impression there was some tension between you—"

"Tension is definitely understating it."

"Has it something to do with your mother? I know she died when you were both young."

Once again, his hesitation was brief but nevertheless there. "She died not long after Tayte's birth."

"And your father for some weird reason blames you for that?"

"No." The smile that twisted his lips held little humor. "Her death was something he celebrated, not mourned. She'd given him two official heirs, after all, and that's all that mattered."

"He has plenty of unofficial ones, if what we've heard is anything to go by."

"Fifteen that I'm aware of, but few are acknowledged unless he wishes to use them in his various schemes. Their mothers are mostly serfs and their offspring considered unworthy."

The bitterness in that statement took me by surprise, if only because it wasn't uncommon for lords to take lovers outside their marriage. My father was a rarity in that respect. "What schemes?"

He shrugged, a casual movement that wasn't. "Remember the

daughters of the trading partners I mentioned? A bastard, however little my father thinks of them, makes a perfect lure in trade negotiations."

"Surely said bastards would not go along with such a scheme if they were so neglected growing up."

"If it meant escaping hostile living conditions? Or because it was either that or the death of someone they loved? Most would. Have, in fact."

"Is that what caused the rift between you and your father?"

"That, and puberty."

I frowned. "I don't understand—"

"You haven't heard the rumors? I'm surprised."

Again, it was bitterly said. "I'd heard you were a spell caster—something you confirmed in Eastmead—but I can't see how that—"

"I'm not just a spell caster. I'm a blood witch."

"And?"

Surprise rippled through his expression. "You do understand what a blood witch is, don't you?"

"Blood is your power and, through it, you're able to create formidable spells. To repeat, so?"

He stared at me for a few seconds longer, then threw his head back and roared with laughter. It was a warm, rich sound that had prickles of desire skating across my skin and a smile tugging at my lips.

"Wife, you have no idea how relieved I am."

"Husband, I have no idea *why* that should be so." I took another sip of shamoke. "You forget what I am—a Strega who can call forth fire and command animals. Why would I in any way cast aspersions on someone capable of calling magic from blood, be it theirs or that of a sacrifice?"

"I guess because that's the only reaction I've gotten for too many years now."

"But why? I'd have thought your father would appreciate having a son with such a powerful weapon at his disposal."

"Except it is *not* a weapon. It cannot be used to kill, only to alter or protect."

Protection would still make it a formidable and worthwhile weapon in any sane person's opinion, surely. "Why?"

"Blood is life, not death. It has always been so." He shrugged. "But there's also the fact that it is considered a 'woman's weapon'."

I let my gaze wander down his magnificent length. "Well, I have to say from the little I've seen, you're definitely not a woman. And thank Túxn for that."

"I'm glad the attraction runs both ways."

My eyebrows rose again even as my heart beat a little bit faster. "Does it? Because there's been little sign of reciprocation."

"And this surprises you, given neither of us had a choice in the matter of our marriage?"

"I guess not." I hesitated, then, because I did not want to linger on the possibility of attraction, added, "I suspect neither of the reasons given are the true cause of the rift."

"You see more than most." He took a drink. "My father now believes he was spelled into bedding my mother in order to produce a son who might one day rule the kingdom her people could not take by force."

Which certainly explained why Aric had never grieved for his wife. "Who were your mother's people?"

"They're from Angola, the largest of the floating islands in the Black Claw Sea."

"I had no idea there was an antagonistic history between Zephrine and the islands."

"That's because history always favors the victor over the conquered."

"So, he trusts Tayte—who bears the same blood—but ostracizes you because you inherited the magic?"

He paused, ostensibly to take a drink, but I suspected there was more behind it. "Yes."

"That really makes little sense. I mean, by doing so, surely he's increased the likelihood of such a plot coming into existence—if ever there had been one in the first place."

The smile that tugged at his lips did strange things to my stomach. "You think with far greater clarity than my father ever has in this matter."

"Your father is a fool."

"On that, we both agree."

I yawned hugely and then took a long drink in an effort to batter away the increasing weariness. "Then why hasn't he made Tayte heir? It wouldn't be the first time a second son has displaced the first on the throne."

He shrugged and drained his shamoke. "I daresay he has his reasons."

I studied him for a moment, sensing the turmoil under the calm surface. He knew the reason; he just wasn't about to tell me. "What about Gayl? Who is she, really?"

He hesitated, his gaze briefly flicking from mine. "She's my aunt, and I asked her here to stand in my mother's place. She never inherited the blood magic, though. I am, in fact, the first in two generations of my mother's line to do so." He placed his cup on the nearby table. "But enough of me for tonight. You, wife, should go to bed before you fall asleep in your shamoke."

"Do you intend to accompany me to that bed?"

Amusement warmed his eyes. "Do you intend to wear your stinger?"

"Indeed. But the bed is big and I'm fully capable of resisting the lure of sexual attraction."

"I'm once again gratified to hear it exists—it bodes well for our future together." He bowed gracefully and motioned toward the platform. "After you, dear Bryn."

I smiled and moved ahead of him. Once I'd removed my dress and climbed under the blankets, I watched with pleasure as he unhurriedly stripped off. There wasn't an inch of fat on the man; he was lean, long, and muscular in all the right places and hung like a stallion. All I wanted to do was explore every glorious inch of him with hand and tongue, to feel the heat of him on me, his thick length in me. To lose myself to fires of passion without the fear of ulterior motives haunting the back of my mind.

But I couldn't so easily erase the years of caution. Not even for the man who was now my husband.

He climbed into the far side of the bed and turned toward me. "Sweet dreams, wife."

"Remember the stinger, husband."

He laughed softly, his blue eyes sparkling in the wash of moonlight filtering down the light tube above the bed. "I will, as long as you remember a man has little control over instinct when he's asleep and the heat of a woman is pressed close."

"As long as you remember a soldier sleeps light and both instinct and training often kick in before full wakefulness."

"It could be an interesting night. I'll see you in the morning."

With that, he turned around. Within minutes, the deepening sound of his breathing suggested he was asleep. I wasn't all that far behind him.

I woke who knew how many hours later wrapped in the warmth of Damon's body and with an odd sense of doom pounding through my veins.

The light tube above us showed gentle wisps of pink beginning to stain the night sky, suggesting it was close to six. The room remained wrapped in shadows, and though several coursers were neighing in the stables, there was little noise coming from the main courtyard.

So, what had woken me? Why did unease pound through my veins?

I slid free from the arm that lightly held me and slipped out of bed.

"Something wrong?" Damon immediately asked.

"I'm not sure."

The platform creaked slightly as he rose from it. I padded across to my wardrobe, quickly pulling on my leathers and boots. After re-strapping my knife on, I headed for the door.

Damon met me there, fully dressed and armed. "If it was the Mareritt, the alarms would surely have sounded."

"It's not the Mareritt. It's something else."

I clattered down the stairs and strode through the empty foyer. Guards appeared and quickly unlocked the doors. The air outside was crisp and cold, the sky bright with the flags of dawn. I ran down the steps, only half watching where I was going, relying on instinct and habit as I scanned the dark mountain that loomed high above us.

Then I heard it—the deep, haunting bugle of a drakkon. One that was moving toward Esan rather than away.

Another call, more urgent than before, and the deep pulse of unease flared into dread.

This wasn't the battle cry of a drakkon.

It was a desperate call for help.

And it was coming from the queen.

5

SHE APPEARED A FEW SECONDS LATER, swooping down the sharp mountainside, her body gleaming with bloody fire, and her wings... Túxn help us, her wings were nigh on *shredded*. How she was maintaining flight, I had no idea.

A warning siren started, the wail ringing out across the still slumbering city. I shouted orders for it to be silenced, then ran out into the center of the courtyard.

"What in Vahree's name do you think you're doing?" Damon stopped beside me, one hand on his sword, his bright gaze on the drakkon sweeping toward us. "We need—"

"She's in trouble, Damon, and you need to shut up while I contact her."

I raised a hand, fingers splayed, and reached for her. Felt another mind chasing mine, and realized it was my mother, though she was leaving the bulk of the contact to me.

The queen swooped low, her claws skimming the curtain wall, sending shards of stone flying as she awkwardly sought to slow her speed and gain purchase. Some soldiers scattered. Others raised swords and crossbows.

"Stand down!" I shouted again. "Under no circumstances is anyone to attack."

She bellowed again, her head snaking left and right, her unease singing through me. Her murderous claws dug into the hard black stone, and she kept her wings outspread and fanning, ready to take off —to react—if attacked. In the brightening light of day, it was very evident it wasn't only her wings that had been nearly shredded—black blood poured from a dozen different wounds across her body.

What's happened? Who did this? I asked.

She bugled again, the sound haunting, desperate. *Attacked. Need help.*

"Bryn—" Damon said, but I raised a hand, stopping the question I had no time for.

For you? I hesitated, fearing I knew the answer before I even asked. *Or for your young?*

Young. No time. Must come.

How?

Carry. Hurry.

I sucked in a deep breath and released it slowly. I'd always trusted her, but this... this was insane.

Please, she added. *They die.*

Oh *no*....

Footsteps had me spinning. Mom ran across the courtyard, one hand clutching her gown and the other gripping a large backpack. My father was behind her, but his gaze was on the massive drakkon who'd claimed the wall, his face a mix of awe and trepidation.

"Trust her and go." Mom tossed the pack toward me. "I'll unleash Veri and follow through her."

I caught the pack with a grunt and slung it over my shoulders. It was damnably heavy, meaning Mom had packed it with everything she thought I might need for drakkon repair—even if repair was not something Esan had *ever* done when it came to drakkons.

"Will someone tell me what in Vahree's name is going on?" Damon said, the slightest hint of command in his voice.

A hint that held echoes of his father.

A reminder that for however different he seemed, he'd been raised in a house and a kingdom that saw women as little better as serfs or Mareritt fodder.

"The queen needs my help."

"With *what*? And why would she come to you?"

Meaning my father hadn't mentioned why I'd been out near Eastmead.

"Long story. Stay here." I looked at my father. "Whatever you do, don't leave—or even react—until we're gone."

"Bryn, you can't—"

"Someone—or some*thing*—has attacked her drakklings. I can't *not* do this."

My gaze returned briefly to Damon, then before common sense got the better of impulse, I rose onto my toes and kissed him. He stiffened briefly, then slipped his arm around my waist and pulled me closer, pressing my length against the warm hardness of his. Our kiss deepened, became far more than what I'd initially intended. He was passion and need and urgency, and it drew me in and swept me away, until there was nothing more than him and me and the desire that threatened to burn out of control between us.

The queen bellowed—a demand to hurry. I pulled back sharply, my breath shallow and quick. I stared at him for the longest of seconds, utterly surprised by what had happened. Never, ever, had I been kissed as thoroughly as that. Never, ever, had it affected me as fast or as deeply.

This thing between us—whether it was mere passion or something deeper—was dangerous.

Not physically. Emotionally.

"While I've never been averse to kissing a pretty woman, especially now she's my wife," Damon said, his voice soft, his eyes glowing with twin fires of desire and amusement, "I still need to ask... why?"

"I just thought I'd better at least taste my husband's offering in case I don't survive this."

"Survive what? What exactly are you going to do?"

It was impatiently said, and I touched his arm. "I'm sure the queen will explain soon enough."

"That is hardly comforting, given I cannot hear her."

"No, but Mom can. Stay here."

I turned and ran for the stairs. Damon immediately followed. The queen bellowed, and her head snaked down, sharp teeth bared in warning and her mind filled with sudden anger. Not at me—at the man behind me.

They kill came her thought. *They always kill.*

Men, she meant, not Damon in particular.

I spun and placed a hand against Damon's chest. Felt the rapid pounding of his heart underneath my fingers. Saw the determination and flick of anger in his eyes. Whether at me or the queen or something else, I had no idea.

"You need to step back, or she will kill you."

"This is insane, Bryn—"

"Yes, it is, but it's also who I am. Now, step *back*."

His gaze cooled, sweeping briefly between me and the queen. Then he nodded and retreated.

The queen huffed, a sound that was an odd mix of amusement and satisfaction. She'd been following the conversation via our mind link, I realized, even though I'd thought it closed. Which meant our connection was not only far deeper than I'd initially thought, but she could initiate it as easily as me.

I turned and bounded up the rest of the steps, then raced around the wall toward her. She shifted, watching me, her black eyes gleaming like diamonds in the morning light. Tears. There were tears in her eyes. The realization hit like a hammer, and it felt like my heart was about to break.

I slid to a halt several yards in front of her. She towered above me, her legs thicker than my torso and the smallest of her claws larger than my head. The wind of her wings streamed my hair behind me, and the stink of her blood hung heavily on the air.

I gulped, swallowing the wash of instinctive fear. *How do we do this?*

I rise. Will grip you.

My gaze darted back to those claws, and I swallowed heavily again. I'd seen what her weapons had done to capras and had no doubt they'd dispatch me just as easily.

Trust, she said. *Need go now.*

I sucked in another breath and then nodded. *Let's do this.*

Her wing sweeps immediately increased in power, and the air swirled viciously around me. I braced my feet then lowered my head in an effort to keep the loose grit and sharp shards of stone out of my face and eyes.

Slowly, ever so slowly, she rose. Her blood rained around me, and her effort and pain swam through my mind, making my heart race in sympathy. Or maybe that was fear caused by the knowledge of what was about to happen.

Her claws reached head height. I held my breath, waiting. Fearing.

Then, with a gentleness that belied her great size, her claws enclosed me. I raised my arms at the last moment, wanting them free, needing to grip on to her top talon even if it was neither necessary nor practical. If she intended to drop me from a very great height, I doubted I'd be able to hold on for very long.

She continued to slowly rise. My feet left the stone, and I briefly closed my eyes, once again quelling fear. When I opened them, I was staring straight into the blue of Damon's gaze. There was little emotion evident in his expression and yet their turbulence boiled through me. It was a whisper of possibilities that would never be explored if I didn't survive this.

My mother was nowhere to be seen, but my father now stood beside Damon, staring up at me. They weren't alone in that—the soldiers on the wall and those coming out into the courtyard all watched as the creature we'd once hunted to near extinction lifted me. Then, with a tip of a wing and a mighty roar, she turned and soared away from the city. And, possibly, safety.

As we rose ever higher, she tucked her talons closer to her body, shielding me as best she could from the turbulent air. That air soon became so cold and fierce it felt like I was inhaling icicles. I reached for the inner flame in an effort to keep warm; leather was a great insulator against the cold and icy winds that often blasted this area, but when it came to warmth, it definitely helped to be wearing one or more woolen or silk garments underneath to help with insulation. In my rush to get out into the courtyard, I'd skipped the latter.

Her grip remained tight but not crushingly so. I nevertheless kept a fierce hold of her scaly talon, not daring to look down, not wanting to see how far below us the ground was.

We swept around the Black Glass Mountains and then out over the wildlands that skimmed the foothills for hundreds of miles before sweeping down to the sea and the port of Hopetown. The area was sparse, and inhabited mainly by longhorns—large, hairy ruminants with horns that stretched at least three feet either side of their blunt heads. While they were by nature intractable, farmers had for centuries crossbred them with bovine to produce an animal that could be used for multiple purposes—neutered bulls to pull carts and plowing equipment, and cows for their fat-rich milk. I had no idea the drakkons hunted here, but it did make sense. If they continually fed in the valley, they would have wiped the capras out very quickly.

Drakkons were a whole lot smarter than many human hunters, it seemed.

Eventually, we left the hills and dropped toward the golden plains. A blob of red became visible in the distance and, as we drew closer, I realized it was the little male. He lay unmoving on his right side, one wing underneath him and the other covering his body. The odd angle at which it rested very much suggested it had been broken in several places. His neck lay stretched out on the ground, and he wasn't moving; there were multiple open wounds across his body, and the nearby grass was stained black with blood.

His sister stood to one side, her bright chest slashed open, the cut seeming as thick as my fist. One golden wing trailed on the ground, shredded and broken. The other wasn't in much better shape, even if the main phalanges looked whole. She whipped her head from side to side, the nubs of her still forming horns gleaming with golden fire in the early morning light. She keened, a sound so filled with anguish and pain that it lanced my heart and brought tears to my eyes.

The queen circled her drakklings, her movements unstable as we slowly dropped height and speed. My grip tightened instinctively on her claw, my pulse rate high as the ground swept toward us. A heartbeat before it appeared we were going to crash, she somehow banked and hovered ten or so feet above the ground.

Will release, she said.

I eased my death grip on her talon. *Ready.*

She opened her claw. I dropped into a crouch and remained there, never so grateful in my entire life to be on solid, unmoving ground. She swept over the top of me and landed next to her drakklings. Her neck briefly looped around that of the little female, and it looked for all the world like she was comforting her. Then she gently—carefully—nosed the little male. He was nowhere near the size of the queen—and males were always smaller than females, no matter what their age—but his angular head was still larger than Desta's entire body.

He was also very dead. I knew that even before her keening joined that of the female. There was simply too much blood staining the ground for him to have survived.

I didn't move. I wasn't a fool. She was a mother who'd just lost one of her young, and I had no desire to risk instinct overriding her need for my help.

As they filled the air with their grief, I bowed my head and silently prayed for Vahree to take the little male's soul and cherish it.

That's when I saw the glimmer of gold.

Not just any old gold, but the tip of what looked to be a feather made of that precious metal.

I carefully dug it out of the ground. Though larger than the feather that had taken Oran's life or the one I'd found in the young Mareritt's treasure pouch, it was very definitely from the same type of creature.

I swore and looked up at the drakkons. Damon had suggested the attack on Eastmead might have been preemptive—a means of testing and perhaps destroying our defenses. Did that explain the attack on the drakkons? They might dominate our skies, but in reality, they had little in the way of defense other than their claws. They killed livestock and, in the bad days during our war with them, men with equal ease, but the ballistas had swiftly proven how easy they were to destroy. But against a flighted creature whose feathers were both a weapon and a shield, they'd have little chance. Not without getting dangerously close.

Was that what happened here? Was that why the queen bore so many wounds? Had she been desperately trying to shield her young against flighted beings unlike any seen before in our lands?

I very much suspected that was the case.

I slipped the feather into a pocket and then rose and took a careful step forward. The queen's head snapped around and, just for an instant, murder filled her eyes and mind.

I instinctively raised my hands, fire flickering across my fingertips, even though I doubted I'd ever be able to flame hot enough to toast a drakkon her size.

You still have one drakkling, I quickly said. *She still needs help.*

For several minutes she didn't move, but the wash of her anger gradually faded, and my breathing eased.

Come, she said. *Help.*

And your drakkling?

No hurt you.

I unslung the pack and cautiously moved forward. A golden head slipped under the queen's neck, and the little female watched my approach with interest, her gaze intent. It rather reminded me of a spider waiting for just the right moment to pounce on its prey. There was certainly no fear in the backwash of her emotions I was receiving via my connection with the queen, but then, she hadn't really learned to fear us. The queen had because she'd been alive—if very young—in the bad days.

I walked under the queen's neck; she shifted, and one massive talon came a little too close for comfort. I sucked in a breath, my pulse rate stuttering for several beats as I forced my feet on. I trusted the queen, but in truth, I was little more than a gnat that could be so easily squashed by one unintended movement.

I came out from under her neck and paused to study her drakkling. The wound on the female's chest was even bigger than it first appeared, and would need to be closed to help it heal. From the little interaction I'd had with injured drakkons, they appeared to heal fast, but I doubted one so young could easily repair a wound so deep I could shove most of my arm into it.

And she certainly wouldn't be able to heal the broken wing. One of the reasons the ballistas had been so successful was because they'd targeted the massive wingspan of the drakkons, bringing them to ground and making them easier to dispatch.

The drakkling snaked her head down and rested it on the ground in front of me, her dark eyes gleaming with sorrow and curiosity. I hesitated, and then slowly reached out to scratch the ridge above her eyes. She jerked back in surprise, her teeth bared in warning. The queen made a low sound deep in her throat, and the little female tilted her head, studying me. Then she lowered it again. I accepted the invitation and scratched the eye ridge one more time. A low sound rumbled from her—pleasure.

I glanced up at the queen. *Will it scare her if I talk directly to her?*

Gria.

I blinked. *Her name is Gria?*

Yes.

I don't know why it surprised me that drakkons had names. They were at least on par intelligence-wise with humans and, for us, names had always been a means of not only differentiating one person from another, but often also their location and ancestry.

Do you have a name?

She studied me for a moment. *Kaia.*

I'm Bryn. I immediately widened my mind beam and then added, *Gria, I need to come closer and look after your wounds.*

She once again jerked back in surprise, her head snapping left and then right, as if looking for the source of the sound inside her mind. The queen rumbled again and, after a moment, the drakkling said, *Hurt.*

Yes.

Fix?

I'll try. I hated to think what the queen would do if she lost both of them. Given the time it took young drakkons to mature and Kaia's age, she had, at best, only one breeding cycle left. *Lift head.*

Gria immediately did so. I walked under her neck and studied the thick, gaping wound. She was lucky in that it appeared no major arteries or muscles had been hit, but one thing was obvious—no mere feather had caused this. Whether it was a claw or something else, I couldn't say. I'd certainly ask the queen that question later, but right now, Gria was still losing too much blood for comfort.

I moved on to her left wing. Two of the main phalanges had multiple breaks. I could certainly straighten and brace them, and then repair enough of the membrane to give her flight, but she wouldn't be able to fly far. The Red Ochre Mountains would be well out of her reach. I continued checking the rest of her body, seeing multiple slashes that spoke of the metal feathers. The leathery membrane on her right wing was loose and flapping, but that was an easy enough fix.

If there was enough sealer spray in the pack, that was. One spray bottle might serve the needs of a dozen soldiers, but whether I could ever carry enough to look after Gria's wounds, let alone the queen's, was doubtful.

I walked back under her neck. First things first—I needed to stop this wound bleeding so profusely, otherwise there'd be little point in repairing the rest.

I squatted and opened the pack. There were a dozen bottles of both the antiseptic and the wound sealer spray, and at least six bone straps. Enough to get her off the ground and mobile, perhaps, but nowhere enough to look after the queen.

Am good, the queen said, obviously following my thoughts. *Gria unsafe on ground.*

I automatically looked around. While there were no known predators around these parts, it wasn't unusual for farmers seeking to replenish stock or hunters after longhorn meat to be out here. Both would certainly view a stranded drakkon as a prize. The ballistas might have fallen silent, but there was no law against hunting drakkons, and the ivory in their claws and horns was still greatly valued for medicine and even jewelry in some wilder parts of Arleeon.

I took out the antiseptic spray, then took a deep breath. *Gria, this will feel cold and sting, but it's necessary to stop the wound getting infected.*

Hurt? came her response.

A question that suggested she didn't entirely understand everything I was saying. No surprise there, given she'd only be ten or so years old and would have been in the aerie for most of that time.

Yes.

Bad?

Maybe.

I could feel her doubt and fear. The queen made a rumbly sound, and Gria's head dropped a little. *Do.*

I immediately got to work. The wound was so deep and gaping that it took a couple of bottles of both the antiseptic and the sealer to take care of it. The seal probably wouldn't hold all that long, given the stress flight would take on it, but it would hopefully last until she was somewhere safer.

But I definitely wouldn't have enough to fully repair both wings, let alone help the queen.

I moved on to her broken wing. After explaining to both drakkons what I needed to do, I carefully straightened Gria's wing out. Her pain rippled through me, but it was the fierce need to snap and kill the thing that was hurting her that had my pulse skipping along erratically. Only the force of the queen's will kept her in check.

With the wing straight, I positioned and then activated each of the bone straps. Once the broken sections were braced, I pulled the silk webbing from the pack and strung it across the bigger sections of the torn membrane in order to give the sealer something to cling on to. It took a while. By the time I moved around to the second wing, only one bottle of sealer and a few strands of silk remained. I repaired the worst of the tears then took a deep breath and released it slowly. Hopefully, it would be enough.

A high-pitched but somewhat distant cry had me looking up. Veri had arrived, and that meant Mom and whoever accompanied her could only be a few hours behind. I told Veri to remain high, then picked up the now very light pack and moved out from under Gria. The queen stared down at me, her jewel-like eyes obsidian in the gray of the day.

That's all I can do for now, I said. *But she will not make it back to your aerie.*

Not safe here.

I hesitated. *What about the old aerie above my city?*

Not safe.

It said a lot about her desperation that she'd risked flying to a city she feared to seek my help. *None will hunt you there. None will hurt you there.*

Used to.

Yes, but no more.

Still have throws.

The ballistas cannot reach you in the aerie, and none venture there now.

Something flared in her eyes, something unexpected. Humor. *I eat if they try.*

I grinned. *Which is why they won't try.*

She blew out through her nose, the sound sharp with frustration and unease. *No been there. Entrance?*

There're two—one high above the city, one overlooking the sea. The second lies at the top of the interlocking basalt columns that run down to the sea.

I sent her an image of the stepping-stone like structures that had been formed by eruptions so long ago.

Know that. Go there. She shifted slightly, once again shifting a clawed foot dangerously close. *You come?*

You don't need my additional weight in flight—

Capra heavier. You easy.

I smiled. *Perhaps, but my kin come.*

Kin?

I waved a hand to Gria and the little male. *They are your kin.*

You kin. You saved Gria.

I'm sorry I couldn't save them both.

Her grief washed through me, thick and heavy. I briefly closed my eyes, battling the tears that nevertheless pushed past my eyelashes.

We go, she said. *See you?*

I nodded. *Gria's wings still need repair, as do yours.*

I heal. We go.

I moved out under her neck and then retreated. Once I was far enough away, she hunkered down and then launched into the air, her wings pumping furiously, sending a maelstrom of dirt and grass my way. I shaded my eyes with a hand and braced against the force of it, my heart in my mouth. She was barely getting enough momentum to rise thanks to the massive gaps in her wing membrane.

Slowly, ever so slowly, she rose. Gria followed, the still loose membrane on her right wing a bright flag that flapped wildly. She was even more unstable than Kaia, and I watched with no small amount of trepidation as they both fought for height.

Eventually, they were high enough to catch the wind, and as one, they swooped around and flew toward the hills and the Black Glass Mountains beyond.

I watched until they were little more than specks on the horizon and then whistled Veri down. I wasn't wearing a gauntlet, so her talons pierced the leather sleeve of my tunic and dug lightly into my skin. I sucked in a breath but otherwise didn't react. Her claws could never do the same sort of damage as the queen's.

She squawked impatiently, wanting her scrap of meat. I squatted down, untied the pack's front pocket, and found not only her treats but also a chunk of travel bread for myself. I handed her some meat, then undid the small message clasp on her right leg. As she hopped off and strutted several feet away to tear her prize apart, I dug deeper into the pocket, found the stylus, and wrote out my message. Once I'd clipped it onto her leg again, I sent her back to Mom.

As she sped away, I walked back to the little male drakkon. His body was a mess of blood and wounds, but it quickly became obvious none had been the ultimate cause of death. That honor belonged to the long piece of wood sticking out of his eye.

I moved past his jaw and clambered up his neck, his scales still slick with blood. I grabbed the nubs of his horns to steady myself and then carefully moved past them and squatted down just behind his eye ridge. The spear was at least an inch in diameter, and its sides were as smooth as silk, meaning it had been created by human hand rather than nature. I rose, gripped the end of the shaft, and tried to remove it. It had obviously lodged deep into his skull—maybe even as far as his brain—because for several minutes it only released in small degrees. Then, with a loud pop, it came free—and, Vahree help me, his eye came out with it.

My stomach threatened to rebel, and I spent the next couple of minutes sucking in air in an effort to maintain control. I'd seen many a gruesome sight over my years of patrolling Mareritten, and some had certainly involved eyes being torn from skulls in various ways—crude if graphic warnings of what the Mareritt would do to us if we were captured. This shouldn't have affected me, especially since he was already dead. Maybe it was the other bits of matter that had come out with it. Or maybe it was simply the lingering aftereffects of my connection with both his mother and sister.

I carefully lowered the spear and its gruesome catch to the ground then climbed down. The spear's point appeared to be made of the same metal as the feathers and was triangular in shape, with two thick barbs on either side. It had clearly been designed for throwing, which confirmed my hunch these birds were not alone. Someone had been astride them—there was no other way such a weapon could be thrown with such accuracy toward a target such as a drakkon. Not from the ground, at least. In all the centuries we'd used the ballistas, there'd been less than a handful of direct kill shots.

But it was a scary possibility, if true. How in Vahree's name could we battle an enemy who not only could control such creatures but, through them, command the skies?

I moved on, studying the rest of his wounds. There were multiple metal feathers lodged in his flesh, but there was no sign of the deeper gash I'd seen on Gria. I guessed there'd been no need for a closer-in assault when the spear had so successfully taken him out.

I walked back to my pack, sat cross-legged on the ground, and munched on the dried meat and crusted trail bread while I waited for the rescue party.

The sun was riding toward noon by the time they appeared on the horizon. I rose, dusted off my butt, and waved an arm to catch their attention, even if that was unnecessary. Mom was well aware of my location, thanks to her light connection to Veri.

There were seven all told in the party—Mom, her four guards, Damon, and, rather annoyingly, his father. Desta ran free beside them and was the first to arrive. She nuzzled me lightly, hoping for a carrot but quite happily settling for a scratch behind the ear instead, then wandered off to eat some grass.

Mom pulled her sweating mount up and leapt off. Her guards remained mounted and fanned out to keep a steady eye on surroundings. She touched my arm lightly. "You okay?"

"Yes, though being carried aloft in a drakkon's claw is not a mode of transport I'd recommend."

"And yet you are your father's daughter and probably enjoyed every scary minute of it."

A smile twitched my lips. "A fact I cannot deny."

She chuckled softly, but her amusement quickly faded. "How did the queen take her drakkling's death?"

"As badly as any mother would."

"I'm surprised she's not here keening. They tend to grieve for days."

"She has another drakkling to look after."

Mom's eyebrows rose. "Two drakklings is rather unusual these days—was it badly hurt?"

"Barely flight capable. I patched her up enough to get her to safety but didn't have enough silk or sealer to fix the queen's wings."

"At least she remains flight capable. Did she say what had attacked them?"

"No, because I didn't ask. I was more intent on getting them to safety. But it appears to be the same foe who attacked our boat—their metal feathers litter the male's body."

Damon and his father dismounted. Aric went to the drakkling, while Damon walked toward us. His gaze swept me, and relief briefly glimmered in the coolness of those bright depths. "No puncture wounds from a careless claw, I see."

I half smiled. "If one of her claws had punctured me, I wouldn't be standing here to talk about it."

"I'm not so sure about that. Resilience and gumption are not lacking when it comes to the females of your family."

Mom smiled. "I'll take that as a compliment."

"You should." His gaze went to the drakkling. "How was he killed?"

"Spear through the eye." I led the way over. Aric was already squatting next to the weapon and its gruesome prize. "The metal in the spear's head is the same as that in the feathers we've found."

Aric glanced up. His blue eyes were cold and held the slightest hint of distaste. But given his apparent abhorrence of women who did anything more than pander to his needs, he was obviously practicing deep control. "Did you question the drakkons about what attacked them?"

"No, because I was a little too busy saving Gria's life."

"Gria?" Damon said.

I nodded. "The young female's name. The queen is Kaia."

"I suppose you gave them those monikers?" Aric's voice was blunt with barely suppressed derision.

"No," I replied evenly. "Drakkons are very intelligent—more so than many men I've met over the years—and are more than capable of choosing their own names."

His gaze narrowed, but before he could reply, Mom stepped forward and pulled the spear free from the remnants of the eye. "This weapon is hefty in both build and length and wouldn't be easily thrown."

"Especially from atop of a flighted bird," I said.

"We have no confirmation that's what we're dealing with, especially if you've no description from the drakkons." Aric pushed to his feet and held out a hand. "May I?"

Mom handed the spear over. He balanced it lightly on one palm. "It's extremely well weighted. Whoever made this knows what they're doing."

"And not just when it comes to making weapons," I said. "These skirmishes definitely reek of testing enemy waters before committing to a full assault."

"Given the destruction of Eastmead and the downing of the drakkons, we must be dealing with a reasonably large force," Damon said. "So where are they stationed? It has to be somewhere within reach of the continent."

"We're talking about *flighted* creatures," Aric said. "We have no idea what sort of speed or distance they're capable of. They could be stationed hundreds of miles out to sea for all we know."

"Yes, but we can presume they couldn't fly much faster or longer than drakkons," I said. "It takes the queen a day or so of flight to reach the coast from the Red Ochre Mountains."

"Even by that reckoning, the five islands would certainly provide a flighted force a suitable base." He glanced at Mom. "Have there been any communications from the communities there?"

His words hit like a punch to the gut. While my grandparents, one of my aunts, and two of my uncles had all made the journey to Esan for the wedding, I still had plenty of kin on Jakarra—including Garran and his parents. They'd stayed to be with Garran and his wife during the birth of their first child.

"If this force hit the islands as thoroughly as they did Eastmead," Damon said, before Mom could say anything, "there'd be nothing and no one left to communicate."

I shared a glance with Mom. Though her expression gave little away, I could feel the sudden fear in her, thanks to our joint connection to Veri.

"It's doubtful any invading force could so utterly erase the inhabitants of an island as large as Jakarra," she said, "but I'll certainly contact them as soon as we get back."

"If not the islands, then what about the Black Glass Mountains?" Damon asked. "You've no watch stations in the peaks around the Throat, have you?"

"No," Mom replied. "Because there's never been a need. The cliffs are sheer and offer no access points from the sea to assaulting forces."

"Regular forces, not flighted," Aric said, "I would suggest the first thing we need to do—"

"Aric," my mother cut in tartly, "neither Rion nor I tell you how to run your kingdom. Please provide us the same courtesy."

He waved a hand. "It was only—"

"I'm well aware what it was." She gave him a tight smile. "A recon team was sent up there this morning—"

"There was?" I said sharply.

Mom glanced at me, frowning. "Why?"

"I've sent the queen to the old aerie. If recon goes near her, she'll kill them."

"Ah. Send a message to your father, then. They'll probably have passed the old nesting grounds by now, but better to be safe."

I nodded and whistled Veri down. After scratching out the note and including the information about both the drakkons and the islands, I fed her another piece of meat and impressed on her the urgent need to find my father.

As she squawked her understanding and flew away, Mom said, "We should be getting back. It's far too open out here if our aggressors still patrol."

Aric nodded, but his gaze was on the drakkling. "We might as well collect the ivory first—it would be a shame—"

"Touch any part of him and I'll burn your ass," I ground out harshly.

So much for getting into the good books with my father-in-law.

His gaze narrowed to slits. Dangerous, angry slits of bright blue. "The creature is dead. He has no use for either claws or horns now."

"I don't care. You'll not defile his body."

Aric snorted. "That will happen soon enough anyway—or do you think the local scavengers will forgo a feast such as this because your feminine sensibilities—"

"I would not finish that sentence," Damon, tone coldly amused. "Because her feminine sensibilities are well armed and very capable of following through with such a threat."

Aric studied me for a second and then, surprisingly, laughed. "And they'll certainly be a worthwhile addition to Zephrine's might." He switched his gaze to my mom and bowed. "I'll await your lead on my mount, Marin."

With that, he turned and walked away. Mom glowered at his back for a second, then glanced at me. "You'll catch up?"

"Unlikely, given I have no idea how long a drakkling's body will take to burn." And no idea what the queen would actually think of me doing so. But it surely had to be a better option than leaving him here for predators to consume, be they animal or human.

"Then I'll see you in Esan."

I nodded. Once she'd mounted and they'd all departed, I looked at Damon. "I have to say, your father's overall response to my threat was unexpected."

"My father is nothing if not capricious," Damon said. "It makes life at Zephrine... interesting. As you'll no doubt discover."

Something to look forward to, for sure, I thought sourly. "Does that mean you're intending to stay at Zephrine rather than return to your studies with your mother's people?"

The smile that touched his lips didn't quite reach his eyes. "That depends on a number of factors."

"Am I one of them?"

"Do you want to be?"

"I want many things I can't have, Damon. You're in the other category."

Something I had but didn't want.

He studied me for a moment, and for the first time in a long time, I wished my ability to hear thoughts ran to humans rather than just animals. The lovely planes of his face were giving very little away.

"No drakkons fly above Angola," he said eventually. "And that is the home of my heart."

"I'm led to believe no drakkons fly above Zephrine, either, though their aerie remains in the Balkain Mountains."

"Yes, but you can at least reach the aeries from Zephrine, a fact I now suspect is important to you."

I raised an eyebrow. "Such consideration is unexpected, husband."

"There is an old saying amongst my mother's people that goes something along the lines of 'happy wife, happy life'. Especially when said wife is armed and dangerous."

I stared at him for a moment and then laughed. "A worthwhile saying indeed, but one that ignores a basic principle."

He raised an eyebrow, the movement lazy and somehow infinitely amused, even if the coolness remained in his eyes. "And that is?"

"For any marriage to be successful, it has to be an equal partnership."

"A principle I heartily agree with."

"I'm extremely happy to hear that."

The amusement finally touched the corners of his bright eyes. "Especially given the man who raised me?"

"I didn't say that."

"You didn't need to."

No, and it was yet another pointer to the fact that we were more of a match than either of us had realized.

I picked up the pack and slung it over my shoulder. "I need to set flame to the drakkling, so you might want to step back."

"Can your heat burn hot enough to dispose of both flesh and ivory? The latter isn't easy to burn."

"I really don't know, but he's only young, and neither his claws nor his horn nubs have fully hardened."

"Ah."

He caught his mount's reins and walked away. I took a deep breath, then reached for the inner fires. They burned through my body and erupted from my fingers, a fierce, white-hot heat that scorched the grass even though the arc of flame went nowhere near it.

Once the drakkling was fully alight, I moved back and mounted up. The force of the fire pulled at my strength, but that was necessary to ensure it remained hot enough to consume the ivory.

When the drakkling's flesh and bones finally began to disintegrate and the fire had burned low, I broke the connection, then turned Desta around and headed home. Weariness ate at me, and a low-grade ache settled deep in my brain. I couldn't be bothered making conversation, and Damon seemed content to keep it that way.

It was nearing dusk by the time we finally rode through the gates into Esan. Torches lined the streets, sending a flickering golden glow across the dark stone. There were few people about, and for very good reason. The air was now cold enough to frost each breath. Luckily for the drakkons, the old aerie was situated close to a volcanic steam vent that not only warmed the sand of what had once been an ancient seafloor, but also heated the caverns themselves. We'd long siphoned similar vents to heat water and keep rooms at an even temperature during the long winter months, but it did of course come with an ever-present danger. The Black Glass Mountains might not have seen an eruption for many centuries now, but that didn't mean they couldn't or wouldn't erupt sometime in the future. Thankfully, the earth witches we now had stationed here would at least give us warning enough to evacuate the city.

As we rode into the main courtyard, Mik appeared. He lightly held Desta's mane while I swung a leg over her withers and slipped from her back.

"Give her a good rub down tonight, Mik. She deserves it."

He nodded and chirruped lightly to get her moving again. I took a deep breath, then glanced across at Damon. "I have to report to my father. I'll meet you in the apartment."

He hesitated, then nodded and walked on. I spun and headed for the metal steps. The two guards stationed at the top saluted and opened the door. I responded and strode through, my footsteps once again echoing in the hall's stillness. It was late, so the building was basically empty, but I wondered if that was a mistake. We had no true understanding of our foe as yet. For all we knew, they preferred night to day—or, at the very least, the indefinite light that came just before dawn. It would certainly explain their predawn attacks on both East-mead and the drakkons.

The shadows got stronger and the air colder the deeper I moved into the wall complex. I tried pushing some heat to my fingertips, but the inner flames remained decidedly weak. It had taken a *lot* of energy to burn the bones of the drakkling to ash, and that led me to one vital question—would they work any faster against flighted foe who were so heavily armored?

And yet, there *had* to be some defense against them—some way of killing them. No enemy was indestructible, no matter how much it might at first appear otherwise. There had to be at least *one* chink in their armor.

But to uncover it, we needed to find them. *See* them.

The guards at the entrance of the war room snapped to attention and saluted. I returned the action and went through the door. The room was full and chaotic, the noise close to deafening.

Something had happened. Something *bad*.

The islands....

I sucked in a breath and released it slowly. Facts first, fear later.

I scanned the room and spotted my parents at the scribe quill whose pair was situated in the ruling council's offices on Jakarra.

I hurried over. "What's happened?"

But I knew, even before my father glanced up. One look at Mom's stricken face told me everything I needed to know.

"We've multiple reports of attacks coming in from the smaller islands." Though my father's voice was flat, his eyes were bright with barely repressed fury. "They were attacked at dusk, just as the boats were coming in from the day's fish."

"Are there many casualties?"

He waved a hand at the nearby desks. "We're still receiving information, but yes, the numbers are high."

"And Jakarra?"

Mom glanced up at that. There were tears in her eyes. Tears she was somehow holding in check.

"We're still trying to raise someone." She hesitated and blinked rapidly. One lone tear escaped and trickled down her cheek. "But from all reports, it's been destroyed. Totally and utterly destroyed."

6

"NO!" The denial was torn from me. "That's not possible."

"According to the missives we received from Zergon before their scribe went down, the capital was ablaze and none of the fleet made it out of the harbor."

Zergon was the smallest of the five islands, and the closest to Jakarra. Garran had once told me a decent enough swimmer could get from one island to the other in little over an hour.

And if they *hadn't* been able to do that, then Garran and every other person on that island might now be dead.

Just as all the inhabitants of Eastmead were dead.

I scrubbed a hand through my knotted hair and wished I could push back the fear and distress as easily. "But Jakarra has multiple watch stations along her harbor—there is no earthly way anyone should have been able to attack her without the siren being sounded."

"It would depend on which side of the island they swept in on." My father's voice was grim. "Remember, vast tracts of the northern side remain uninhabited."

"But surely someone could have—" *managed to send a warning before the invasion force swept in,* but I spotted Mom's expression and kept the words back and gripped her arm instead. It was a somewhat useless gesture of comfort but all either of them would allow in a public situation such as this.

She smiled—an extremely pale refection of its usual robust self—and added, "We *will* know soon enough, though."

"Rescue boats have been sent?"

Rion shook his head. "Six cutters. They should be small enough to escape detection from any enemy patrol that remains aloft. Once we get a full report on the situation there, we can decide our next move."

I drew in a breath and released it slowly. "Any word from the patrol you sent into the Black Glass Mountains?"

"Not at this point."

I frowned. "They should have reached the Beak by now, even without using the more direct older caverns."

The Beak—so named because it rather weirdly resembled a kayin's slightly hooked beak when viewed from the sea—was one of the smaller peaks in the Black Glass range, but it was the closest to Esan and gave a good line of sight to the Throat. If our enemy had set up camp on that treacherous peak, they should be able to see it. Weather willing, of course.

"I know, and at this point, I'm not willing to risk anyone else going after them."

"I'll go," I said. "I need to see the queen anyway."

"You need to rest—" Mom said, then stopped when my father touched her arm.

He knew, like I knew, that I was the logical choice. Very few people knew those tunnels as well as me, thanks to my long years of wandering them as a child. I'd often wondered if my inherent need to explore was part of the reason Mom had insisted I learn sword and bow. They never expected me to move into the military from there, but hadn't fought the decision either. Maybe Mom's often reticent seeress abilities had foreseen a future where it would come in handy.

"You cannot go alone," he said.

"But—"

"No," he said bluntly. "You're bone-tired, and that's when mistakes happen. If we were not so desperate for information I would not agree, but we both know you'd disregard orders and do it anyway."

"On the pretense of tending to the queen, of course," my mother added. "But your father is right—you cannot and will not go alone."

I nodded. I knew that tone from my childhood. Even the soldier in me wasn't about to gainsay it. "Then I'll take Damon and Kele."

A party of three wouldn't scare the queen, and we'd be able to move quicker and easier through the tunnels than a full patrol.

"Ensure you at least eat something first," Rion said. "I'll send orders to Kele to meet you at the cavern entrance in an hour."

I nodded, lightly saluted, and returned to my apartment.

Damon was standing at the air slit, but turned as I entered. "I've ordered us both a meal. It should be here shortly."

"Good." I slung off my weapons and headed for the bath. A quick hot soak would ease the worst of the aches even if not the tiredness. "The islands have come under attack. First reports are of mass destruction."

Damon swore. "Boats have been sent?"

I opened the water pipe and let the heated water spill into the bath as I stripped off. "Just cutters at this stage. We have no idea what they might be sailing into, and they're not as easy to see in the darkness."

He walked across and sat on the nearby stone bench. Though his demeanor was all business, his eyes glimmered with appreciative heat as I stepped naked into the steaming water. "I take it you're planning to be on the boats when they are sent?"

I recapped the pipe and reached for the soapweed. "No, I am not."

"But you want to."

"Yes, but I need to make good on my promise to heal Gria."

He studied me for a moment. I rather suspected he was seeing what few others did, and not just physically. "But that's not your first priority now, is it?"

I sighed. "No. We've lost contact with the patrol my father sent into the Black Glass Mountains. I leave in an hour to retrace their steps and hopefully find them. Well, you, me, and Kele will be, because we both know you'll not be stopped from accompanying me."

A smile tugged at his lovely lips. "I do like the level of understanding we've reached so early in our relationship. It bodes well for our future."

"You've yet to view me in a shamoke-deprived state."

He laughed softly. "Nor you me, I'm afraid."

Another thing we had in common, then. "This may well delay our departure for your city."

He shrugged. "Our departure is delayed anyway. My father has decided to forgo the traditional celebration of consummation—"

"Which hasn't happened."

"Whether the marriage has been consummated or not plays no part in festivities. You should know that by now." A decidedly wicked smile briefly teased his lips. "Of course, an hour does still lend us time."

"If our marriage is consummated in a mere hour, I will be mightily miffed."

He threw back his head and laughed. Desire skittered across my skin, warmer than the water itself.

"I am, my dear wife, mightily pleased to discover your sex drive appears to be as... vigorous? ... as my own."

"And I, dear husband, certainly hope you can live up to the promises made in that statement."

My gaze caught his and silence fell for several seconds. And yet the air burned with things unsaid, and hopes too new and raw to explore as yet. I barely knew this man, but there was already a connection—an understanding—between us that went far beyond the physical.

Dhrukita, something within whispered.

But that was a tale told to little girls growing up. A belief that while not everyone would achieve happiness in their lifetimes, everyone *did* have a perfect partner—a soul that was the other half of their own. A destiny of the heart, if you will, that echoed down through every life.

It was also a belief I'd never really subscribed to.

This was nothing more than the natural attraction between two healthy, sexually active people. Or in my case, a natural result of being *less* than sexually active in the long lead-up to our marriage.

As for that connection? I was a Strega, and it wasn't unknown for the ability to connect with animals to sometimes bleed over into certain people. It had happened once before, when I was much younger, but he'd died in an attack while on patrol in Mareritten, robbing us of the opportunity to discover if our fledgling connection could ever have led to something more than bone-melting pleasure.

I pulled my gaze away and started scrubbing my skin with the soapweed, breaking the gathering tension between us. "When does your father leave?"

"Tomorrow morning." Amusement ran through his reply, and it wasn't hard to guess why. I'd retreated from what lay unspoken. He hadn't. "He'll send another longship to retrieve us."

"I take it he wants to prepare Zephrine for possible battle?"

"That is certainly the excuse he's given your father."

I glanced at him sharply, eyebrows raised. "It's a lie?"

His smile made a brief appearance but failed to warm the chill from his eyes—a chill that always appeared when he was speaking about his father. "He hates the bleakness of this place. The unrestrained blackness of it. Zephrine glows. Esan glowers."

"That is nature's dictate, not ours." I paused. "Do you feel the same way?"

"It's not unlike the topography of Angola, so in many ways, it feels like home." He held out a hand. "Do you wish me to scrub your back?"

I hesitated, then handed him the soapweed. He knelt behind me and, with long but gentle sweeps, scrubbed away the grime I couldn't reach. It was an exquisite form of torture, having him touch me so intimately and yet so impersonally.

"You've a rather nice collection of scars back here." Though his voice was conversational, it held an edge that spoke of barely contained desire. "The one near your spine is particularly glorious."

"And not a result of battle, sadly, but rather riding bareback in the rain and stupidly falling off onto rocks. Túxn was smiling on me that day, because by rights, I should have broken my back."

"It happened when you were a wild and wandering child, I take it?"

"More like a wild and wandering adult."

He laughed, placed the soapweed on the edge of the bath, then rose and moved across to the nearby shelf holding the drying cloths while I ducked briefly under the water to rinse my hair.

Someone knocked at the door, the sound echoing. "Your meal, as ordered, milord."

Damon bid the man to enter before I could. As our meal was brought in, I stepped out of the bath and into the thick body wrap he held out for me. As he drew it closed, he brushed his knuckles slowly —deliberately—across my breasts. My nipples pebbled, and desire stabbed through me.

I stepped closer, rose onto my toes, and kissed him. It was a gloriously intense exploration of mouth and tongue, one that heated my soul and made my body ache in all the right places.

As the soft click of the door being closed indicated we were once again alone, I murmured, "Touch my breasts like that again without invitation, and your balls will become acquainted with my knee."

He threw his head back and laughed. It was a warm, rich sound that filled the room with delighted anticipation. "Then I shall start wearing appropriate protection."

I raised an eyebrow. "Is there such a thing?"

Surprise flitted through his expression. "Your male soldiers do not wear a box?"

"It would hardly be practical on the back of a courser." I reached past him to grab a smaller drying towel for my hair.

"Not all your scouts are sent out on coursers, surely?"

"Well, no, but wouldn't they be uncomfortable even when walking?"

"They are, but better to be protected than not."

"To which I can only say, thank Vahree breastplates are far less cumbersome."

I wrapped the smaller cloth around my hair and then walked across to the seating area. A number of stews and fortified breads had been laid out on the small table, along with a flask of shamoke and a thick glass of green goop—the healing and revitalization potion Mom made when wounds or weariness were not deep enough to bother the healers with. It was a recipe prized by her family and one handed to each new generation—a tradition I would *not* be following. Despite the fact she swore by it, in my experience it actually had little effect. Worse still, it smelled like a sulfur pit and tasted as foul as I imagined the water from those treacherous places would.

I nevertheless gulped it down, then drowned the bitter aftertaste with shamoke and food. As the time for our departure drew close, I dressed, strapped on my knife and my sword, and then led the way out of the palace and across to the supply stores. I stuffed two packs with everything I needed to heal the drakkons while Damon filled another with trail rations, water, several small but empty vessels—for who knew what—and rope. Then we headed across to the point where the black curtain wall met the blacker mountain. The path that zigzagged upward from that point was long, steep, and barely wide enough to hold capras. Even if we hurried, it would take hours to reach the vent that led into the mountain and the old aerie grounds.

Kele waited close to the path's beginning. My parents stood on one side of her, Aric on the other. He didn't look happy, but I was beginning to suspect that was a normal state for him.

I stopped and saluted. My father acknowledged me and then said, "The recon team were using the blue vein lava tube, so even if the queen had arrived, they wouldn't have disturbed her."

Surprise flitted through me. The blue vein was a small but spectacular tunnel system that gave them a direct run up to the Beak. Unlike many in that section of the mountain, however, it was not the result of a lava flow but rather centuries of fractious earth movements. Consequently, it was at best passable, and at worst, extremely dangerous.

But the fickle nature of the blue vein tunnel wasn't the only danger you had to worry about, because that area was *not* uninhabited. The olm—a sightless, wingless miniature drakkon that could grow up to five feet in length—called those tunnels home. While they fed mainly on mosses and the small vertebrates that lived within the many pools and lakes dotting the underground system, they were also opportunistic hunters. If any of the team had been injured in a rockfall or earth movement, the scent of blood would not only draw the olm, but drive them into a feeding frenzy.

"Where did the last communication place them?"

"A mile south of the Hassleback system."

Which meant they'd been more than halfway through the tube and well beyond the scribe pen's "dead zone." We should not have lost communication with them.

Something had happened. Something *other* than the dangerousness of the tunnel.

Something unforeseen.

"What of the tracer stones?" I asked.

"We're not picking up anything with the receiver," Mom said.

Meaning either the scouts were dead—the tracer's magic somehow used the body's heat to transmit—or the tracers were. All magic could be countered, and the spells on tracer stones were amongst the simplest.

"Given the fickle nature of lava tunnels, how do you intend to ensure this team doesn't befall the same fate?" Aric's voice was clipped, his annoyance barely concealed.

Granted, he was facing the possible loss of his heir if things went wrong, but given the antagonistic nature of their relationship, I doubted he'd really care. Which meant it was either disapproval of my parents' approach to ongoing communications difficulties, or simply his distaste for this place becoming harder to conceal.

"Bryn knows these caves—and these mountains—better than most," Rion said. "She won't get lost."

Aric's grunt somehow conveyed disbelief. "And if the first team are not lost, but rather yet more victims of your unknown foe?"

It was interesting that he said "your" rather than "our." He obviously wasn't seeing this as a country-wide threat as yet, which was rather odd. Why would he think our winged attackers would restrict themselves to only our half of the country? Or was it said merely to annoy my father?

I suspected it might be the latter, especially given his early retreat. Whether he hated this place or not, it was a break in protocol.

But then, Aric had a long history of doing that when it suited him or benefited Zephrine.

"Veri can be sent aloft close to dawn," I said. "I can pass on any images of what we find through her to my mother."

"Meaning the volcanic nature of the stone doesn't interfere with Strega abilities as it does the tracer?" he asked.

"No," Rion said, somewhat curtly. "It does not. And Strega is not a term we appreciate in these parts."

"I meant no offence, Rion."

It was formally said, and my father accepted it with a nod of acknowledgment. But his eyes were cold and his expression set. It was the first time I'd ever seen him show a glimmer of anything approaching distaste for his Zephrine counterpart.

Mom handed me a small pouch that held the scribe quill, writing tablet, and the slightly larger receiving stone. I gave her a quick smile, then stepped back, saluted my parents, nodded to Aric, and motioned Kele to proceed. Once we were underground, I'd resume the lead. As my father had said, there were few around these days who knew the old passages as well as me, thanks to the many years I'd spent here as a kid, dreaming up multiple schemes and stories about the drakkons repopulating the old aerie.

And now the drakkons were here for real.

It might have been brought about by a tragedy, but my inner child couldn't help but smile.

It was well past midnight by the time we reached the vent. It was little more than a three-foot-wide jagged slit in the otherwise smooth rock face, but the air rolling out of it spoke of the heat and danger that still bubbled deep under the mountain's heart.

I slung off my pack and took a drink, my gaze scanning the darkness that shrouded these peaks. Nothing moved through the night; there were no sounds, and no stars, thanks to the clouds blanketing the skies.

And yet, I couldn't escape the sense of wrongness.

It was the same wrongness I'd sensed in the few minutes before the boat had been attacked. While I doubted our enemy would risk attacking Esan before they'd fully understood our strengths and weaknesses, a scouting flyover would not be out of the question. And with the moon and stars hidden, it was the perfect night for it.

"What's wrong?" Damon asked softly.

He'd stripped off his coat halfway up the mountain, but sweat darkened the collar and underarms of his undershirt. The scent stung the air, sharp but not unpleasant.

"I don't know." I flicked the droplets of moisture from my forehead and looked toward the peak we couldn't see from where we stood. "I think something comes."

"A scouting mission on a night such as this would make tactical sense," Damon said. "As would a test skirmish. Keeping the enemy in disarray is a strategy that has proven its merit time and again."

"Yes," I said, "but they're attacking us using flesh-and-blood creatures, and there must be limits in what they can and can't do."

"We have no idea what the origins of those creatures are, or how warped or strengthened by magic they might be," he replied. "Normal limits of flesh and blood—even when it comes to the drakkons—might not matter if altered in such a way."

I wrinkled my nose and scanned the sky once again. Still nothing, but that unease was sharpening.

"Limits or not," Kele said, "it wouldn't hurt to send Esan a heads-up."

"At the very least," Damon said, "they can ready the old ballistas. If they can bring down drakkons, they can surely bring down whatever these things are."

"As long as they don't get too trigger-happy and start aiming at drakkons again, because that would seriously annoy our captain here." Kele squinted up at Damon, mischief teasing her lips. "You haven't had the pleasure of seeing her in a mood yet, I take it?"

"No, but I do look forward to it. A bit of spice is always good in any relationship."

"Spice indeed." Kele laughed and glanced at me. "The man has much to learn about you, doesn't he?"

"We can worry about *that* once we uncover what is happening right now." I tugged the scribe quill and small tablet from the pouch Mom had handed me, and wrote a quick message.

Once it was sent, the tablet cleared, but I didn't immediately put it away. My father, at the very least, would still be up. He'd always been a night owl.

A few minutes later, his reply came through. *Will alert night watch. Have already recommissioned the ballistas and issued standing orders that under no circumstances can they be used against drakkons.*

Relief ran through me. I sent back an acknowledgment, then shoved the tablet and quill away and rose. "We should get moving. It'll take us at least an hour to reach the blue vein system."

Damon nodded and motioned me to precede him. I carefully

squeezed through the vent's entrance, then slung my pack over my shoulders and flicked on a light cylinder. The pale yellow beam speared the darkness, lending warmth to the rough black walls. This wasn't a lava tube and, as such, much narrower than the ones we'd reach higher up. It was, however, easy to move through, lacking the moisture and mosses we'd strike later on. It meant we reached the first of the feeder tubes relatively quickly.

It had been a long time since I'd been in any of these old tubes, but little seemed to have changed. This particular one was spectacular, thanks to the forest of lava stalactites that hung from the roof, and the thick black "high lava" lines that ran its length. The air was warm and still, smelling faintly of sulfur and damp earth. The latter came from the main tube, which was the oldest and biggest of all the tunnels and had long ago been reclaimed by mosses and string ferns.

It took us a good hour of climbing to reach it, and by that time, I was sweating profusely and wanted nothing more than to sit and rest for an hour or so.

But time was against us.

Or rather, against the missing recon team. The olm couldn't harm a drakkon, small or large, but an injured man, however well-armed, would not outlast their tenacity.

"Vahree himself would feel right at home in this place." Kele placed her pack on the ground and stripped off her jacket. "Can it get much fucking hotter, or what?"

"Oh, it can, and does." I stopped and untied my water bottle. "The old breeding grounds are basically a sauna."

"Oh, something to look forward to, for sure."

I smiled. "It's not necessary for you to accompany me there. Once we uncover what has happened to the scouts, you can head back."

"What? And miss the only chance I might ever have to get up close and personal to a drakkon? No way."

I smiled and glanced at Damon. His undershirt clung to his torso, emphasizing the muscular planes underneath, but the man looked decidedly unfazed by the heat. Which wasn't to say he didn't look hot —he did. Totally, utterly, deliciously so.

Thankfully, he was studying the ragged carpet of moss that covered the nearest wall rather than me, so missed my momentary slip into wanting.

Or so I thought until he looked at me. The faintest hint of knowing tugged at his lips, and his eyes were bright with awareness.

All he said, however, was, "None of the tubes within Zephrine have this sort of biodiversity."

"Our earth mages believe the combination of flowing water and heat has created ideal growing conditions." I took a long drink, though it didn't do a lot to ease the thirst—physical or sexual. "At one point I think they were investigating the possibility of developing a greenhouse system here, but were thwarted by the impossibility of getting light this deep into the mountain."

"It would indeed be a massive feat of engineering." He accepted the water bottle I offered him with a nod of thanks. "How far away is the aerie from here?"

I wrinkled my nose. "Another half hour, perhaps, but the blue vein will spin us away from it."

"But the drakkons will still be there?"

"They've nowhere else to go right now. Not until Gria can fly again."

"I'm really looking forward to seeing the little one," Kele said. "You don't often see drakklings these days."

"Given how many mature drakkons we've killed over the centuries," Damon said, "it's a wonder they're not walking the edge of extinction."

"They were at one point," Kele said. "But according to our resident expert here, their numbers have steadily risen over the last few centuries."

Damon offered the water bottle to Kele, then glanced at me, his eyebrows raised. "And here I was thinking you were two years younger than me."

I rolled my eyes. "It was once the duty of all archivists to record drakkon numbers. Esan's still do, though it's a task made harder by the fact they no longer fly over Esan or use the aerie. I generally head out on the annual pilgrimage with them, just to ensure nothing untoward happens."

"Untoward being code for them becoming lunch?"

I wrinkled my nose. "We're more a snack. Not much meat on human bones to satisfy hunger, from what I've been told."

Kele looked at me, eyes a little wider. "Seriously? The queen told you that?"

"No, it was a comment made in passing by a young red I healed some time ago. She was debating the merits of eating humans with me."

"While you repaired her?" Kele looked horrified. "That's kinda ungrateful, is it not?"

"I managed to convince her bovine and capras were on the whole a far more worthwhile meal than us."

My voice was dry, and she shook her head. "Seriously? You're insane."

I laughed and stripped off my jacket. My undershirt, like Damon's, clung to my skin. Unlike his, mine just emphasized my overall lean flatness rather than lovely planes of muscle.

Damon's gaze did a slow tour down my length and came up... well, amused. I had no idea why, because he'd seen me naked a number of times now and was well aware of my lack of womanly curves. I glanced down to check there wasn't something strange hanging off me—a random lichen or crater crawler, perhaps—and then mentally shrugged and bent to tie my jacket onto one of my packs.

"Does that mean the reds still have aeries in these mountains, even if Esan's has been abandoned?" he asked, tone holding none of the amusement I could see. Feel.

"There're a couple of smaller ones deeper in the wildlands they use, but most now roost in the Red Ochre Mountains. They still hunt here, though." I slung the pack over a shoulder. "This way."

I moved out, following the bank of the small stream that had carved out a deep channel in the lava tube's floor. Greenery flourished either side of it, and crawlers darted for the safety of the water, their eye stalks shrinking back to their crusted bodies until we'd passed.

The slope gradually increased, and chunks of stone littered the ground, victims of the tremors that continued to shake this area.

We were about five minutes away from the entrance to the blue vein system when the queen's presence sharpened in my mind.

You come?

Later. We've men missing in a tunnel and need to find them first.

Not eat. Not that hungry yet.

I grinned, though it was such an echo of my earlier conversation with Kele and Damon that I couldn't help but wonder if she'd been listening in.

Once we find what happened to our people, I'll come back and finish repairing Gria's wings.

Good. She paused. *Like here.*

It was once an old aerie.

Know.

Just as she undoubtedly knew why it was no longer used.

Why men missing? Gilded ones?

I frowned. *Gilded ones?*

Images flooded my mind, so fast and sharp that I stumbled and would have fallen had Damon somehow not caught me.

His gaze scanned me in concern. "You okay?"

I nodded. "Kaia just sent several images of the birds that attacked them, and I wasn't expecting it. Hang on for a sec."

I pulled my arm from his grip but didn't step away. The birds were about half the size of drakkons, with a shorter wingspan and stubby, powerful necks. Their legs were long, black, and scaly, their talons thick daggers, and their beaks hooked. The metallic feathers cloaked the top of their bodies but not their underbellies, which looked to be regular feathers of a rich, bloody hue.

On top of them, in what very much resembled the type of saddle we used on our coursers—but with girths around the base of each wing and a connecting leash under the barrel—was a short stocky figure wearing what looked to be chain armor made of golden feathers. This covered them from head to foot, and they wore both a helmet and gauntlets—the latter, I couldn't help but note, five fingered, not six.

The Mareritt weren't behind any of this.

Which wasn't much of a relief. At least with the Mareritt we'd have some idea who we were dealing with.

Kaia, when the birds flung their feathers, did new ones slip into their place?

Unsure. Fighting, not looking.

Censure ran through her mental tone. Understandably so. *Could your claws penetrate their armor?*

Armor?

I sent an image of the golden feathers.

Yes, but hard to get close. Belly better. Unprotected.

What of the rider?

Armed. Killed Ebrus. Flung him.

Ebrus being her male drakkling. *The rider? Or Ebrus?*

Ripped free. Threw to ground.

My heart began to beat a whole lot faster. If the rider had been fully armored, it was unlikely predators could make an easy meal of him. And that meant, if we could find him, we might finally get some idea of who or what we were fighting. At the very least, if their armor was made out of feathers, we could study and test it for means of destruction.

Would you be able to find him again?

Could. Why?

We need to see who kills your kin and mine.

She considered this for a moment. *I help. When?*

Need to find our missing men first.

After heal Gria?

I hesitated. *First we need to head up to the Beak to see if the gilded ones roost nearby.*

Beak?

I sent her an image.

Not seen before.

Unless she flew out across the seas—and few drakkons did these days—she likely wouldn't. *I'll come to you and Gria as soon as I can.*

Hurry. Hates waiting.

I couldn't help but grin. Impatience very obviously was another emotion drakkons shared with humans.

Hunt now, she added. *Gria hungry.*

Has your wing fully repaired? I asked, surprised.

Some healed. Membrane loose. Flight still unstable.

I'll fix that when I fix Gria.

Good.

As the mental connection faded, I refocused on Damon and updated him. "She tore one of the riders off during the attack. He wouldn't have survived the bite or the fall, but if we can find his body—"

"We can finally get some idea as to who is behind the attacks," Damon finished for me. "Do you know where we'll find him?"

"The queen said she'd show me." I hitched my pack into a more comfortable position and walked on. "The birds do have one weak point, though—their underbellies aren't covered by the feathered armor. She just couldn't get close enough to take full advantage of it."

"Should we scribe Esan?" Kele asked. "The sooner they get a description, the better chance they'll have of designing a counter."

"The pen won't work this deep into the mountain. We'll have to wait until we're closer to the Beak."

"Well, that's damn inconvenient," Kele said.

"If that's the only inconvenience we strike under these mountains," Damon said dryly. "I'll consider us lucky."

"A truth I'm unable to argue with, sadly," she replied.

I felt rather than saw the sharp rise in Damon's amusement—another indicator of our growing connection. "And do you argue often?"

Kele chuckled. "Why do you think I've never gotten my captain pips?"

She actually *had* been offered a promotion, but it would have meant moving to another regiment, as it had for me, and in the end, she hadn't wanted to leave her many friends there.

It had taken several long, heartfelt drinking sessions between the two of us before she'd reached that conclusion, though.

Up ahead, the entrance into the blue vein tube loomed. It was a formidable sight, vaguely resembling the sharply protruding snout of the badulf, complete with sharp lava "fangs" not unlike those of the wily plains scavenger. From inside the snout came a faint blue glow—the rock veins that gave this system its name.

"We won't need the light tubes in there." I switched mine off and clipped it to the pack I was carrying on my left shoulder. It was easier to reach than the one on my back. "But keep your hands close to your swords. I've no idea what olm numbers are like these days."

"If the scouting team is injured or, Túxn forbid, dead, then we could be dealing with a frenzy," Damon noted.

"I know." My gaze met his. "I hope they taught you more than magic in the home of your heart."

"I'm well able to handle myself," he said, his voice mild but the faintest flicker of annoyance evident in his blue eyes. "With steel or without."

"In bed and out, too, I'd wager." Kele's gaze unhurriedly scanned his length. "You do have a look of proficiency about you."

His eyebrows rose, expression coolly amused. "And what does such 'proficiency' look like?"

"Oh, you know, big hands, big"—her gaze dropped to his crotch—"feet."

"Kele," I said dryly, "stop flirting with the man. He's taken. At least, he is for the time being."

"Does that mean you intend to use and then discard me, wife?"

"I haven't yet decided what I'm going to do with you, husband."

But it definitely depended on what he intended this marriage to be. I was happy to give us a chance, but if he wanted to continue his wanton ways, fine, as long as he realized there would not be one rule for him and another for me.

I was a soldier. I was not built to meekly sit at home waiting for my husband to give me a second of his time.

And one look at him said he was very much aware of this. What he thought about it, I couldn't say. His expression gave little away, and the tenuous link that sometimes flared between us remained mute.

And that was annoying.

As was my own inconsistency.

I turned from his all-too-knowing but beautiful gaze and strode into the blue vein's mouth. The tunnel beyond narrowed sharply, and the heat became a thick blanket that wrapped around us, constricting movements. The walls ran with slickness, and sharp daggers of rock lined the two main veins, ready to tear at flesh the moment you slipped. None of us did, but progress was tediously slow.

When we reached the first of the cross tunnels, I pulled the receiver stone from its pouch and held it out in front of me. After a second or two, an intermittent pulse ran through it—three beats followed by a short pause—an indication only three of the five who'd started out were alive.

But if three remained, why had no one moved beyond the scribe's restrictions and sent for help? Were they immobilized? Or surrounded?

The stone couldn't give me that information, which was damnably frustrating.

I moved on through the narrow tunnel, clambering over rockfalls and spotting the occasional boot print in the moss hugging the tiny trickle of water running along the floor.

We'd passed the halfway point and were closing in on the area where Esan had lost contact when I heard the soft snuffling.

"That," Kele whispered, "sounds an awful lot like an olm."

"One that's feeding," Damon said. "And the scent of death rides the air."

It certainly did. I raised a hand and splayed my fingers, warily reaching for whatever lay ahead.

And hit minds filled with nothing but blind, bloody ecstasy.

There wasn't just one olm up ahead, there were at least eight.

And they were indeed in the middle of a feeding frenzy.

7

I SUCKED in a sharp breath and resisted the urge to deepen the connection and force them away from both the living and the dead. Aside from the fact there was very little reasoning with *any* animal in such a manic state, it was also very dangerous. Even the strongest mind could be swept away by a tide of bloody lust.

I'd never seen it happen, but there were stories, and they never ended well.

I clenched my fingers around the receiving stone. Three beats remained, even if one was rapidly fading. There was hope yet.

"There're at least eight olm in the junction up ahead," I said grimly. "This tunnel remains single file until we near that junction, and there's no way we can get around them from here."

"What about the junction itself?" Damon asked. "Is there anything that might provide cover for those people or us?"

I hesitated. "We've had a few tremors recently, so it could have changed since I was last here, but overall, it's tear-shaped, with an exit at the point to our left and another directly opposite. A partial shelf that's five or so feet off the ground runs along the wall between our tunnel and the one opposite, but otherwise, it's relatively flat."

"A five-foot-high shelf won't give those soldiers much protection,"

No, it certainly wouldn't. An olm could leap twice that height without any effort at all.

"If they *are* in a feeding frenzy," Kele said grimly, "at least they won't notice us until we start burning their asses."

I glanced at her. "Which we can only do if they're not close to our people."

"If those men are close enough to be burned, they're probably already olm food and way beyond caring."

A truth I didn't want to think about. I once again glanced down at the stone still in my hand. "We've three still alive, but we'll need to move fast."

Damon unsheathed his sword, the blade a deep blue stone. The Blue Steel Mountains were the only place in Arleeon producing stone of that color, and while it was prized for its strength and imperviousness to weather, it was also extremely difficult to mine. Few went to the bother, though I knew Zephrine often used it for spears. This was the first time I'd seen a sword made of the stuff, though.

But then, he was Zephrine's heir, so it made sense that he had the best weaponry available.

"If we split up," he said, motioning with his blade to the junction ahead, "it'll give us the best chance."

I nodded. "I'll go right, and Kele can go left, which should give us better flame coverage."

"Meaning I'm straight down the middle." He glanced at me then added, the seriousness in his expression blunted by the wicked glimmer in his bright eyes, "Please do resist the temptation to 'accidently' cinder the unwanted husband in crossfire."

"You have absolutely nothing to fear from my flames." Amusement danced through me, but I managed to keep my tone serious. "Unless, of course, you do not live up to a certain... shall we say energetic?... reputation."

"What the whispers actually say," Kele corrected blandly, "is that he has great stamina *and* ardor in the bedroom—and that is definitely a good thing. It's all well and good being energetic but a certain amount of intensity and passion is required for a truly great experience."

"The gossips in Esan definitely have sharper ears than those of Zephrine," Damon said, tone dry. "But I'm relieved they apparently approve of my bedroom endeavors."

"I shall also point out that if it is just bedroom endeavors, our girl will be disappointed."

I rolled my eyes at Kele, then glanced at Damon. "Ready to go?"

"Always."

He obviously wasn't referring to the task at hand, given that wicked glint, but I let it slide. Save our people first, drakkons second. If we survived all that, then maybe we could get down to that much needed discussion about what we both wanted—or expected—from this marriage.

Or, better yet, just do what Kele had originally suggested and ride each other senseless.

My hormones were currently leaning toward the latter option. No surprise there, given how little sex there'd been in the lead-up to the marriage.

I tucked the receiver away, then drew my sword and padded forward. The noise up ahead sharpened with every step, changing from a confused babble to something more definable—soft growls, teeth snapping, flesh and cloth tearing, the clang of metal hitting stone. And, ever so faintly, the occasional whimper.

The last had my stomach churning. I had no doubt it belonged to that fast-fading third pulse in the stone. If we didn't get in there soon, he or she would die.

But if we hurried, we could die. The dagger-sharp rocks between the two blue veins were ready and waiting for the slightest slip, and the ground underfoot remained slick.

The tunnel widened as we neared the cross point. I paused, slipped my packs from my shoulders, then held up a hand and slowly counted down on my fingers.

When the last one dropped, we moved in as one.

I called to my flames and ran right. Saw, in swift succession, a man and a woman on the platform, braced against its rear wall, and two olm pacing underneath them; three more olm were in the middle of the junction, tearing into the two bodies lying there, while another paced back and forth just beyond the sword reach of the man sitting next to the other exit. His back was pressed against the wall, and his legs were a shredded, mangled mess.

Six olm. Where were the other two...?

A faint stirring of air across the back of my neck gave me a heartbeat's warning.

I spun, saw two in the air, their razor-sharp teeth bared and blind eyes pinpointing me with surprising accuracy. I flung a noose of fire, caught the first one around its neck and threw it hard back into the tunnel, then jumped sideways and raised my sword, bringing it down onto the second creature's snout, severing a good portion of its mouth and a chunk of tongue in the process. It hit the ground on all fours and shook its head, spraying thick drops of blood and flesh through the air, its roars of pain and fury filling the air. Then it leapt at me again, its speed frightening. I swung the sword, but it somehow twisted away from the blade and lashed out with its claws. They skittered across my right arm, slicing through leather but not into flesh. It had barely hit the ground when it lunged at me again. I quickly backed away, fashioned my flames into a rope, and flicked the lasso toward it. It settled around the creature's neck, and I snapped it tight —not to kill, because the scales on these things were as thick as a drakkon's, and it took more than an instant to burn, but to control. I swung it around, gathering momentum, then released the rope and threw it against the nearby wall with as much force as I could muster. Bones crunched, and fire now crawled over the length of its body, but it didn't seem to care. It simply struggled to its feet and leapt again.

I stood my ground until the very last moment, then jumped out of its way and swept my sword along its body, severing limbs and slicing open the entire length of its barrel. It hit the ground and stumbled forward, its insides spilling onto the stone underneath.

And *still* the bastard wouldn't die.

I sucked in a breath, created another leash, and once again whipped it against the nearest rock face. This time, it didn't get up.

One down, several more to go....

The thought had barely crossed my mind when something hit me from behind and sent me sprawling forward. Teeth tore into my shoulder, while needle-sharp nails scraped frantically at my leathers, as if desperate to reach the flesh that lay underneath.

I bit down hard on the scream that rolled up my throat and went full flame, directing every scrap of heat and fury that remained within me into the heavy creature hanging off my shoulder. It was cindered from my flesh in an instant, but I nevertheless kept the flames alive, chasing its ash down to the ground, just to be sure. Then I drew the flames back into my body, cauterizing the wound in the process.

Cauterizing wasn't healing, however, and Vahree only knew how badly it hurt.

I sucked in another, somewhat quivery breath, caught the sound of sharp nails on stone, and spun. The two olm who'd been pacing the base of the shelf were now coming straight at me. I threw up a hand and unleashed a wall of flame. Pain flicked through my brain, but I knew it was a result of tiredness more than lack of strength. I was a long way from running out of "juice".

The threat of fire stopped one. The other simply ran around it. I raised my sword, but before I could cleave the creature in two, it was caught in a rope of flame and smashed upward against the roof with such force that its head shattered and brain matter exploded.

Kele, her timing as impeccable as ever.

Another olm had leapt up onto the ledge and was now charging at the two people standing there. As the woman raised her sword, I threw mine; it pierced the olm's chest with enough force to throw it sideways and pin it to the wall. The woman then plunged her blade down through the base of the creature's neck, killing it in an instant. I called more flames to my hand and turned, just in time to see Damon kill the last of the three olm who'd been devouring the dead. Another two lay between him and the junction's second exit, one burned, the other missing limbs and a head. Kele now knelt beside the wounded soldier, a medikit—not hers—on the ground beside her. She, thankfully, appeared unhurt.

My gaze returned to Damon. There was a cut on his forearm and a graze on his chin, but neither appeared bad. We'd been lucky. If the olm hadn't been in a feeding frenzy incited by the blood of their victims, it might have turned out very different. They generally hunted in packs and were very canny fighters.

The woman standing on the ledge pulled my sword free from the creature's body and handed it to me hilt first. Then she straightened and saluted. The large cut running down the side of her face bled profusely, her short blonde hair was matted and stringy with sweat, and her blue eyes narrowed with pain even though little of it reached her expression.

I knew her, I realized. She'd been in my team for a few years as a base soldier before being promoted to scout with another team. I returned her salute. "Good to see you, Suzi."

"Good to still be here, Captain."

It was wryly said, and I smiled. "What happened?"

"We hit a barrier of some kind in the tunnel running up to The Beak—literally, in Randel's case." She pointed toward the man Kele was looking after. "It flung him back onto the damn spikes and shredded his legs."

"You couldn't get around it?"

She shook her head. "It wasn't a physical barrier, more a magical one, though I'm no expert in such things. We were coming back here to take the longer route when the damn olm attacked."

"They obviously caught the scent of blood," the soldier standing beside her said. "We'd bound Randel's wounds and stopped the bleeding, of course, but it doesn't take much to attract them bastards."

No, it didn't. "How badly are you both wounded?"

Suzi now had a hand pressed against the dark stain on her side, and her partner had a palm-sized chunk of flesh flapping at his left thigh. While both were at least upright, I doubted either would be walking very far. Or at least, not far enough to get out of these tunnels before more olm appeared.

"We're mobile, Captain, but I doubt Randel will be."

"Definitely not" came Kele's response. "The spikes might have shredded flesh and muscle, but the olm have broken bones."

I met her gaze. Though she didn't say anything, her expression told me everything I needed to know. Even if we could carry Randel, he wouldn't survive the trip out of the tubes, let alone down the mountain. Not without proper medical help. One look at his gray, sweating features was enough to confirm that.

I returned my attention to Suzi. "How far up that tunnel did you hit the barrier?"

She hesitated and glanced at the other soldier. He wrinkled his nose and said, "Maybe a quarter of a mile?"

A quarter of a mile should give us some scribe coverage... I frowned. "Why didn't you scribe for help when the accident first happened? Was there no coverage there?"

"We would have, but Randel was carrying the scribe and quill in his pack, and it was shattered when he hit the rocks."

"Which is probably the only reason he's still alive," the other soldier added. "The force of the impact should have broken his spine, but his pack took the brunt of it."

"It would seem Vahree wasn't yet ready for his soul," Suzi added.

I wasn't so sure of that, given Randel's current state, but I simply nodded. "I'll head there and make the call—"

"Not alone, Captain," Damon said. "It's too dangerous, given we have no idea who or what made that barrier."

I glanced at him, nodding imperceptibly at his use of my military title. It was appreciated, even if not necessary in his case. "What we can't do is leave these soldiers without protection. Between you and Kele—"

"You forget what I am," he cut in again. "I can raise a protective barrier using the blood of the olms to enhance its strength. With Kele stationed here, you and I can head into that tunnel, make the call, and then investigate the barrier."

I hesitated, if only briefly. It was a practical move under the circumstances. "How long will the protective barrier last? It's going to take at least four hours for assistance to get here."

And whether even that would be fast enough to save Randel was debatable.

"The blood of two olms should create a six-hour protection period. If we restrict the area needing coverage—using the wall behind Randel as the base—to a semi-circle around our survivors, it should give us an hour or so longer."

"Do it." I offered Suzi a hand. "Let's get you two off that ledge and over to Kele. She'll be able to treat those wounds you're not mentioning."

"She's a trained medic?" the soldier asked.

"No, first aider." Every company had at least two soldiers trained in field treatment; recon teams generally had one.

Suzi grimaced. "Harri was ours. Poor bastard was the first one hit."

She took my hand and carefully eased herself off the edge. Though she didn't say anything, fresh blood seeped past the fingers pressing against her right side. I suspected the tightness of her leathers was the only thing currently preventing her from bleeding to death.

The other soldier waved my offer of assistance away, eased down, and then limped over to the dead. "We can't leave them here, Captain. Not like this. Aside from the fact they'll only attract more olm, I can't—"

He stopped and shrugged, but there was fury and deep agony in his eyes and expression. One of the dead had meant something to him, that much was obvious.

But moving them would be next to impossible. Very little

remained of their leathers or their flesh, and what did simply wouldn't be enough to hold their bodies together.

"I'm sorry, soldier." My voice was flat, though my heart ached for him. "But they're already at Vahree's gates, and care not for what happens to their flesh now. Our main priority now has to be the living."

"Can you at least burn them? That would surely be a more fitting end for them than being torn apart any further."

Suzi lightly touched his arm. "Their bodies are the only reason we're alive now, Jace, and we both know it. If the captain ashes them, it will simply mean the olm will return their attention to us." She glanced down at the bodies and then added softly, "Mills would understand our choices, believe me."

Jace didn't say anything for a long moment, then nodded and continued on toward Kele. As Suzi followed, I returned to the entry tunnel and collected our packs. After dropping them in the middle of the junction, I walked over to Damon. He was collecting the blood of the olm Kele had smashed against the ceiling in one of the empty vessels he'd brought along.

"Is there anything I can do to help?"

He glanced up, his eyes dancing with a power that gave his irises a bloody hue. He might not have called to the magic that ran through his veins as yet, but it was nevertheless there to be seen in his gaze.

"You can cut a semicircle into the stone around our group. We need to give them a physical indication of the barrier's location, and your sword will do it easier than mine."

I nodded, drew my sword, and walked back. Kele met me halfway and picked up her pack. "That soldier has lost a lot of blood and muscle," she murmured. "Even if he does make it, he may never walk again."

I touched her arm. "Do what you can to keep him going until the healers get here."

She frowned. "I'm not staying—"

"You have to. You're the only trained first aider here."

"But—"

"Suzi and Jace are also injured. I need you here to keep an eye on things until we get back."

She drew in a deep breath and released it slowly. "I do not agree with this decision."

A grin broke free. "You never do when it means you being left out of the action for even the most practical of reasons."

"Truth." She sniffed. "As long as I get to see the drakkling, I won't complain."

"Oh, you will, and we both know it," I said dryly. "I will just ignore as per usual."

"Another truth."

With a smile, she turned and walked back to her patients. I moved over to the exit near the tear's sharp point and stopped, mentally "feeling" for any more olm. None were close, but that didn't mean much, given how fast they could move. The scent of blood and death might take a while to filter into the deeper tunnels, but they would eventually scent it. And to them, meat was meat; it wouldn't matter if the bulk of that scent belonged to their own kind.

I stepped closer to the edge of the exit and placed the tip of my sword against the hard stone of the floor. The Ithican blade had as little trouble biting through stone as it did flesh, and in very little time, I'd carved out a fine, semicircular line around Kele and the recon team.

Damon finished siphoning a second olm, then walked over and stopped beside me. "That line marks the no-crossing zone. If any of you step beyond it, the protective curtain will fall."

"Will the olm be able to break through?" Suzi asked, doubt evident. "They're tenacious enough to keep battering at it, and no magic lasts forever."

"No, it doesn't, but this spell should give you a good seven or so hours, as long as no one breaks the seal."

"What about the rescue party?" Jace said.

"They won't get in unless you step out. Creating a complete barrier is faster and easier than creating one with exceptions."

"And if the barrier starts fading before rescue gets here?" Kele asked.

"We should be back by then," I replied. "But if we're not, well, flame for as long as you can and don't get dead."

She smiled and lightly saluted. "Sound advice, Captain."

I stepped back and motioned Damon to proceed. He drew in a deeper breath, then slowly released it. The bloody glow in his eyes sharpened, and the air around him briefly shimmered and pulsed.

He walked over to where I'd started my line, pushed up his left shirt sleeve, then began to spell, his voice taking on a deeper, softer note that vibrated through my entire being. I didn't understand a word he was saying—the language sounded Angolan, which made sense, given that's where his mom and her kin were from—but his phrasing was older and far more formal. It was also hauntingly, almost heartbreakingly, beautiful.

He raised the water flask and slowly walked forward, continuing to spell as he dribbled blood with surprising precision onto my line. With every step, every drop, the power in the air grew, making the tiny hairs at the nape of my neck rise even if the only visible indication of the curtain he was building was the faintest shimmer that briefly appeared after each drop hit the stone.

When he reached the other side, he dropped the flask onto the ground behind him, then unsheathed his knife, raised his left wrist, and sliced it open.

I barely contained my gasp. I knew he was a blood mage. I just hadn't expected him to use his own when he was already using olm.

He turned his wrist around and let the blood fall onto that of the olms. The melodious spell briefly rose in tempo, then stopped with an abruptness that had my breath catching in my throat. For a heartbeat, nothing happened, then a faint stream of scarlet rose from the point where his blood had smothered the olms'. The smoke thickened as it raced back along the line and fused the droplets together. When the smoke hit the far side, there was a short, soft explosion. The blood along the entire length of my trench turned black, and that faint shimmer disappeared.

Damon pulled down his sleeve and glanced at me. His eyes were once again blue, though their whites remained stained pink. "The barrier is raised. We're good to go."

"If it exists, why can't we see it?" Jace asked, expression a weird mix of doubt and fear.

Understandable given there hadn't been a blood witch in Esan for decades—at least, not as far as anyone knew—and this was a new experience for us all.

Damon shrugged. "It is the nature of the spell and the reason I asked for the stone to be marked. Captain, we should get moving."

I nodded and glanced past him, my gaze briefly meeting Kele's. There was fear in her eyes, though I doubted it had anything to do with the man or his magic.

"Be careful," she silently mouthed.

I acknowledged her plea with a slight nod, then spun, collected my packs, and walked into the other tunnel.

Once we were far enough away from the others, I stopped and turned. "Show me your wrist."

He raised an eyebrow, but nevertheless held out his arm and pushed up his bloody sleeve. His skin from wrist to elbow bore a multitude of faint scars, but there was no sign of a fresh wound.

I ran my finger across the many cuts decorating his dark skin. Felt the slight jump in his pulse and its echo in my own. I swallowed and looked up. Caught the flick of desire through his still-bloody gaze before coolness replaced it.

"How is that even possible?"

He shrugged. "It is part of the magic—and not, I'm guessing, dissimilar to your own ability to cauterize a wound."

"Cauterization seals and disinfects. It doesn't heal and, let me assure you, it still hurts."

"Then why didn't you ask Kele for a pain dampener?"

"Because those three soldiers needed them far more than me."

He smiled, caught my fingers, and raised them to his lips. His kiss felt like a brand. Felt like home. Which was utterly ridiculous given how little I really knew about the man.

"Even a commander is entitled to pain relief, Bryn. Especially when a clear head is needed."

"A clear head is the *other* reason I didn't take a potion. They can affect the speed of your reactions in dangerous situations." I drew my hand from his, but couldn't help instinctively curling my fingers to retain the heat of his touch. "In case you haven't noticed, we are in the middle of one such situation."

He raised that eyebrow again. It was a very expressive eyebrow, I decided, conveying all manner of emotions in one elegant movement. This time, it was amused disbelief. "Would you expect such stoicism from the people under your command?"

"No, but they do expect it of me." Because I was a princess and it had taken me far longer than most new recruits to win respect. I wasn't about to risk its loss by taking a potion that could affect my judgment and endanger the lives of others.

I turned and continued on. He followed, a big warm presence I was far too attuned to.

Every five minutes I tried to scribe, but the connection remained nonexistent.

"If this barrier is magic," I said, after the fifth such attempt, "will you be able to sense it before we hit it?"

"It will depend on its type and construction. I'm not, for instance, able to sense Mareritt magic."

"Well, that's damnably inconvenient." I glanced over my shoulder. "Why not?"

"Their mages pull on their own *life* energy—the electricity of the body, if you will—and that of their land, rather than their blood. It's hard to differentiate between the magic that comes from the energy of the land and that which they call from within."

"Fascinating."

"You'd be one of the few who think so," he said, tone dry. "Most find the subject... tedious, at best."

"I'm not most people."

"That has become increasingly evident over the last few days."

I glanced over my shoulder again. "Is this a good thing or bad?"

"Oh, definitely good. I suspect life will never be boring while you're in it."

"While I'm in it?" Amusement twitched my lips. "You planning to get rid of me at some point in the future?"

"Were you not the one who claimed only a few hours ago to be uncertain as to what to do with me?"

"Oh, I know what to do with you," I said lightly. "I'm just not sure it's wise. I mean, there's the previously mentioned reputation to consider, and I, well, I'm a lowly soldier who will probably never live up to certain expectations for very long."

His laugh was soft and warm and rolled across my skin as sweetly as any summer breeze. "With what already lies between us, I believe said expectations will be well and truly blown out of the water. Whether it will retain enough heat to last is another matter entirely, and something only time and proximity can answer."

"Proximity being code for madly passionate sex?"

"More day-to-day living, but I can certainly live with a relationship being based on nothing more than madly passionate sex."

"At least for a few years," I agreed.

His warm laugh teased my senses again and had my hormones dancing. "Sounds like I'm going to need to keep my strength up. Want to try scribing again?"

I did, and this time, the pen lit up to indicate there was a viable connection present. I quickly detailed what had happened, then emphasized the urgent need for medical assistance. At the end, I told them Damon and I were continuing on to the Beak.

Stay wary came the response a few minutes later. *Keep in contact.*

Once I'd signed off and had tucked everything back into the pack, we walked on. This section of the tube hadn't suffered as badly in the tremors, so we were able to move at a fairly good clip.

We were almost at the quarter mile point when Kaia said, *Stop*, her warning so loud my brain just about rattled.

I immediately did so and said, *What is it?* even as Damon asked, "Something wrong?"

His gaze scanned the tube ahead, and his hand was on his sword, but there was nothing to see—nothing beyond the blue veins and the wickedly pointed rocks jutting out between the two strips of pale light.

Magic, she said. *Ahead.*

Surprise flitted through me. *You can feel it?*

See through you.

How?

She did the mental equivalent of a shrug. *Why matter?*

I guess it didn't. I glanced at Damon. "Kaia says the barrier the recon team mentioned lies just ahead."

He tugged the light tube from his pack, then raised the light and shone it directly ahead. "There's absolutely nothing to indicate that."

"Should there be?"

He grimaced. "Depends on the practitioner, but generally, when it comes to barriers it's best to pin the magic onto something solid. It prevents a strong wind from causing the spell to wander about randomly."

My eyebrows shot upward. "And has that ever happened?"

"All the time." His serious expression was undone by the twinkle in his eyes, and I nudged him lightly. He laughed. "Unpinned magic is harder to raise. It can be done, but it's easier if there's a foundation."

"I wouldn't call blood a solid foundation."

"Then you'd be wrong. How far ahead is she talking?"

I relayed the question.

She hesitated. *Half one wing.*

I did the mental gymnastics—math was never my strong point. "A little over thirty-five feet."

"Let's move closer, then, and see what happens."

"If I hit that barrier and get flung into razor rocks, I'm not going to be a happy soldier."

"I suspect my bigger worry will be your unhappy drakkon."

"She's not mine—"

You kin came Kaia's reply. *Belong.*

It would appear that having connected our minds on a deeper level than we had previously, there was now no stopping it—something that had never happened before with any other animal. But having her in my head, watching everything I did and hearing everything I said, was going to take some getting used to.

Warn me if we get too close.

Should stop. Safer.

Safer doesn't get us through that barrier. Safer won't find us the gilded ones.

She mentally sniffed. It was a very unimpressed sound.

I grinned and returned my attention to Damon. "She'll warn us when we're close."

"Good."

He shone his light on the ground, no doubt looking for the pins he'd mentioned. I followed, studying the tunnel ahead but still not seeing anything untoward. Then the edge of Damon's light caught a slight flutter. I touched his arm, and he immediately stopped, his muscles tensing briefly under my fingers.

"Point the light left—there's something there."

That something turned out to be a thin strip of leather coated with a black substance. Dried blood. This must be where Randel had hit the rocks after being thrown by the barrier. It had to be just up ahead, and yet there remained no sign.

I edged on cautiously, but had barely gone a dozen more steps when Kaia snapped, *Stop.*

Damon bent, picked up a loose, fist-sized stone, and tossed it.

Four feet in front of us, something flashed, and the stone rebounded with such force it could have caused serious injuries if it had hit our heads or limbs.

"It's odd that I can't see or sense this shield. I should if they are indeed using blood magic."

"Maybe it's a different type to what you use."

He glanced at me, his expressive eyebrows raised and suggesting amusement. "Blood is blood, no matter what creature it comes from."

"Well, obviously not." I motioned to the barrier neither of us could see. "Do you think my Ithican blade can counter the barrier's magic?"

"The actual barrier rather than the pins? No. Ithicans do use magic in the creation of their weapons, but as far as I'm aware, they cannot counter it."

Can.

I blinked. *The sword* can *counter magic?*

No. The reply was annoyed. *Me.*

Hate to point this out, Kaia, but you're not here at the moment, and you're too big to fit in these tunnels.

No need.

Why?

Can help you through. She paused. *Not him. Not kin.*

"Huh." I refocused on Damon. "Kaia says she can get me past the barrier but not you."

"Separation isn't a good idea, given we have no idea what waits beyond the barrier. Just because the tunnel appears to be empty of threat doesn't mean it is."

"I'm aware of that, but we need answers fast, and this might be the only way of getting some."

"We could backtrack and take another tunnel."

"That'll take hours we might not have." I paused. "Once I'm on the other side, I can look for the pins you mentioned and destroy them. That should bring the barrier down, shouldn't it?"

"Unless they've countered that possibility with another spell."

"Why would they?"

"Why would their first attack be on an outpost like Eastmead? These people are *not* following expectations when it comes to the tactical rule book." He studied me through narrowed eyes. "If you can't break the pins, how long will it take you to reach the Beak from the other side of the barrier?"

"Presuming there're no further traps or waiting guards? Half an hour."

"If you're not back in an hour ten, I'll be taking the other tunnel and heading up to find you."

"I'll inform Kaia not to eat you, then."

He did not look amused, and I somehow managed to contain my grin. "I've been roaming these tunnels for years, Damon. I really *will* be fine."

"The gilded birds and their riders haven't been here for years, though, have they?"

"No, but a fire hot enough to burn the body of a drakkling should be able to cinder a rider, with or without their golden armor."

And I hoped that in saying that, I hadn't snagged Túxn's interest. The goddess of luck could sometimes be very fickle with her favors.

"And how much fire do you actually have left after everything you expended in that cavern?"

"Enough."

"That is not a comforting statement."

I smiled. "I have a drakkon to heal, remember, and besides, there's the promise of hot passionate sex to claim."

"I love that the drakkons come first over everything else." He shook his head. "We really will have to find an active aerie for you in Zephrine, won't we?"

"Well, it would not only get me out of your hair, but also your father's. A double bonus, I'd say."

He raised his eyebrow again, the movement somehow both mocking *and* amused. "I don't keep enough hair to worry about these days, so don't let that bother you."

I laughed and gripped his arm. He slid his hand briefly over mine and gently squeezed it, and I did my best to ignore the desire that surged at the simple touch. But there was a big part of me that wished I'd taken time to explore the muscular perfection of this man before... I shut the rest of that thought down.

There was plenty of time ahead for such exploration. Besides, sexual arousal wasn't uncommon after a near death experience, and this "surge" could surely be put down to that.

And if I kept telling myself that, I might even end up believing it.

"If I can't break the barrier, I'll return as fast as I can."

"I would prefer you be as careful as you can, but given the propensity of your family to throw themselves headfirst into the middle of trouble, I won't be waiting with bated breath for that to happen."

A statement I didn't bother refuting. I tried pulling away, but his grip tightened, preventing me. I frowned up at him, saw the devilment and desire in his eyes.

Fires sparked within, a deep-down heat that had nothing to do with flame.

"What?" I said, voice edged with a huskiness I couldn't quite control.

Though he hadn't appeared to move, he was somehow so much closer. "I believe the custom you started in Esan's courtyard should be continued."

His breath brushed heat across my lips, and I swallowed against the sudden rush of wanting. It was insane to be kissing this man right now, given we had no idea what dangers might even now be approaching, and yet... and yet, was that not also a good reason for doing so?

I softly cleared my throat and said, "What custom would that be?"

"A kiss goodbye before you fly away with your drakkon."

"I'm not—"

His lips met mine, stealing the rest of my words away. Stealing thought and breath, leaving nothing but sweet sensation as the kiss deepened and our tongues tangled, tasted, teased.

God, the man could *kiss*.

The deep-down fires burned to life once more, and I pressed my body harder to the length of his, wanting more, needing more, wishing we were flesh-on-flesh so I could explore the glorious length of him. But leather lay between us, and that was probably just as well. A cold stone tunnel really wasn't the best place to consummate our marriage.

As if he'd heard that thought, he groaned and pulled back. His blue eyes were afire with desire, but there was amusement there, too.

"This kiss confirms desire will never be a problem between us, but I believe our timing could certainly be better."

"I believe you're right. Perhaps we should—" I paused and waved a hand at the seriously impressive erection visible even through the leathers. "—discuss your current inconvenience once we return to Esan."

"I believe the same inconvenience affects us both."

His voice was dry, and I grinned. "Yes, but mine's a whole lot less obvious."

"I shall enjoy exploring and tasting your less... obvious... inconvenience once we have the time."

"I believe I would enjoy that."

"I shall ensure that you do." With the smile of a man well used to pleasuring women, he bowed and stepped back. "And you had best be on your way, before your drakkon becomes impatient again."

I laughed, but turned to the barrier we couldn't see and said, *Ready when you are, Kaia.*

Deepen bond, she said. *Must be one.*

I frowned. *To share immunity?*

Mesh with young. Protects them, will protect you.

I blinked. *When have you had to protect drakklings against magic?*

The only magic we ever employed against them these days was

from the weather mages, and that was simply a means of forcing them into retreat on the few occasions they did fly over.

The white ones use.

The white ones being the Mareritt, according to the image that accompanied her reply. *I had no idea drakkons flew into Mareritten.*

Good hunting in warm times. Risk worth. Bond.

I drew in a breath, then deepened the connection between us. Her mind was deep and vast, alien and yet not, and it opened to me like a flower, as mine did to her. My connections with other animals had been surface level only, so the difference here was to be expected. But this was much, *much* more than deepening the ability to read thoughts and feel emotions. It was a sharing of our very *beings* —of all that we were, all that we had been, and all that we could be. It was a sharing of memories, of power, and of joy, but it was also pain— of friends killed, love betrayed, and dreams diminished on my part, and on hers, mates and drakklings lost, some to humans, some to wind and weather, and some who simply weren't strong enough to survive the harshness of the lands we'd driven them into. Grief rolled through me, through *us*. Then there was a brief twist of senses and mind, and I was looking through her eyes and she through mine.

We were one.

It was a weird sensation, and my brain scrambled to cope with the multiple points of view now hitting me—not only what I was seeing and sensing here, but what Kaia was, both here and in the aerie, where Gria slept with the bloody remnants of a capra scattered around her.

Kaia obviously *wasn't* having the same difficulty as me. But then, if she'd done this with drakklings, she was obviously familiar with the dual points of view.

Walk now, she said.

I did so, every sense I had—hers and mine—tuned to the barrier I could now see. It was a fierce golden wall through which hundreds of fiery ribbons shimmered and roamed.

Magic, Kaia said. *No stop.*

I hit the barrier. It briefly resisted my presence, then the threads on either side of me melted away and I stepped through. It felt like what I imagined walking through a tar pit would. It enveloped me, smothered me, making breathing difficult and forward movement harder and harder. Fear rose, as did flames. I clenched my fingers against the need to react and forced my feet on. Kaia remained a bright presence in my mind, and there was no concern in her thoughts.

I'd trusted her before. I could do no less now.

I moved on, each step slow and steady, for what seemed an eternity. Then, with a suddenness that tore a gasp from my throat, I was through.

I stopped and scanned the tunnel ahead for any sort of threat, then drew in a deep, somewhat shuddering breath and turned. The barrier continued to burn bright, and there was no sign of Damon through it.

"Bryn?" he said, voice sharp and very distant.

"Here, safe," I replied. *Thank you, Kaia.*

Welcome. She retreated from my mind enough that we regained our individuality, but not so far that I couldn't see the barrier. *Not felt this magic before.*

They didn't use it on you when they attacked?

No.

Perhaps their magic was protection-based rather than attack, and if that were true, it was at least one point in our favor. Right now, they seemed to have too many other advantages.

Damon said if we can find the pins that keep this barrier in place, we might be able to bring it down.

Who he to you?

I hesitated. *He's my husband.*

Husband?

Mate.

No cinder?

I smiled at the slight note of amusement in her mental tones. *Definitely not.*

Will tell Gria. He magic?

Thank you, and yes. Protective magic, not attack. He won't hurt either of you. I promise.

No like them, but trust.

Men, she meant, rather than Damon. And I could hardly blame her. Women might long have been a part of Esan's military might, but in truth, we were but a fraction overall. It definitely took a certain mindset to want to risk life and limb in order to protect greater society.

"Have you spotted the pins?" Damon asked. "They'll likely be on either edge, hidden from obvious sight. Destroy one, and it should short the spell and take out both."

I wrinkled my nose and studied the nearest wall for several seconds. After a moment, I realized there was a pattern to the swirl of ribbons or whatever the hell those things actually were—they dove down into the corner, swam back up the wall, then raced across half the barrier before turning around in the middle and doing the whole loop again. I drew my sword and cautiously moved forward. In a crevice at the point where the wall met the floor was a small metallic feather. The threads were rolling around the outer edges of the feather before crawling up the wall.

"I think the pin is one of those metallic feathers," I replied. "I can't think of any other reason for it to be shoved into a hole in this tunnel."

"Are you able to get your sword into the crevice?"

"Yes." I paused. "What sort of reaction can I expect?"

"Unknown."

"Well, that's always fun."

"Cleave it from a side-on angle if you can. If the pin is set to explode most of the force will go to the front rather than the sides."

"'Most' is not a comforting word right now."

He laughed. "Best I can do under the circumstances."

I stepped sideways until only half of the feather was visible, then knelt and pressed the tip of the sword into the crevice, onto the feather. There was no response, but then, I hadn't yet tried to damage it.

With one of those breaths that didn't do a whole lot to calm the inner nerves—I really would rather fight a half dozen Mareritt than do something like this—I thrust the blade tip through the glittering leaf, hitting the base of the rock underneath. A sharp, bell-like chime rang through the air, and the movement of the ribbons became chaotic. Then, with a surprisingly soft and yet powerful *whoomph*, the barrier exploded. The force of it was a foul wind that sent me tumbling.

I landed on my back a good ten or fifteen feet away, staring up at the dagger-like rocks only inches from my forehead. Fuck, I'd been lucky—*so* damn lucky—that I hadn't ended up in the same damaged state as Randel.

"Bryn?" Damon dropped to his knees beside me. "You okay?"

"Yeah, just winded. Move back so I can get up."

He shuffled back and rose with me, one hand hovering near my elbow, as if ready to catch me should I waver.

"I'm fine, Damon, really."

"You look fine, but magic can sometimes have detrimental effects that are not obvious at first glance." His gaze swept me critically and came up looking relieved. "I can't see any evidence of post-spell fragments clinging to you."

"Which maybe suggests they didn't expect us to be able to break through."

"And we wouldn't have, if not for your drakkon." He reached out and plucked something from my hair. "There is this, though."

"This" was a semi melted, blackened remnant of the gilded feather. "Is there magic clinging to it?"

"Enough to tell they *are* using blood magic, so it is strange that I cannot see it." He raised the fragment a little, allowing the blue light to flow across it. "If this remnant is anything to go by, they are not restricted to mere protection as we are."

"You said your magic could also alter—isn't that what they're doing with the gilded birds?"

He shrugged. "It's possible that's the birds' natural state—perhaps they are their country's equivalent to our drakkons."

"Theoretically, though, it *is* possible to physically alter a living being such as these birds?"

He hesitated. "Theoretically, anything is possible with enough will and skill, but such wide-scale alterations on such large creatures might well require more blood than the mage can spare."

Which wasn't much of a problem when you could use the blood of others. "Then, presuming the birds *are* altered by blood—could you or your Angolan kin undo them?"

He dropped the remnant onto the stone and ground it underneath a heel. "Not to kill—as I said, our blood magic is protection based rather than attack. It *is* possible that if we caught one, we could figure out what has been done to it and maybe even return it to its natural state, but that is an unrealistic task if we are dealing with a squadron or more of them."

I adjusted the position of my pack, picked up the one that had slipped from my shoulder when I'd been thrown, and then moved forward again. Despite the quiet fierceness of the explosion, it had caused a fair bit of damage to the walls either side of the crevice. Chunks of blue glowing stone lay scattered throughout the tube, along with multiple bits of the black rock's "teeth." No wonder Damon had asked me if I was okay. By rights, the explosion should have blown me apart as easily as the rock. And might well have, had I been standing in front of the crevice.

We made good time and soon reached the point where the tube met a much older system. From here, it was only a ten-minute walk through a small cavern, and a sharply inclined but shorter tunnel to reach the Beak.

We paused at the edge of the tunnel and studied the small cavern. At first glance, it appeared empty, then Damon lightly nudged my arm and pointed to the right, near where the entrance to the Beak's runner tunnel was.

I studied the area, initially seeing nothing but a series of odd-shaped rocks. Then I noticed their oddly formal structure. They *weren't* rocks. They were concealment cloaks hiding what looked to be a series of differently sized boxes.

"They've obviously started setting up some sort of supply depot," I said.

He nodded. "There doesn't seem to be much here yet."

"It might also be but one of a number scattered across the Black Glass Mountains or even the Throat. With winged access, there're plenty of places for them to use."

And it wasn't like we could find every one of them, given how large—and how dangerous—the range was. Besides, it would take far longer than we probably had.

"True." He paused. "There's no sign of a guard here. What does Kaia say about magic?"

None came her immediate response.

She was still following along with our adventure, obviously.

Bored, she said. *You more interesting.*

What did you do before I came along to relieve said boredom?

Fly. Dangerous here. Can't leave Gria too long.

A good point, given the stash we'd just uncovered. I returned my attention to the cavern. "Kaia isn't sensing anything."

"Good." He rose. "Let's go investigate those boxes."

I nodded and padded out after him.

We were five steps into the cavern when I heard the voices.

Damon grabbed my arm and pulled me back into the tunnel. I knelt in the deeper shadows, keeping close to the wall to present a less noticeable shadow, one hand clenched against the fire burning at my fingertips and the other on my sword's hilt. Damon knelt beside me, pulled his knife free from its sheath, and sliced open a fingertip.

He rapidly spelled, his singsong words so soft I could barely hear them despite our closeness. As the blood dripped onto the ground, shadows roiled up from it, deepening and thickening as the spell reached its peak. He closed it off with a sharp motion, but this time there was no explosion.

"The veil will prevent them seeing us," he murmured, his breath a sweet caress across my ear. "But do not move, as the spell will ripple in response, and that might attract attention."

I nodded, my gaze on the still empty cavern as the voices grew closer. I had no idea what they were saying, because it wasn't any language I'd heard before. While there was a common language shared by Arleeon and all her trading partners, this was something else altogether.

There were at least ten in the group, which normally wouldn't present much of a problem given there were two of us and I could take out at least half of them with fire—presuming, of course, their armor wasn't fireproofed. But killing or capturing these men would only warn their commanders that we knew of their existence, and both instinct and common sense said that wasn't a good idea. Their unawareness gave us the chance to learn more about them and prepare, whereas reacting now could lead to an immediate and full-scale attack on Esan and maybe even Arleeon itself.

We needed time.

Time we didn't have, instinct whispered yet again.

The voices stopped with an abruptness that made my skin crawl. I didn't move, barely dared to breathe, as tension locked my body and heat pressed harder against my fingertips.

Then, on the soft stirring breeze, came the sound of footsteps. Two men appeared, each holding what looked to be narrow tubes of very thin metal. A small pouch was connected to the base of the tubes, and inside this, visible thanks to the sheerness of the metal, was some sort of dark liquid.

They were both wearing the chain armor Kaia had shown me, but only one had a helmet on. The other had it lashed to his waist belt, revealing brown features with a flat wide nose, high cheekbones, and a mouth that was a thin dark slash. His hair was short, spiky, and a rather shocking green.

Definitely not a race we'd ever traded with.

They scanned the cavern carefully, their weapons raised and their fingers resting on what I presumed was the release button. The helmetless man's gaze paused at the entrance of our tube for several incredibly long seconds before moving on again.

The first man growled something in that guttural language we'd heard earlier, and then two of them took up sentry positions, one remaining near their tunnel, and one walking across to the right side of ours.

He looked in briefly, his gaze skittering across the deeper shadows that surrounded us, then grunted and turned around, the tube still held at the ready. But this close, I could smell the stuff, and it very much reminded me of that faintly sweet but musty scent evident whenever I entered the cages holding our gray hawks. *That* suggested it was a liquefied form of their gilded birds' shit. After what it had done to the boat, I hated to think what it would do to human flesh....

In a two-by-two formation, six more armor-clad men moved into the cavern, each pair carrying a large box. The first pair flipped the concealment blanket back, then placed their box on top of the nearest. The other two pairs followed suit, then, after pulling the blanket back down, they all retreated. Conversation faded as they moved deeper into the other tunnel.

We didn't move, not for another five minutes. Then, warily, Damon dismissed his shadow spell and rose, offering me a hand. I placed my fingers in his and allowed him to pull me upright, even if it wasn't really necessary.

Except it somehow was, because there was a part of me that hungered for his touch. *Any* touch, however brief. A part whose demands had only increased after our last kiss. We just needed time...

but instinct was whispering that if I wanted this man in my bed, I had best get him there soon, before the world blew apart around us.

I pulled free from his grip and flexed my fingers. Mom's seeress abilities had never really been a functioning part of mine—at least to date—so instinct's warnings were probably based on nothing more than fear.

Probably.

I ignored the tension that rippled through me, then dropped the pack looped over my shoulder onto the ground and drew my sword, edging warily to the cavern's entrance. There was no response to our movement, and the tunnel opposite remained empty of any indication it was occupied.

I motioned to the boxes. "You check them out; I'll head up the tunnel and investigate."

"How much farther on is the Beak?"

"A couple of hundred yards, if that. Kaia's still with me, so if there's any sort of magic, she'll warn me."

Hope is. Am bored.

I grinned and repeated her comment to Damon. His eyebrows rose. "I never really gave much credit to drakkons being so intelligent, let alone them having so many human emotions."

Same with us to them, Kaia muttered.

A laugh bubbled up my throat but thankfully didn't make it past my lips.

"Don't tell me," he said dryly. "She just applied the comment to me."

All males, Kaia corrected. *Have brains, just don't use. Think with breeding stick.*

This time, the laugh escaped, though I managed to raise a hand in time to at least keep it partially smothered.

Damon raised his eyebrows again, an unspoken demand I share.

I grinned. "She basically just said that all males, no matter the species, think with their cocks rather than their brains."

"Well, she's not wrong."

Rarely am, she said, somewhat smugly.

I smothered another laugh, then touched Damon's arm and moved out. The air whisked lightly around me, and there was the faintest hint of murkha within it. It was a weed cultivated and smoked via clay pipes by some of our more distant trading partners, a practice that had never taken off in Arleeon, mainly because murkha was difficult to grow here and expensive to import. My father did have a supply, but it was only ever used during trade negotiations.

If these invaders were using it without any sort of restriction, then maybe they grew it, or at least came from the same region as those who did.

I moved into the other tunnel, my steps light on the ground and every sense alert. The stirring air strengthened, but it brought with it no sound, and no suggestion the men we'd seen remained at the Beak. That wasn't really surprising—the Beak wouldn't hold ten men, let alone the birds they probably flew in on.

The closer I drew to the Beak, the more the faint strains of pre-dawn light infused the shadows. I slowed my pace and kept my flames at the ready. The distant sound of crashing waves and the occasional cry of a kayin greeting the rising of another day remained the only sounds to be heard.

The tunnel swept left and made its final rise toward the Beak. I pressed against the wall, eased forward the final few inches, and then peered around the corner.

No soldiers, no armed birds, and nothing more than footprints on the gritty ground.

Tension remained, however. I'd been in too many close calls with Mareritten ambushes to believe the quiet emptiness of this place.

Kaia? I asked. *Any magic?*

Not sense.

I guess that was something. I flexed my fingers against my sword's hilt, then moved on. The breeze stiffened almost immediately, filled with the salty scent of the sea. I remained close to the wall, my gaze scanning the opening ahead and the curving rock that gave this place its name. I knew from past adventures up here there was very little room for anyone to stand either side of the entrance—the cliff face was simply too sheer. Even a capra would have trouble scrambling up and down the thing.

But these invaders were flight capable, and that meant they could easily perch somewhere above and simply swoop down the minute I poked my head out.

Which I did, of course, but carefully, quickly checking either side before twisting around so I could study the dark sweep of mountain above me. Nothing.

With the sword still held at the ready—though it was unlikely to be much use against these birds given how close I'd have to get to the things to damage them—I stepped out. The wind tugged at my braid and the roar of the sea far below filled my ears. Dawn had broken across the skyline, her long plumes of red and gold tinting the gathering clouds and promising a stormy day. The Beak's stone—once a smooth, shiny black—was heavily scarred, the trenches littering its length at least six inches deep.

Birds heavy, Kaia said. *We not damage that badly.*

No. I squatted next to one of the newest-looking scars and ran my fingers around their edges. They were V-shaped, the wider end—where two claws were—scored deeper that the tip that possessed one solitary shorter claw.

Land hard, no hover, Kaia commented. *Front claws sharp, slice deep.*

I slid my fingers into the toe section of the cut. It was a good hand deep. *Their claws have to be pretty damn strong to slice through stone like this.*

Claws not natural. Birds not natural.

And if they could damage the Beak like this with so little effort, what could they do to Esan's walls? The Mareritt, for all their magic and sometimes superior technology, had never breached the city. These creatures, twisted and strengthened by magic, could well achieve in days what the frost scum hadn't been able to in centuries.

I rose, looked toward the Black Glass peaks, and caught the faintest glimmer of gold. I swore and lunged toward the cavern's mouth, pressing close to the shadows that still hugged one side of it, my gaze sweeping the color-wrapped skies for any indication I'd been spotted. A few kayin hung on the breeze, lazily circling; if there'd been any threat or unusual activity, they wouldn't be doing that. They were in general timid souls.

I sheathed my sword and then swung my pack around and undid the small long viewer lashed to its side. I didn't use it all that often, because we generally relied on scouts rather than these things. They had a limited focus range and tended to take a while to refocus when moving from point to point, which made them a little dangerous in tight situations needing a fast response.

After dropping my pack, I edged partially out. The gold glimmer remained where it was, bright against the black of the mountain behind it. I raised the long viewer to my right eye, closed the left, and adjusted the small ring halfway down the tube until everything jumped into focus. It took me a minute to find the source of the glimmer and... Vahree save us, these things were *monstrous*. Not in size so much as form. I might have already seen them in the images Kaia had shared, but somehow physically seeing them made them all the more real. All the more dangerous.

This one appeared to be tethered with a chain attached to the chest plate holding the wide leather saddle on its back in place. It wasn't trying to escape, and it probably could—claws that could carve such deep trenches into the Beak could surely shatter chain just as easily, however thick. It was also wearing some sort of hood over its head and eyes, and it appeared to be rocking lightly back and forth, as if moving to some invisible tune.

The wind, Kaia said. *It follows the ebb and flow of wind.*

That's odd, isn't it?

Perhaps wishes to fly. Can't, so imagines.

Surprise rippled through me. *Do drakkons ever do this?*

Young dream fly.

146   KERI ARTHUR

I centered the long viewer on the bird again. I had a feeling this one *was* young, though I had no idea why. It was just a suspicion that the natural weight of the bird, combined with that of a fully armored rider, would take a toll on them physically. It would make sense to use those in the prime of their lives rather than risk the strength of an older bird failing at the wrong time.

Not drakkon, Kaia said. *Even Jagri lift you, metal covering or not.*

Jagri?

Old male. Guards breeding grounds in red mountains.

A mate?

No. Can't catch in flight. Not worthy.

I smiled. Drakkons mated on the wing, and only the strongest, fastest males were allowed to breed with the queens. *I wasn't wearing armor when you lifted me.*

Can carry hair beast with ease. You nothing.

Hair beast being a longhorn, if the image that came through was anything to go by. *Carrying in claws would be different to carrying on your back. It would affect your flying dynamics, would it not?*

What dynamics?

I hesitated. *The ease with which you move through the air.*

Horns and spines larger than you.

And I guessed if I was sitting behind them, the flow of air wouldn't really be disrupted. I hesitated. *Would you be willing to carry me on your back if it was needed? It would leave your claws for defense.*

If bank, you fall.

You could catch.

If miss?

How often do you miss prey?

You not prey. Matter more.

A statement that utterly warmed my heart. *What if I was roped on? Or had some sort of saddle to keep me on?*

Not that we actually had a saddle that would *fit* her back. It would have to be made, and I doubted we'd have the time to do that.

She was silent for a minute. *I think.*

Thank you.

I refocused on the invader and carefully swept the area. There were no cave entrances on that plateau that I could see from this angle, but it was obviously a sentry point, as what looked to be a triangular metal tent was set up behind the golden bird and a tied down privy pot sat farther away. Talk about a seat with a view, I thought wryly.

I scanned the other peaks within the range of the long viewer, but couldn't spot any other sentry stations. Which didn't mean they weren't there—if they'd gone to the trouble of setting up one, there would undoubtedly be others. Hell, maybe the Beak was meant to be their next one—it would explain the boxes and the barrier we'd come across.

If that were the case, though, we needed to find a means of preventing them from gaining ground here without giving them a reason to suspect we were aware of them.

Movement caught the edge of the long viewer's glass. I turned the ring a fraction to sharpen the image again and saw the bird's rider exit the metal tent, a bottle of some sort of green liquid in one hand and a long pipe in the other. He walked around the bird and took a seat on its claws; the bird shifted fractionally, and its chest feathers ruffled around the man, cloaking a good portion of his body. The man relaxed back, alternating between drinking and smoking.

These birds might be altered by magic, but the bond between rider and bird appeared to be a mutual one rather than enforced by magic.

Wear bands, Kaia said.

Bands?

On leg. Saw when attack.

The image of a metal ring encircling a scaly red leg flashed through my mind. *It glowed; bird reacted.*

I focused the long viewer on the bird's legs, but it was partially sitting and its under feathers were fluffed up, concealing its legs. But there was a silver band similar to the image Kaia had sent on the rider's left wrist.

Only one bird had ring, Kaia commented.

I frowned. *How many attacked you?*

Three.

Three of them. It was a wonder she and Gria had even survived. *If only one had the ring, it's possible it's a communication device of some kind. Perhaps it's a means of the lead bird and rider giving orders to the others.*

Especially given the man wrapped in feathers had a similar band on his wrist.

Birds no speak? Drakkons smarter then.

Drakkons are definitely smarter, I agreed.

Something close to smugness rolled down the line between us. I smiled and shifted my stance, checking the peaks closer to Esan. I couldn't see anything that caused alarm, but perhaps the Beak was their first foray into the mountains closer to Esan. I couldn't help but wonder yet again why—given their superior air strength—they were being so cautious.

But maybe we were reading too much into the two attacks that had happened on our settlements. Maybe the force that had attacked Eastmead and the islands was the only force they had here, and they were simply testing our strengths and weaknesses while they awaited the arrival of their main force.

If that were true, then we needed to figure out a means of combating their winged battalion before the rest got here.

I glanced down at the gouges in the rocks again, then spun and walked back into the tunnel. After tying the long viewer back into place, I swung my pack on and headed back down to the cavern.

"Wife incoming," I said as I neared.

"Husband warned and standing down."

"Shame," I said with a laugh. "I was looking forward to seeing you at full attention."

"That could very easily be arranged if you'd stop flitting about after drakkons and armored birds." His voice was dry. "But given the needs of the former appear to come before yours or mine, I suspect it might be some time yet before that happens."

"I suspect you are sadly right." I walked over to the large crate he was standing behind. It hadn't yet been opened, but the others had, and they contained a variety of unmarked boxes and leather-wrapped goods. "What have we got?"

"A selection of food and camping items in the other boxes, if what I've pulled out is anything to go by."

He sliced apart the leather strap binding the final box, then nodded for me to grab the edge of the lid. As one, we lifted it and slid it off the end. Inside was a selection of those metal tubes and several tubs of the dark liquid, and a collection of the smaller, translucent metal pouches.

"Weapons. They're obviously in the process of setting up a supply station here."

"Yeah." I reached down and picked up one of the tubes. It was light and simple in design, with little more than the trigger and the attachment point for the metal pouch. There was no sight and no guard against possible splash back, making me wonder how useful these weapons would be in any sort of wind. "I wonder if we can use these things to bring down the tunnel and block this point of entry?"

"It would be better to use magic to destabilize the roof and bring it down that way."

"Won't they be able to sense your magic?"

"It's a possibility, though likely a remote one, given I can't sense theirs."

I nodded. "I take it, then, that you are able to bring the roof down?"

"Wouldn't have suggested it if I couldn't."

I glanced at the tunnel for a second. "Will it take much energy?"

Amusement glimmered in his bright eyes. "Worried I won't have the strength to rise to the occasion later on?"

I grinned. "From what I've witnessed over the years, a man could be three-quarters dead and still be erect and ready to go if opportunity arises."

"If it was your luscious body they were reacting to, I am not surprised."

"Luscious? Perhaps you need to get your eyes tested, husband, because I'm as far from luscious as you can get, especially in the breast department."

"Your breasts are small, granted, but they are perfectly formed. And more than a handful is a waste—"

"Said no man ever," I cut in dryly, even as desire stirred. My breasts had been called many things—pimples, stone fruit, a waste of time—but never had anyone called them perfect. "And there's no need to sweet-talk me—I have already decided to taste your wares."

"And I do like a good tasting." His slow smile was decidedly sexy, and my pulse skipped up several beats. "Rest assured I will return the favor."

"Excellent." It came out a little husky, and the heat in his gaze increased. I cleared my throat and did my best to ignore it. My pulse nevertheless skipped along in happy abandon, no doubt anticipating what was, at best, hours away. "Why I asked is—I was wondering if you could create some sort of barrier shield on the two internal entry points into the old aerie. Gria won't be able to fly for a few days yet, and I'm worried about these invaders—or someone from Esan—randomly finding their way in."

Eat if do came Kaia's thought.

Eating isn't the answer to every problem.

Is when men come hunt.

Have you ever eaten anyone?

Too gristly, no taste came the response. *Better to bite and drop.*

I smothered a laugh. *Seriously?*

Yes. No meat on bones.

"I gather Kaia is commenting on the proposal?" Damon said, voice dry again.

"More on how gristly people are as a meal. Why?"

"Because you get this very distracted expression when you're listening to her." He paused, frowning. "She really said we're gristly?"

"Too gristly, no taste, and no meat on our bones, apparently."

"I'm not sure whether to be worried by that comment or amused."

"You're safe from being taste tested," I said with a grin. "And she's promised to make Gria leave you alone."

"Hmmm," he said, in a gravelly, surprisingly sexy way.

But I suspected I'd find anything he did sexy right now. Rahtee—the goddess of lust, passion, and sexual pleasure—might have spent too many years overlooking my needs, but she'd definitely decided to hit me with the desire stick hard and heavy now.

I only hoped reality could live up to imagination. I suspected it would, but I'd been disappointed before far too many times.

"So, you *can* raise the barrier?"

"Yes, although my blood alone will not be enough."

"I could ask Kaia if she could bring in a capra."

They close. Can collect. Gria eat meat.

And with dawn rising, she should be safe from the gilded birds and their riders.

Hunt now? she added.

I repeated the question to Damon, and he shook his head. "The fresher the kill, the stronger the spell."

Wait then. Tell when need.

Will do.

Damon walked around the crate and headed toward the tunnel. I trailed after him. "Is there anything I can do?"

"Stay here. Spells don't often go wrong, but this one can be... touchy."

"Because you're destroying rather than protecting?"

He nodded. "It's a bit of a gray area. It can work if the intent is to protect, but backlash is not unknown."

I frowned. "Backlash?"

He nodded. "If I come tumbling out of the tunnel a raw and bloody mess, that's backlash."

Alarm flicked through me. "I'd appreciate you avoiding such an occurrence."

"Oh, I plan to, if only because it'd play havoc with my seduction plans." He swung off his pack and handed it to me, then brushed his lips across mine—a barely there caress that had me hungering for more. "Back in a few minutes."

I nodded and watched him disappear into the gloom, then swung his pack over my shoulder and moved back behind the largest of the boxes. I had no idea how much of the tunnel would be affected, but it should be safe enough at the back here.

And hoped that I hadn't just tempted Túxn to withdraw her favors and look the other way.

Time seemed to tick by extraordinarily slowly, but it was probably only five or so minutes later when a gentle vibration began to run through the ground. Stone dust began to sprinkle down from the ceiling, and I glanced up sharply. Tiny fissures raced across the ceiling, some of them meeting and merging, creating ever larger lines as they were drawn toward the exit tunnel.

Foreboding pulsed, and I turned, then hesitated, reaching back into the box to grab a handful of the metal tubes and a small tub of the liquid before hurrying toward the tunnel. I doubted Damon intended collapsing the whole cavern, but he'd also mentioned how unstable the spell could be. Better to be safe than sorry.

I stopped a few yards inside our escape tunnel, dropped my haul onto the ground near my feet, then crossed my arms and leaned against the rough wall. For several more minutes, nothing more happened. The needle-fine cracks continued to run together, creating a dangerous network of splinters across the cavern's ceiling and the dust in the air increased, a red haze that quickly decreased visibility. A soft *whoomph* echoed, then the walls around me shuddered violently. Large slabs of stone began to rain from the cavern's roof and, barely visible through the haze, a thicker cloud of dust and rocks ballooned out of the other tunnel.

Damon emerged from its middle, running hard. A heartbeat later, I saw why. Boulders chased his heels. Bounders big enough to crush.

The force of his spell hadn't just collapsed the tunnel, it was about to take the whole damn cavern with it.

8

HIS GAZE SWEPT the cavern and landed on mine. He veered toward me, running across the avalanche's surging frontline, leaping over boulders, and somehow avoiding the deadly rain coming from the ceiling.

As he hit the cavern's mouth, the stream of rock crashed into a line of boxes. Bits of wood and metal flew in all directions, deadly spears that could pierce skin as easily as they did the air. Dark liquid sprayed high, splashing across the growing network of cracks in the cavern's ceiling.

"Go, go," Damon said, his voice hoarse with weariness. He swept up the tubes and the tub I'd salvaged, then grabbed my arm and pulled me along with him. I shook free, scooped up my other pack, and ran on, leading the way through the dust, the gloom, fear pounding through me as cracks splintered the ceiling above us.

From behind us came a series of heavy thumps; more of the cavern's ceiling had come down, and it sent a thick wave of stone grit chasing after our heels. Then an odd hissing began. It sounded like a shamoke pot steaming, only a thousand times louder.

The liquid, I realized suddenly. The avalanche had crushed its receptacles, and it was now reacting—violently, if the increasing volume of that hissing was anything to go by—to the stone.

A heartbeat later, there was another loud *whoomph*, and the whole tunnel vibrated.

"Lose the packs, now!" Damon commanded, dropping the tub and the tubes and racing away from them.

"Why?" I said, not looking back as I hastily obeyed.

He didn't answer, just dove at me. Surprise tore a gasp from my lips as his arms wrapped around me and he took us both down, somehow twisting in the air so that his body took the brunt of the heavy fall. He grunted, a sound filled with pain, but rolled the two of us toward the base of the tunnel wall. My shoulder hit it hard enough to split open my cauterized wounds, but any sound I might have made was lost to a wave of rock and heat so loud, so fierce, it felt like we'd briefly stepped into Vahree's hellish domain.

For too many seconds, we simply huddled together, our hearts beating in terrified unison as the air burned and chunks of rock thudded all around us. Nothing hit us, though, which made me suspect he was using a shield to protect us. It would certainly explain his miraculous avoidance of being crushed in the cavern.

The rain of heat and stone gradually eased, and though dust still swirled, it was nevertheless easier to breathe. I sent a sliver of fire across to my shoulder to seal the wound again, and then moved my face away from his chest and looked up. "Did you intend for all that to happen?"

He laughed, though it was a rough, somewhat wry sound. "Would you be very surprised if I said no?"

"Then what did happen? Was that the backlash you mentioned?"

"No. One of their containers must have had a leak, though I didn't notice its presence until I'd finished and activated the spell. A spell spark hit the thin stream, and that's when it all went south."

"Meaning the acidic stuff is also explosive? That is not good news."

"No." He shifted slightly and skimmed his hand from my waist to my hip. Awareness flared in his eyes and echoed through me. "Are you hurt?"

"I daresay I'll have a charming array of bruises happening tomorrow, but otherwise, no." I raised a hand and lightly traced a finger around the shallow wound slicing his cheek. Desire deepened, both in his eyes and within me. "If this is your only wound, then you were damnably lucky."

"I think my luck changed the moment I stepped off a boat and met my reluctant bride. Túxn was definitely in a playful mood that day."

"Given everything that has happened since, it might be more accurate to say she was in a foul mood."

He laughed, pulled me closer, and kissed me. He tasted of dust and sweat, of blood and desire, and heated promises of a future longed for but never expected. A future I might not get if the winged riders— I pushed the thought away, not wanting to consider the possibility.

I slipped a leg over his hips and pressed against his muscular body and the glorious length of his erection. This was neither the perfect time nor place for any sort of consummation, but rational thought wasn't having much luck against the almost violent need to finally give in to the desire that burned between us.

The kiss deepened, intensified. I rubbed against him, the throbbing heat of his cock pressing against my mound, the leathers that lay between us little barrier to the fierceness of desire. It wasn't skin on skin, but it nevertheless set me alight. His lips left my mouth and trailed down my chin, my neck. I gasped, shuddering in delight at each tiny press of his lips against my skin. Then he shifted and, with one hand, began to undo my jacket's clasps. I should have objected. Should have told him the last thing I wanted was to make love on the cold, hard cavern floor. But that would be a lie because, right now, I didn't care. I wanted him, all of him. Any damn way, any damn where.

The last clasp came away, and he pushed the jacket aside, his fingers brushing the aching tip of one nipple. I jerked, even as desire speared my entire body. He laughed softly, his breath warm on my skin even through the silk of my undergarment. His lips slowly followed the path of his hand, then he caught the aching nipple gently in his mouth and lightly sucked on it. I gasped again and rocked against him more urgently, rubbing his thick length against me, feeling the pooling heat, and increasing wetness. I wanted him. Lord how I wanted him....

"Bryn?" came a distant call. "Damon? You out there?"

Kele.

Túxn was no doubt laughing in delight right now.

"Here," I replied, then groaned softly and rested my forehead against his. "I'm not sure whether to laugh or scream."

"Scream. Definitely scream." He tucked a finger under my chin and gently raised it, kissing me deeply and unhurriedly. "But perhaps it is for the best, given where we are."

I moved my leg from his hip but remained pressed against him. "There's definitely one part of your body disagreeing with that statement."

"And it would definitely have overridden common sense if we'd not been interrupted." He brushed a hand down my cheek, then across well-kissed lips. It felt like I was being branded. Felt like heaven. "But what we started here deserves more comfort and time."

If we had it, that inner voice whispered again. I swallowed the trepidation that rose and simply said, "Agreed."

"Then we fix your drakkon and retire to more comfortable quarters?"

"Perhaps a bath should be our first stop. We're both a little... grimy."

"Grime neither of us were worried about only a few seconds ago."

"True, but imagine the fun that could be had in a bath—"

"I've been doing nothing else ever since I sat by said bath and watched you only a night ago."

It was wryly said, and I smiled. "The same night I threatened your balls with my knee? I'm pleased to inform you such a threat is no longer on the table."

"I'm relieved to hear that, wife." He paused, wickedness flickering through his eyes. "Though there is great delight to be had on a table, I can assure you."

I raised an eyebrow. "Is there now? I hope you're prepared to follow that statement with a physical example."

His eyebrows rose. "You've never ventured beyond a bed or a bath?"

"I'm a soldier," I said dryly. "For most of my time in the military, quarters were shared, tables nonexistent within them, and privacy never assured. Sex was a fun but necessarily unadventurous event."

"Then it will be my great pleasure to educate you on this particular matter."

"And mine, I would hope."

"That I can promise."

He pushed to his feet, then offered me a hand and helped me up. He caught the edges of my jacket and did it up, causing havoc with every—probably not so accidental—brush of his fingers against my currently oversensitive skin. I glanced down at his still very evident erection. "That's going to cause a whole lot of conjecture and comments, especially given Kele is one of those who approach."

He shrugged. "Let them talk. Desire for my wife is something I will never feel ashamed of."

Another statement that warmed my heart. Once the jacket was done, he turned and picked his way through the rubble littering the floor, heading for the tubes he'd abandoned. By some quirk of fate, he'd rolled us just past a slab of rock that jutted out several feet into the tube, and given the tide of rubble sitting on the other side of the protrusion, it had obviously helped protect us from the worst of the explosion.

I looked around for the packs and spotted them a few yards away.

Damon's was half buried under a few rocks, but my two were just dusty. I walked over, dug them out and shook them off, then did a check inside mine to ensure everything remained in a usable condition. After tugging the light tube free, I switched it on, then slung one pack on my back, the other over my shoulder, and carried the third over to Damon.

"Did the weapons survive?"

"The tubes were crushed, but your weapon master should still be able to dissect and study them. The tub is fine—a good thing, considering if it had gone up like the others, we might not be here talking about it."

He exchanged his pack for the tubes, putting it on before picking up the tub of liquid. "Lead the way, my dear captain."

I couldn't help smiling again. "You just want me in the lead to hide the impressive length of your erection."

"No, I want you in the lead so I can watch the delicious sway of your ass."

I laughed. "That is not going to help said erection."

"Do I look as if I care?"

He certainly did not. I impulsively rose onto my toes and kissed him, then pulled away before it could get too heated and led the way through the rubble-strewn tunnel and into the connecting tube.

Five minutes later, Kele and three soldiers from her squadron appeared. I raised my hand against the brightness of their lights and stopped.

Once they were close enough, I said to Kele, "I take it the rescue team arrived?"

She nodded. "About half an hour ago. It took a while to stabilize Randel enough to move him, but all three are being escorted back to Esan as we speak."

"Good." I glanced past her to the oldest of the three men. "Grant, we'll need you and your men to take the weapons we found back to the commander."

He saluted. "Yes, Captain."

I retrieved the tub from Damon, then handed both it and the tubes over. "Be wary of the liquid. It's explosive."

"Is that what caused the blast we heard?" Kele asked.

I nodded. "It destroyed the tunnel leading up to the Beak."

"Not a bad thing, if our attackers were using it."

"They were." I flicked my gaze to Grant again. "Move out, Lieutenant, but be wary of the olm. They'll still be hunting through the blue vein tubes."

He and his men spun and quick timed it down the tunnel.

"We heading to the drakkons now?" Kele asked, anticipation in her voice.

I nodded again. "I have a promise to fulfil."

"Excellent." Her gaze slipped past me. "You can come out of the shadows now, my lord. The men have gone, and we women are never likely to mock such a deliciously rigid rod."

"It's hardly rigid," he said mildly. "It has been a good ten minutes since it received so much as a longing gaze."

"If that's hardly rigid, our girl is going to be one happy woman."

He laughed. "Only if she deigns to stop playing with drakkons and start playing with me."

"Seriously? I am here. I can hear you both."

Kele clapped a hand on my arm. "You can hear, but will you take notice? Because that fine man behind you is obviously in need of some tender ministrations."

"And if you had timed your arrival ten minutes later, he might well have gotten them."

My voice was dry, and she laughed in delight. "Well, that certainly explains the state of your jacket and the flush on your cheeks."

I frowned down at my jacket. "What state—" I stopped. The buttons had been done up wrong. "Obviously, my husband is more used to undressing women than dressing them."

"I cannot answer that statement on the grounds that I may incriminate myself."

I rolled my eyes, fixed my jacket, then brushed past Kele and once again led the way. It didn't take us long to reach the still faintly glowing remnants of the barrier spell. I stopped and pulled out the scribe quill and tablet, knowing I had better send my father a message before he sent out a secondary rescue team. I quickly described what we'd found, then let him know we were sending our scavenged tubes and liquid back with Grant's team while we headed for the drakkons. His reply simply said, *Keep safe.*

I hesitated, then sent back, *The islands? Any news yet?*

No. Contact remains lost.

And the cutters? They should have arrived there by now, should they?

They were sleek and fast, even in rough seas and weather, and at the very least, should have reached Manderlei, the closest island, just before dawn started stretching her bloody fingers across the sky.

No word from them as yet. Scribes may be down.

That was unlikely, and we both knew it. The scribes had been tested under the most trying conditions, and generally the only time they stopped working was when the tablet had been shattered—and it took a good deal of force to do that—or it was beyond a usable range. Jakarra was well within that range.

I wrote back, *And the tracker stones?*

Eighteen signals remain, but they weaken.

Meaning death was closing in, because the trackers were fueled by body heat—no heat, no tracker. Any rescue launched was now on a tight deadline.

It also meant they'd been attacked and that three of the six boats had been lost. But if three did remain, why hadn't they reached Jakarra yet?

Have sent out a rescue team, my father continued. *Should know more once the ship reaches their location.* There was a pause, the tiny ink blot that was the quill he was holding pulsing gently as it waited to relay more information. *Have told them to find shelter before dusk, no matter what.*

Meaning he'd ordered them not to risk their lives to save the lives of those in the cutters. I closed my eyes. That would have been a hard thing to do. It was a hard and fast rule within Esan's military ranks that we never left anyone behind—not even our dead, unless it was absolutely necessary.

But we couldn't risk losing any more people and boats to this threat, either. Not until we found some way of countering their weapons.

I hesitated again, not entirely sure what to say, then simply signed off. It was pointless to keep questioning him when so little was known. Hopefully that would change by the time we arrived back. Hopefully the rescued men and women would be able to shine at least a little light on what was happening.

I packed the quill and tablet away, then rose and continued on. As we neared the cavern in which the olm had attacked, I sent Kaia a message, letting her know we were on our way.

Know came her reply. *Hunt.*

Meaning she was well aware of our location and had acted accordingly once we were close enough.

Am queen, she said, her tone almost condescending. *Am smart.*

We finally reached the cavern in which the scouts had been attacked, and the first thing I noticed was the lack of bodies. The rescue team would have retrieved what was left of our dead, but they certainly wouldn't have done anything to the olm.

"We dragged them into the right tube," Kele said, obviously seeing my frown. "Figured if they were going to come for a feed, they'd tackle their dead first before they came after us."

"Good thinking."

"It does happen occasionally."

I laughed and moved on, leading the way through the tube until we reached the side tunnel that snaked up toward the old aeries. The heat gradually increased, and sweat trickled down my spine. Though no one truly understood the reason why this section of the range was so much warmer than the rest, it was thought to sit above a deep but still active lava tube, and that this area, with its multiple fissures, allowed the overheated air to rise more easily. The old aerie in Zephrine apparently had similar properties, but I had no idea if the one in the Red Ochre mountains did. As far as I was aware, there were no pockets of volcanic activity in that region. Maybe it wasn't necessary, given that range wasn't plagued by the violent swings of weather that could hit both Esan and Zephrine, thanks to their closeness to the sea, and tended to be more temperate.

I slowed as we neared the aerie. *Gria? We're coming in. Don't attack.*

Not. She paused. *Who we?*

Me, Kele, and Damon.

Mate fix cave? Make safe?

Yes.

No eat?

I smiled. *No eat anyone.*

She sighed. It was a very put-upon sound. *Hungry.*

Kaia will return soon. Was, in fact, already returning if the strengthening buzz of her thoughts was anything to go by.

I stepped into the aerie and paused a few yards in. The main chamber was a vast high space that could easily have held more than a grace of full-sized drakkons. There were also eight chambers running off it—smaller C-shaped areas of deeper warmth in which eggs could be safely laid and hatched, and which were more easily defended if raiders came. For too many years, we had. And for too many years, the blood of drakkons and Esan's soldiers had stained the gritty soil of these caverns.

Gria was hunkered to our left, half in, half out of one of the larger hatching caves. She was too big to entirely fit into it, but her tail and haunches were resting on the warmer sands, and contentment ran through the back reaches of her mind.

Damon and Kele stopped on either side of me. Gria eyed them, her thoughts abuzz with curiosity. It struck me again just how little fear she truly had of us. Of course, she'd been raised far away from any settlement, resulting in very little interaction with us, but I still found it surprising none of Kaia's distrust had leached over to her daughter. But then, Kaia had never shown any animosity toward me, either, despite her awareness of where I came from. Drakkons were obviously more magnanimous than we humans.

"Can I get closer to her?" Kele whispered, as if frightened speaking too loudly might spook a reaction. "Would she mind?"

No mind, Gria replied. *Must scratch.*

I grinned and unslung my pack. "She said as long as you promise to scratch the ridge above her eye, she promises not to eat you."

Kele's gaze cut to mine, her expression a mix of uncertainty and amusement. "She said that?"

"Not in so many words, but yes."

"Huh."

She followed me across, her fingers flexed and her expression a mix of wonder and awe. Though Gria was a third the size of her mother, she still towered above the two us. The drakkling watched us approach, her eyes black jewels in the faint glow of the light tubes. Then she lowered her head, her snout landing a few feet away from Kele's side. It was an obvious invitation, and after a brief hesitation, Kele reached up and scratched the ridge. Gria rumbled in contentment, and Kele laughed in delight.

"Looks like the drakkons have snared another heart," Damon said dryly.

"Easily done." To Gria, I added, *Stretch your right wing out. I need to finish patching it.*

Hurt?

Shouldn't this time.

She grumbled in soft disbelief, and Kele jumped back. "What did I do?"

"Nothing. She was just responding to me. Keep scratching her while I repair her wing."

I dumped the packs on the ground, dug out the silk webbing and sealer, and then began the slow process of repairing the remaining sections of torn membrane. After checking the repairs I'd made earlier and seeing—with some surprise—that even the breakages were almost healed, I came out from under her wing and checked her chest. It, too, was healing well, though it was unlikely she'd be able to fly for at least a couple of days without the risk of tearing it open again.

I left Kele scratching the drakkling's eye ridge, picked up my packs, and walked back to Damon. In the soft glimmer of my light tube, the pink nature of his sclera was very noticeable. "Will you still be able to raise the shields over both entrances? It's a big area, and you've already expended a lot of energy."

"Yes, which is why I'm using the capras. It won't cost me as much." Devilment twitched his mouth and danced through his eyes. "Still afraid I won't have any energy left to perform my duties tonight, wife?"

"No," I said dryly. "As I noted earlier, apparently not even death can stop a man getting an erection."

"There is more to consummation than a mere erection."

"I would hope so, or I shall be peeved." I glanced around as awareness stirred within. "Kaia's on her way back."

He swung off his pack. "I'll start getting ready then."

I nodded and walked over to the entrance tunnel. It was by necessity wide and high, with a ridge of thick stone that jutted out into emptiness, giving the drakkons a perfect landing and take-off pad. The stone was deeply scratched by the hundreds of drakkons who'd used this place over countless centuries, but time, weather, and disuse had softened many of the harsher lines. I couldn't help but hope that she and Gria would continue to use this place, even once I'd relocated to Zephrine.

An aerie deserved to have drakkons.

They deserved a safe place to breed and fly.

I dropped my packs out of the way, then rubbed my arms against the wisps of old rage. I couldn't change the past. Couldn't change what had been done to these magnificent beasts. Couldn't even change the attitude of Arleeon's people, who saw the drakkons as nothing more than pests that needed eradication for their stock to remain safe.

But there was a part of me that wanted to try, at least when it came to the latter.

The wind of Kaia's approach intensified, and I braced against the force of it. A few seconds later, she appeared, her wings gilded in the growing sunshine and her scales afire. She was gliding toward the landing stone, two capras clenched in her murderously large rear claws, but she didn't land. Instead, she banked, dropped one of the capras onto the pad, then flipped the other into her jaws and circled around. I ran forward, grabbed the capra by its hind legs, and dragged it back into the main tunnel, out of her way.

She made a rumbly sound deep in her chest that echoed the appreciation spinning through her thoughts then, with her feet outstretched, she landed neatly and lightly. After tucking her wings close to her body, she strutted forward, a queen reclaiming her home.

Or at least, that's what it looked like.

She dropped the second capra next to mine, then ducked her head for an eye ridge scratch. I obliged, and that deep-chested rumble echoed again.

Mate make Gria safe now?

Yes. And I've patched the rest of her wounds. She should be fully healed in a few more days.

Good. Her gaze shifted, and her head rose, her eyes glittering and wariness in her thoughts.

I looked around. Damon approached, his hands held partially up. "Tell her I mean no harm."

"She knows."

He lowered his hands and stopped several feet away, staring up at her. "They are magnificent beasts, aren't they?"

"They are, but they're as vulnerable to our winged attackers as we are. We need to find a way to protect them, Damon."

He glanced at me, his expression wry. "I never thought I'd be saying this, but I agree. And not just for your sake, but theirs. Arleeon would be poorer for their loss."

Not thought that in past, Kaia grumbled. *Many not think that now.*

No, but if we can make this place safe, then these ranges will at least give you some protection from what comes.

Must fight, she said. *No hide.*

You have Gria to look after.

Gria die—we die—if winged ones not fought.

That was a truth that could not be denied. I refocused on Damon. "I know your magic can't be used offensively, but is there any sort of spell that can be used to give the drakkons some protection?"

"I don't know, but when we get back to Esan, I'll scribe home and see if a search can be made through the archives." He motioned to the capra at my feet. "Let's get these over to the entrance so I can build the shields."

We tugged them across, the two drakkons watching with interest and more than a little anxiousness on Gria's part, mainly because she feared not getting her food, and hey, she was hungry.

"Do you need me to mark out a line in the stone with my sword again?" I asked.

He shook his head. "That was nothing more than a visual reminder of where the barrier was. In this case, the drakkons don't need it, and it's better if anyone coming in from the other side doesn't know about it until they hit it."

He bled the two capras, this time collecting their blood in two vessels rather than one, then glanced up at me. "I'm going to need a contribution from both you and Kele."

"Me?" Kele squeaked. "Why?"

Damon raised an eyebrow. "Don't tell me you're squeamish about a little blood?"

"Hell no, not if it's drawn in battle. But willingly sticking a knife in my own flesh? Hell yes."

He laughed. "Well, your blood isn't actually necessary for the spell, but it will mean you won't get through the barrier I'm about to raise."

She glanced at Gria, whose gaze remained on her meals rather than any of us, then sighed. "Fine. You can drain me of all life and energy."

"It's only a couple of drops from you each," he replied, amused. "I can assure you, you won't even feel the knife."

She snorted but nevertheless walked over and held her finger out. "Best get it over and done with, then, before I change my mind."

He shook his head, then, after rinsing his knife off, made a motion over it with his hand then took her finger and pressed the knife point into it.

Blood instantly welled, and surprise flitted across Kele's expression. "That didn't hurt."

"Told you it wouldn't." He turned her finger around and let her blood drip into a third, much smaller vessel. By the time he released her hand, the wound was already closing.

"If blood mages have the ability to make an incision painless," Kele said, stepping back, "why isn't it more widely used? It'd sure make surgery a lot easier."

"You forget blood mages are held in even less regard than Strega. Besides, sticking a knife in someone takes no skill, whereas repairing does." He took my finger, his touch gentle, almost impersonal, and yet my body reacted almost violently. This really was getting ridiculous. The sooner I got this man into bed—or bath, or even on the goddamn table—and satiated desperate hormones, the better.

He repeated the process with my finger, then raised it to his lips and kissed it, his gaze on mine and eyes burning with promises.

"Preferential treatment happening there," Kele noted.

"Totally," Damon agreed sagely and rose. "I'll need to do one shield at a time, so it may take a while."

"Meaning I get to scratch Gria more? Excellent."

"Let's feed her first," I said wryly. "Otherwise, she may forget her promise not to chow down on you."

Kele grinned. "And she'd probably spit me right back out again, given I'm probably gristlier than most."

I laughed, and then we each grabbed a rear leg of the nearest capra and dragged it over to the young drakkling. Gria instantly reached for it, but at Kaia's warning rumble, snatched her head back. We ran back for the other capra and dragged it over to the first. Only when we were both well out of the way did Kaia let her daughter eat.

Although eat was a relative term, given her teeth barely touched the capras. She basically swallowed each beast whole with barely a pause to break their bones.

As Kele returned to scratch Gria's eye ridge, I walked across the cavern, tugged off my pack, and then asked Kaia to extend her wings so I could fix them. While most of the tears had begun to heal, several large sections of leathery membrane remained loose and would never heal properly unless given a frame on which to do so. As Damon's magic rose, I once again tugged out the silk webbing and stretched it across the tears, then carefully sealed the loose skin to it. After that, it was simply a matter of giving the drakkon's natural healing ability time to work.

Won't take long, she said. *We fast heal.*

They certainly did. Most of the wounds that had scored her body only a few days ago were now little more than faint scars.

Once she'd tucked her wings back against her body, I folded one now empty pack into the other, then sat close to her and crossed my legs, leaning back against the wall of one of the hatching alcoves. Pain flared briefly as I pressed a little too much weight against my damaged shoulder, but the warmth emanating from the stone went some way to easing the aches through the rest of my body.

It was, however, a sharp reminder that the first thing I'd have to do when I got back was not report to my father or bed my husband, but rather see a healer and get some numbing salve. My fires might have sealed the wound and burned away infection, but it would be days before the pain faded—I knew that from experience.

The words of Damon's spell filled the air, a rich, melodious sound I could listen to all day. As before, he'd spanned the arch with the siphoned blood, added several drops from the vessel that held mine and Kele's blood, then drew his knife and sliced open his left arm. The minute his blood joined the darkly glistening line on the stone, smoke rose and fizzed back along it. But again, there was no explosion. Instead, Damon raised a hand, and the smoke followed his movement, filling the entrance's void. When he closed his fist, the smoke briefly solidified. Then it simply disappeared. The only indication of its existence was the slightest shimmer, and even that was fading fast. There'd been no evidence of the spell he'd raised in the olm cavern, either, but for some reason I'd just thought something this big would be at least partially visible.

Winged ones magic not, Kaia said. *This no different.*

I looked up at her. Dark eyes gleamed back at me, filled with what I swore looked like tolerant amusement. *So the winged ones do use blood magic?*

Same darkness, different feel.

Blood magic feels dark to you?

Yes.

Interesting. *In what way does the winged ones' magic feel different?*

No life.

Which made sense given Damon's magic was all about protection rather than destruction. Even if our attackers *did* use it for protection, its base—philosophy?—was very different.

I watched him walk over to the next entrance, noting the weariness that now haunted each movement and the slight gauntness in his cheeks. All magic had its costs; for blood magic, that cost was obviously physical strength. And one man could only do so much—protect so much.

Worry slipped through me, but I pushed it aside. The man would surely know his own limits, and given he appeared far more sensible that me, I doubted he'd push them too far.

I dragged the small flask from one of my packs, took a drink, and then squinted up at Kaia again. *How many other drakkons are there?*

Not know number of sun beasts, she said. *Most nest on drifting land beyond black shore.*

Sun beasts being Zephrine's golden drakkons, and the drifting land the floating islands that lay deep in the sea beyond Zephrine's fortress. *None remain in Zephrine?*

I sent her an image of the fortress, and she huffed. *That place kill. They always kill.*

My gut clenched. *Even now?*

Few remain to kill. Would.

I swore and scrubbed a hand across my eyes, trying not to think about my impending move there even as I wondered how in the wind's name I was going to survive. No matter how attracted I was to Damon, it would never be enough. Not for me. Aric may hate Esan's bleakness, but at least a beating heart lay underneath it. I was beginning to think that was not the case in Zephrine.

What about in the Red Ochre aeries? I sent her an image, so she knew I was talking about the mountains she called home.

Nine flights.

Images accompanied the answer—a flight was basically what we called a grace, and consisted of a queen, the other, generally younger, breeding females, a gaggle of males who vied for the attention of the smaller females, and the elders who helped tend and protect the eggs and the drakklings.

And in the Black Glass Mountains?

I knew drakkons existed here, I just had no idea how many.

Reds scattered. Warm caves big enough hard find here. Two flights known. Why ask?

Curiosity, mainly. I scrubbed a hand over my eyes. If I was doing the sums right, that meant there were twelve, maybe thirteen, queens in all, if we included her. *If Damon can come up with a means of protecting drakkons, do you think any of them would trust him enough to allow the magic?*

Not trust him. Trust me.

Surprise rose. *They would listen to you?*

Am queen.

Yes, but not the only one.

Biggest.

The arrogance in her reply made me smile.

Could mate protect us? she added.

Possibly only the queens—

If we safe, easier to protect flight and young. I like this plan.

So do I, but I can't promise it'll happen.

I trust.

She was putting a whole lot of trust in me already, and that in some ways was scary.

Not, came her reply. *We kin.*

I smiled. *We are.*

I reached back into my pack, grabbing some jerky to munch on while I watched Damon. His spelling was close to culmination now.

I think, Kaia said, after a few minutes, *will allow.*

I raised an eyebrow, wondering what in the wind's name she was talking about.

Saddle, she said. *Can use. Ride atop, behind neck spines. Leave claws free.*

My heart began to beat a whole lot faster—and while there was no denying some of it was based in fear, most of it was excitement. To soar high in the sky astride her would be... Well, it would be the realization of a long-held fantasy.

I cleared my throat and somehow kept my voice on an even keel. *It also means I can more easily use my fire to protect us both.*

Fire kill winged ones?

Don't know yet.

Hope do.

So do I. I climbed to my feet and stretched my limbs—immediately regretting it when my shoulder protested and sent pain spearing down my left arm. Painkillers were immediately added to the must-get list. *You should rest the night, Kaia, to give the patches time to work. I'll see you tomorrow morning.*

We fly? Check dead rider?

I hesitated and then nodded. My father might not be happy about the prospect, but he'd also realize that getting hold of their armor was a vital step forward in finding a means to get through it.

Kaia rumbled her satisfaction, then lowered her head for a final eye ridge scratch. I happily complied, then picked up my pack, walked over to grab Damon's, and continued on over to Kele. She was perched on one of Gria's outstretched claws, leaning back against the edge of one nostril, her expression a mix of delight and disbelief.

"You're game, resting so close to a drakkling's mouth." I stopped and offered her my right hand. "If she dreamed about swooping down after capra and opened her mouth to capture one, you'd be dinner."

She laughed, caught my hand, and bounced up. "No doubt, but hey, what a way to go."

"Says the woman who fussed about a little knife stab."

She laughed again and picked up her pack, trailing behind me while I walked around the sleeping Gria and across to Damon. He turned as I approached and smiled wearily. His face was pale and so drawn it was almost skeletal, and his eyes were sunken pools of faded blue and red. He didn't say anything, he simply caught my hand, drew me into his arms, and held me. His weariness washed over me, a cloak so thick it was almost stifling.

"That was a lot harder than I thought it would be." His voice was cracked and whisper soft. "It usually takes two of us to raise a shield of that magnitude."

"For Túxn's sake, Damon, you should have said—"

"Perhaps."

"There's no perhaps about it, husband. Next time, mention it."

"Perhaps." He chuckled softly, though it held little of its usual vigor. "Tell Kaia the shield will flash gold if you, me, or Kele approach, and red if anyone else does—"

"Will it stop weapons?" I cut in.

"Yes, although anything we carry will get through. If the shield is continuously flashing, it means someone is magically attacking it, but it'll hold long enough to give them time to leave."

Is good. Thank.

I repeated it, and he smiled. "We males do have some uses, Kaia."

Some, she grumbled, amusement heavy in her tone.

I handed his pack to Kele, then I swung around and slipped my right arm around his waist. He half raised his left arm, as if to rest it around my shoulders, then obviously remembered my wound and wrapped it around my waist, under my pack, instead.

"You want me to take the lead?" Kele said, shouldering his pack. "You can shout directions from behind if I go the wrong way."

I nodded, and she continued on, happily humming as she went through the tunnel. The barrier rippled briefly as she went through it, but didn't flash any particular color. Its energy briefly caressed my skin as we followed her, though I suspected I only felt it because I was holding on to Damon. "How long will these barriers last? Because it hardly seems worth the cost if they're only going to last eight or so hours."

"A question you perhaps should have asked before I expended all that energy."

"Probably." I glanced at him. "Does that mean you'll have to keep coming up here to reenergize them?"

"No, because I leashed these spells to a couple of steam vents. The spell should draw on the earth's energy to regenerate. In theory, anyway."

"You've never done it before?"

I couldn't help the surprise in my voice, and a tired smile tugged at his lips. "It would be fair to say that the last few days has provided a number of firsts."

"For us both." I paused, easing us both past a narrower section of tunnel. "How long will it take you to regain your strength from your exertions?"

He quirked an eyebrow at me, devilment in his eyes. "And once again the specter of me being unable to perform my husbandly duties arises."

"No, it's simply a matter of practicality," I replied dryly, though I couldn't deny that *was* a part of it. "We've been on the go for over twenty-four hours now, and I was hoping we could use it as an excuse to get out of the consummation feast. That's on tonight, remember."

"I doubt us being unable to attend would stop the celebrations, anyway. It's basically just another excuse for our friends and family to have a party."

"True." Though in times past, when virginity was far more prized than it was now, the consummation feast came after an inspection of the bedding to see if the wife had bled when penetrated. Too bad if she happened to be a rider because, hey, that scrap of skin designating so-called purity was easily torn when riding, especially bareback.

At least it was one custom that no longer existed, even if arranged marriages did.

Our pace through the mountain was by necessity slow, and while Damon's condition didn't deteriorate, it also only improved in small increments. We stopped a number of times to eat and rest, and that helped, but his weariness remained evident. He kept reassuring me he'd be fine once he slept and had a decent meal, but I'd heard too many tales of witches pushing it too far to be convinced.

Although by the time we finally reached Esan, he wasn't the only one shaking with tiredness.

Guards met us with sets of orders—one for me to report to my father, and one for him to report to his. I told Kele to go rest, then turned to Damon.

He brushed my cheek with his knuckles, a featherlight caress that had my breath catching. "Whoever gets to the room first orders the meal."

I nodded, my gaze dropping to his lips as the urge to kiss him hit.

But our fathers were waiting, the guards were watching, and I was a soldier more than a princess or a wife. There were protocols to follow.

At least some of the time, anyway.

A smile twitched the lips I was desperate to kiss, an indication he knew exactly what I was thinking, but he didn't say anything. He let his hand slide from my skin, then stepped back and, after giving me a somewhat formal half bow, left. I drew in a deep breath and made my way through the various gates, then up the stairs to the administrative and military building. My boots echoed on the polished stone floors, and the guards at the far end had the door opened by the time I approached. Which was good, because I think if I'd stopped, even for a fraction of a second, I might well have fallen.

I nodded in acknowledgment of their salutes and strode into the semi-darkness. My father was standing at the far end of the long table, studying the maps scattered in front of him. Mom wasn't there, but Vaya and Jarin were, as was Harris, our master of the fleet.

The maps, I noted, all appeared to be of the isles and the seas around them. They were obviously discussing various options for rescuing whomever might survive there.

If anyone survived there.

Maybe that was why Mom wasn't here. Maybe she simply couldn't confront the reality of losing everyone and everything she had loved growing up. Her immediate family might be safe here, but she came from a large extended family, and many, including my cousin Garran, hadn't been able to make the journey. Mom was the strongest, most sensible person I knew, but even she could be swamped by a tragedy this large.

And it wouldn't be the first....

I pushed that thought away determinedly. We would find a way to stop them. We had to. The only other choice was to cede them our lands, and that was never going to happen. Not while any of us had breath left to fight. Not while *I* had breath left.

My father glanced up as I entered, his gaze sweeping me and

relief briefly evident. But there was a tension in him, a sadness, that had my skin twitching. Something else had happened.

"Report, Captain Silva."

I did so, fleshing out the details I'd scribed earlier. When I'd finished, he nodded and said, "I'll contact our trading partners and see if any of them have had contact with such a race. We'll also post guards in the blue vein and main tunnel—that will at least give us some forewarning of an attack. What of your drakkons?"

"Protected."

"Good. Good." He glanced down at the maps, and tension rippled briefly across his shoulders. When he looked up again, the tension within me increased. He really didn't want to ask whatever it was he was about to.

"Captain, this is a question rather than an order.... Can your queen fly over the five islands and give us an aerial report?"

Surprise flickered through me. Surprise and concern. "What else has happened?"

"They've blocked our harbor," Harris said. "We drove them off before they could destroy the fleet, but we nevertheless lost two galleons in the attack and a dozen men."

The fact that we *had* been able to drive them off was at least something. "And the ship you were sending to pick up the survivors from the cutters?"

"Found fourteen and recovered four bodies. They are on their way to Hopetown."

Hopetown was a long way from the islands, but in current circumstances, might be the only safe port left in this section of East Arleeon. "How in the wind's name did they block the harbor?"

"Magic. Blood magic," my father said heavily. "By the time our earth witches were aware of the spell and tried to counter it, it was too late. They destroyed half the peninsula and dumped all the rubble into the harbor's mouth."

"It's going to take days for our witches to remove it all," Harris added. "We need to know what the situation is for the survivors over on those islands."

Presuming those islands hadn't suffered the complete decimation of their population that Eastmead had, of course. He didn't say that, but he didn't have to. We were all thinking it.

Then I frowned. "What time did they attack?"

"Just before dawn," my father said. "Why?"

"When I saw the armored bird and its rider, it was just after dawn, and the creature had what looked to be some sort of hood over its eyes. It might well mean they're sunlight sensitive and therefore unable to hunt during the day."

"Not necessarily," Jarin said, his voice a low rumble that matched his stout figure. "Hooding is a commonly used procedure on gray hawks to calm them down, especially when they're young and new to training."

"Yes, but every attack so far has either been at night or just before dawn. That does suggest some limitations."

"Meaning a flight over to the island might be safely done during the day." The glance Vaya cast my father suggested they'd been arguing over that point, and I wasn't entirely surprised. He might be my commander, but he was also my father, and those two halves would always be at war when it came to ordering me into dangerous situations. "We must risk it, Commander. We have no real choice here."

"Except the question was not answered." His voice was flat, but his gaze and his attention was on me. "And I will not make it a command, simply because there is only one person in this room who can command your drakkon. Additional air witches have been called in. It remains possible that by combining their powers they could transport a small scouting force to Jakarra."

"And it could yet take days for those summoned to arrive," Jarin said. "Depending on the level of destruction that has happened on those islands, it's possible those who remain may not have that much time left."

My father didn't reply. He just held my gaze, willing me to refuse, *wanting* me to refuse, even though he utterly agreed with everything being said. Because he knew, without a doubt, that I would not ask Kaia to do this alone. I would go with her, protect her, as much as I could.

"I will ask her when I check on her tomorrow morning. The decision is hers to make, not mine."

Will, she said. Her mental tones were distant but nevertheless determined. *White hair feed Gria?*

I briefly closed my eyes. There was a part of me that had wanted her to refuse, because she was risking everything for us, and we so didn't deserve it. *Yes, Kele will ensure Gria is fed.*

Good. We fly.

I opened my eyes and met my father's again. He knew the decision had already been made. That was evident in the brief flicker of guilt and understanding through his gaze. But all he did was nod. "Until then, get some rest, Captain. You look dead on your feet. Oh, and tonight's celebrations have been canceled."

Because it was wrong to celebrate when so much death had happened recently. Again, he didn't say it, but we were all thinking it.

"And what of my impending move to Zephrine?"

"Postponed. Until this problem has been resolved, I will not lose one of my better captains." Or indeed risk his daughter on the long sea journey to Zephrine's warmer shores.

He didn't say that, of course, but I could nevertheless see it in his eyes.

I ignored the thick surge of relief, stepped back, and with a salute that wasn't as crisp as normal, turned and made my way out of the administration building and across to the hospital quarters. Maree—a rotund woman with thick blonde hair and ruddy cheeks—greeted me as I walked in the door and led me without question into the nearest curtained booth.

"Strip off and let's have a look at that shoulder of yours," she said, as I perched on the edge of the bed.

I obeyed. "Did my father contact you?"

"No." Amusement danced in her blue eyes. "Your husband did. And he's a rather gorgeous specimen of manhood, if you don't mind me saying."

"Nothing wrong with the truth." I winced a little as she lightly ran her fingers across my shoulder and then down my back. She wasn't a healer as such; her skill lay more in divining what was happening within the body, thereby providing a clearer picture for those who healed or repaired with magic or knife. But she also was a skilled herbalist, and her numbing potions were second to none. "Was that all he came here for?"

She cackled. "Indeed not. I ended up giving the lad a revitalization potion. It'll stave off the tiredness long enough for you two to have some fun. Because, girl, that man is made for fun."

"Indeed, he is." Even though we hadn't yet gotten that far. Hopefully, tonight, we'd remedy that. "Which is why I need something to stave off the shoulder pain."

"Easy enough to do. Good job on the shoulder, by the way. Ain't sensing any sign of infection, and the beasties that bit you didn't tear anything vital."

"I was lucky."

"You've made a habit of that, I would say. Túxn obviously favors you." She moved across to the glass-fronted cabinets that lined the rear wall and were filled with all manner of tubs, jars, and herbs, pulled out a squat bowl of what looked like pale clay, then returned. "This will numb the pain for eight hours, and it's also waterproof. Apparently he has seduction plans involving a bath."

My head snapped around, and she laughed, a deep and bawdy sound.

"He *told* you that?"

"Not in so many words, but I've been around a long time, and I've learned to read between the lines." She scooped the muck onto my skin and rubbed it in, her movements quick but sure. The slow throbbing ache quickly eased. "Better?"

I nodded and then hesitated. "I've got to head over to Jakarra tomorrow—"

"Heard about the attack on the islands," she cut in. "Any news as to how bad it is?"

"Not yet—the communication lines are down. I'll be traveling light, but I was wondering—do you have anything transportable that I could take with me? Painkillers, numbing lotion, stuff to battle infection? I'll be taking the bone straps and sealer, of course, but that might not be enough."

"If it's bad over there, whatever you can carry will not be enough."

"I know, but it's a start, and it'll be better than arriving with nothing."

She nodded. "What time are you leaving?"

"Dawn?"

"I'll have a bag ready and waiting for you then."

"Thanks, Maree."

"No problem at all." She shuffled over to another cabinet and retrieved a small vial of greenish goop. "Now drink this, then go have fun with that sexy man of yours."

"Oh, I very much intend to." I accepted the vial a little dubiously but nevertheless uncorked it and gulped it down. A shudder ran through me. "That tastes horrible."

"But it'll work miracles on your stamina, trust me on that," she said, with another bawdy laugh followed me out the doors.

With a grin on my face, I strode across the courtyard and ran up the steps to the palace, acknowledging the guards as I headed to the first floor. I hesitated, glanced down toward my parents' suite, then followed the twitch of instinct and headed down. However badly I wanted sex, I needed to make sure Mom was okay first.

The guard outside their door watched me approach, a smile touching his lips. He was a bull of a man and had manned her door for as long as I could remember. "She said you'd be here in ten. She's ordered shamoke and a meal for you."

"How is she, Lenny?" We'd long ago dispensed with formalities, at least in situations where there were few others around.

"Coping. You've only just missed your grandparents."

"Damn. I would have liked to see them."

He opened the door for me. "Plenty of time, Lady Bryn."

I wasn't so sure of that, but I nodded my thanks and entered the room. In many respects, it echoed my own quarters, only twice the size. My parents also had additional rooms—such as a dining and a living room—attached, so they could entertain guests less formally.

Mom was standing near the window slit that looked out over the courtyard, but turned as I entered. Her face was pale, drawn, and there was grief in her eyes, but overwhelmed she definitely wasn't.

"You heard?" she asked softly.

I nodded. "I've just made my report to Father. He also mentioned that my move to Zephrine has been postponed."

"Yes, and it was, surprisingly, Aric's idea."

"I thought he was keen to get his heir home?"

"I suspect he's decided he needs a more reliable source of information temporarily based here."

I snorted. Yep, that definitely sounded like something Aric would think.

She motioned me toward the table, then poured me a large cup of shamoke. I sipped it gratefully. Unsurprisingly, it was just the way I liked it—sweet and black. "I take it your father has asked you to journey across to Jakarra?"

"Well, he asked me to send Kaia, but he was well aware I'd be going with her."

"He was against it."

"I picked that up while we were talking." I studied her for a moment. "You're the one that suggested it, weren't you?"

She nodded. "Yes, and I know the risk to both you and the queen, but we must do this, Bryn. I—*we*—must know the situation there before any further plans can be made."

And that was the practicality of the woman who'd once been the bow master speaking, rather than my mother.

She picked up a bowl and spooned the thick stew sitting on the warmer tray into it before handing it to me. "If there are survivors, you will not find them in any of the towns, if such even exist anymore. They would have retreated to caves high in the Karthling Mountains."

I raised my eyebrows. "I had no idea there were caves up there." And I'd certainly spent enough time chasing Garran through that area over the multiple summers I'd spent there as a child.

"Few do. It was a well-guarded secret, known only to those who'd be responsible for evacuation in a time of crisis."

And *this* was certainly a crisis. "If they are up there, why wouldn't they have scribed?"

"Because the area is volcanic, and much like parts of the Black Glass Mountains here, the ability to scribe is restricted."

"How big are the caves?" My stomach rumbled in sudden hunger, and I hurriedly scooped up some stew.

"They once held drakkons. They could hold all of Jakarra if needed." She looked away, though not before I'd seen the sheen of tears. "That would not be the case here. We'll be lucky if half the inhabitants survived."

"Is there anywhere in that area for Kaia to land and bunker down? I can't direct her into the heart of the island without risking an attack from whatever ground forces the gilded riders have, or even our own people."

"You should not go to ground. It is too dangerous."

"I'll have no choice, and you know it."

She knew. The guilt that flashed across her features said her objection was perfunctory—a statement that had to be said but never meant. She reached for one of the scrolls sitting at the end of the table —there were three, two large and one much smaller—and unrolled it. It was a detailed map of Jakarra, one I'd not seen before. After putting a couple of cups on either end to stop it from curling up again, she pointed to the large, U-shaped mountain range that ran around the western edge of the island.

"This is the Karthling Mountains. This section here"—she pointed to the longer of the mountains' two arms—"is the Helvede Range, and holds the network of caves any survivors would have retreated to."

I leaned forward with a frown. "That looks dangerously close to the main port and Illistin. The gilded riders would have seen their retreat."

"Yes, but between Illistin and the main cavern entrance lies a series of old, deep crevices that can only be crossed by bridges. They will have been destroyed in the retreat."

I nodded. I remembered those bridges, and they'd scared the life out of me as a child. They were basically an arc of stone just wide enough for a wagon to pass over, and had nothing in the way of protective railings, which sometimes made crossing tricky with the fierce winds that often hit the island.

"Destroying the bridges won't stop a flighted enemy."

"No, but the nature of the mountain itself will. The entrances to the caves are hidden and narrow. Their birds won't get in. That gives survivors a fighting chance."

Not against a blood mage capable of moving rock, it didn't. But I didn't give voice to that thought. Mom would know that just as well much as me. "Where is the old aerie, then, if not in the Helvede arm of the mountains?"

She pointed to the leeward side of the shorter arm. "Here."

"Meaning Kaia will have to drop me off and then retreat while I head in and look for survivors." I scooped up more stew and munched on it contemplatively while I studied the map. I might have roamed through the forests and foothills of these mountains, but my overall knowledge of them wasn't great. "Obviously it'd be too dangerous to dismount anywhere near Illistin, so where do you suggest?"

She pointed to the windward side of the mountain's longer arm, near the point where it joined the trunk. "There's a wide ledge underneath the summit's peak here. There shouldn't be too much snow up there at this time of year, but our winters sometime linger, and it can at times be deep, so ensure you're wearing appropriate boots. There's a series of caves midway between the ledge and the peak but you can't miss the right one—it looks like a bent key. The others are shallow caves that aren't part of the main system."

"And once inside? How am I going to find the survivors without wandering through the tunnels for days?"

"With this." She reached for the second scroll and unrolled it. It was a detailed drawing of a tunnel system.

I glanced at her. "Where in the wind's name did this come from?"

"Esan's archives. This is where you'll enter." She pointed to the left side of the map, then traced her finger along a series of tunnels until she reached a large, oval-shaped cavern. "You'll likely find the bulk of survivors here. It was adapted long ago as a storm shelter, and provisions regularly rotated to keep them usable."

"Meaning as long as they can keep our winged foe out of the system, they can survive for weeks or even months."

"A month would be pushing it, but in theory, yes."

I finished my stew and picked up the cup of shamoke. The southern exit was remote, and it was unlikely our gilded foe would or even could check every cavern entrance in that area to find our survivors—so why hadn't the survivors made their way up to that peak and scribed us? Surely any well-provisioned storm shelter would have included a couple of scribe pens, even if they couldn't be used within the mountain itself.

If they hadn't attempted it, there would likely be only one reason —they had no one fit enough, uninjured enough, or familiar enough with the deeper tunnel system to do so. Mom would be well aware of all that, but I still had to ask, "Do you think they'll have posted guards at the southern entrance?"

She hesitated. "Unlikely. They will be concentrating on

protecting the main entrances, though I have no doubt watchers will be posted at the three tunnels leading into the shelter cavern."

Her use of the term watchers rather than guards suggested she didn't believe many of Jakarra's fighting force had survived. It was logical that those who *had* would be posted to the more likely access points.

"Can I take this?" I had a fairly good memory for directions, but too much was at stake right now to make a mistake and go the wrong way.

"This one would be too cumbersome, but I drew up a smaller one and marked the right path." She handed me the final scroll. "I have one more thing for you."

She turned and walked across the room to the large alcove that held all her clothing. After a few minutes, she returned with a black-wood short bow and a quiver full of arrows.

Blackwood bows were rare here in Esan, as the trees really only grew well in the five islands, but they had a natural elasticity, a sweetness of draw, and a cast second to none, and those three things made bows crafted from them prized possessions. This was Mom's bow—one she'd been gifted when she became bow master so long ago.

She placed them on the table next to me. "I want you to take these."

"Mom, I have a bow—"

"But you do not have a bow like this, nor do you have arrows as deadly as these." She drew one free of the quiver and held it up. Even in the wan light filtering through the light wells overhead, the decidedly crude glass arrowhead gleamed with a deadly blue-white light.

"Ithican glass?" My gaze shot to hers. "How?"

"They are shards—waste, if you will. Jakarra imported them from Ithica for decades, using the larger flints for fishing spears and the smaller for arrowheads. If anything can penetrate the winged ones' armor, it will be these."

Because there were few things Ithican glass *couldn't* penetrate. "How many of these arrows have we got?"

"What we have—both in arrows and in spears—I brought with me from Jakarra. I have no idea what supplies remain there, but it is a long time since they used spears to hunt sea life."

"And Ithica? Have they been approached to buy more?"

"Indeed yes, but we have not yet received a reply. Even if we are able to purchase enough to cover our needs, the distance between our two continents means it could take weeks for it to arrive. I fear we do not have that time, Bryn."

I feared the very same thing. "Does Father know you're giving me these?"

She smiled. "We keep no secrets from each other. No married couple should."

"Your marriage is far different to mine. You love Dad, whereas I —" I cut the rest off and shrugged. I had no idea what I actually felt for Damon. Yes, he was attractive and sexy, and I liked what I knew of him so far, but we were still strangers in so many ways that really mattered.

"He is a good man, Bryn, even if he comes from bad stock. When the darkness comes, you should trust him, even when common sense suggests otherwise."

Alarm slithered through me. "You're dreaming again?"

She half raised a shoulder. "Whispers, nothing more."

"What have those whispers said? What haven't you told me?"

"All I know is that Aric lies. About what, I cannot say. Not yet."

"Aric, not Damon?"

"The whispers have only said he can be trusted."

That was something. Mom's dreams, while few and far between, were rarely wrong. I just had to hope this wasn't one of those rare occasions. "Why is Aric still here? I thought he was going home before the feast?"

"He decided to wait until we knew more of the situation at the Beak before he did."

"You believe him?"

"In that, yes."

I finished my stew and leaned back, feeling better if no less tired. "Anything else?"

"No." A smile tugged at her lips. "Go play with your husband, while you still have the time."

I pushed to my feet. "Because a comment like *that* isn't going to raise any concerns about what the future brings."

It was wryly said, and she chuckled softly, catching my hand and drawing me closer to drop a kiss on my cheek. "It was not meant to be anything more than a reminder that war gathers on the horizon, and we must take our pleasure where and when we can. Go. I will talk to you tomorrow morning before you leave."

I nodded, picked up the bow and quiver, and then left.

The time had come to seduce my husband.

9

NOT THAT I for one minute suspected that would, in any way, be hard. All evidence so far suggested the exact opposite. Still, I wasn't about to go in there smelling of blood and grime, either. I might be looking forward to the promised bath seduction, but the last thing I wanted was for it to be happening in water as foul as I currently smelled.

I quietly bypassed my room and headed down to the thermae, placing the bow and quiver on a nearby bench before stripping off and climbing into the spring.

As the bubbly water tingled across my skin, a young bathing attendant appeared and placed a towel on a nearby bench. "Can I get you anything else, ma'am?"

"A scented soapweed—the verum, I think—and a robe. My clothes are... well, worse for wear."

A small smile tugged at her lips. "Shall I send them for cleaning?"

"Yes. Thank you."

She fetched the soapweed, then gathered my clothes and silently left. I quickly scrubbed the grime from my skin and hair, then tossed the soapweed into the refuse bin and climbed out. As I toweled myself dry, she reappeared, several robes held over her arms. After a moment, I chose the one that was all but sheer aside from a few discreetly placed panels. I did have to walk back to my room, after all, and while as a soldier I might be well used to walking around naked, there were the sensibilities of the palace guards to consider.

After retrieving the bow and quiver, I headed out. The corridors remained empty of traffic aside from the few discreetly placed guards who studiously looked the other way as I passed. Once inside my room, I tucked the bow and quiver into the storage cabinet to the right of the door, then swept my gaze across the room. Shamoke steamed lightly on a heating pad sitting in the middle of the table, and there were also breads, cheeses, and a covered tray of what smelled like roasted meat. The bed platform was empty, so I headed toward the bathing facilities, discovering Damon lounging in steaming water, his arms resting on the sides of the bath and his eyes closed.

"Whoever approaches," he murmured, "you smell too good to be my wife."

"I do love the way compliments simply drip from your lips." I walked past the bath over to the shelving to grab the soapweed. "Did you really tell Maree that you intended to seduce me in the bath?"

His eyes cracked open. "She told you that?"

"There are no secrets when it comes to Maree."

"Huh." Though his gaze remained thin slits of blue, I had the distinct impression I was being very thoroughly examined. "I like that gown, by the way, but it hides entirely too much for my liking."

"The gown is almost sheer," I said dryly.

"It's the 'almost' that disappoints."

I laughed. "Would you like me to wash your back?"

"I would rather you join me in this bath."

"I will. In time."

He closed his eyes again. "Rest assured I will hold you to that promise."

I smiled and knelt behind him. After dipping the soapweed into the steaming water, I started washing him, slowly brushing the balled netting across his right shoulder and then down the muscular length of his arm. "What did your father want?"

"Are we really going to discuss our parents at such an important moment in our relationship?"

"Indeed we are, because the consummation celebrations have been canceled and we have the entire night ahead of us. Is it not better to get words out of the way, so our mouths can be put to better use?"

He chuckled softly, a sound that reverberated deliciously through me. "Put like that, I have no option but to agree."

"Wise man." I swept the matting across to his other shoulder and then down, keeping my movements slow and rhythmic. "Why didn't your father leave?"

I already knew, but there was a tiny part of me wanting to know if he'd answer honestly. A part stirred to life by my mom's comments.

"He wanted a report, as the guard said."

Tension rippled briefly through him, telling me that wasn't all his father had wanted. "And?"

"And he ordered me to keep him updated on events. He even handed me a scribe tablet linked directly to one in his private chambers."

I frowned at the deeper edge in his reply and swept the matting across his right shoulder again, then down to his chest and the sculpted magnificence of his abdomen. A soft sound escaped his lips, but he didn't move, and he certainly didn't open his eyes.

"That suggests he doesn't trust my father."

"He doesn't trust anyone."

"Even his sons?"

"Particularly his sons. Or, at least, this son."

"But you're his heir."

He shifted fractionally, resting his head between my breasts. "I'm both his greatest asset and his greatest bane. Something he needs but does not want."

"Then why not disown you and simply make Tayte his heir?"

One shoulder rose fractionally. "As we've both noted, his decisions sometimes make no sense."

An answer that really wasn't. He knew the reason. He just wasn't willing to tell me yet.

I ignored the sliver of disappointment and continued washing him, sweeping the netted soapweed across every inch of his washboard perfection, leaving no part of his torso untouched. But when I finally followed the sharply defined V that led down to his groin, he caught my hand and tugged me around the side of the bath.

"Time for you to join me, I believe."

"But I've already had a bath."

"So the divine scent emanating from your skin would suggest." He opened his eyes and pinned me in a sea of blue. Just for a moment, it felt like I was falling, drowning, and there was definitely a part of me that wanted to do nothing more than lose myself in promises so visible within that glorious sea.

But shadows haunted the deeper depths, and until I knew their source, I could not risk falling. I would not set myself up for heartbreak. Not again.

Then devilment flicked through the blue, and his grip on my hand tightened. Before I knew what was happening, he'd dragged me into the bath with him. I came up spluttering and coughing, shifted position so that I straddled his lower thighs, then whacked his chest with the soapweed.

"That was *not* polite."

"No, but you're now in the bath with me, so I don't really care."

His fingers trailed up my waist and circled my left areola, then the right, both of which were now very visible through the robe's wet material. His touch was so light and yet so heated, and my nipples hardened as desire curled through me. It was all I could do not to press into that teasingly delicious caress.

I swallowed heavily, dunked the soapweed back into the water, and continued my ministrations. This time, when I swept down the

V to his hips and on to his groin, he didn't object. I gently washed around the base of his cock but ignored his magnificent length, instead sliding back on his legs to wash his thighs. His fingers caught the robe's ties, stopping me from retreating any further.

"My calves and feet do not need your tender ministrations," he murmured, tugging at the ties until they came undone.

My breath caught as he parted the robe and his fingers brushed my skin, making me shiver in delight. "You don't like you calves or feet being touched?"

"Oh, I do," he said, voice seeming to come from somewhere deep in his chest. "But right now there are other parts of my body needing your attention more."

I smiled as he slipped a hand around my waist and slid me back up his legs.

"And what would they be?" I whispered, leaning forward and brushing my lips across his mouth. "This?"

"No."

I moved my mouth down to his chin. "This?"

"Definitely not."

"What about this, then?" I shifted and caught his right ear between my teeth, lightly nipping as I pressed my mound against the hard heat of his erection and gently rubbed up and down.

He sucked in a quivering breath and then said, "No."

"Ah." I trailed kisses down his neck and shoulders, then continued on with my hands, sliding down his torso, gently caressing every glorious inch before once again following the deeply cut V to his groin.

He caught my hands before I could touch. "That way lays danger."

I grinned. "And this is bad because?"

"Because I suspect I am more primed than you."

"I wouldn't bet on that, husband."

"I'm not one for betting. I *am* one for ensuring." Wickedness gleamed in his eyes as he raised my hands to the top of my head and held them there. "My turn to touch and tease, wife."

"Oh, please, feel free."

He smiled his devilish smile, brushed his lips across mine, then proceeded to echo my earlier movements, kissing my cheeks, my neck, my ear, each sweep of his lips a delicious torture. His kisses drifted down my neck and along my collarbone, branding me, making me shiver. When the water prevented him from going any further, his switched lips for hand, and plucked and teased my nipples breasts with the precision of a maestro conducting a band of one. The shivers grew, and the deep-down ache bloomed, curling upward through my body, demanding and needy.

He slid his fingers down my stomach, brushing across the line of hair as he shifted his thighs, forcing mine wider, giving him easier access. When his finger slid across my clit, I shuddered, a deep moan of delight escaping my lips.

He chuckled softly, his grip on my hands shifting, drawing me close enough to claim my lips and kiss them hungrily as his fingers continued to tease and explore. When they finally slipped inside, I gasped in pleasure and rocked against him, wanting more. Needing more. He chuckled again, and the heated rhythm increased, first with one finger, then with two as his thumb grazed my clit, causing havoc. I moved with him, riding his fingers, my shudders increasing and my breathing harsh and fast. Then my orgasm hit, wave after wave of pleasure fiercer than anything I'd ever experienced. I shuddered and shook and moaned, barely even aware that his touch had left me, too caught up in the backwash of pleasure. Then his hands found my hips and he lifted me up and on to him.

And oh, it was glorious. *He* was glorious.

Thick, and hard, and so damn big it felt like he was slipping inside forever.

And yet it felt so right. Felt so perfect. Like I'd been specifically designed to sheathe this man.

"Look at me," he whispered.

I opened my eyes and stared into the blue of his. Saw the hunger there, the recognition of perfection. Saw, deeper in those glorious depths, the surprise and perhaps even a little fear—a realization that this moment, this exquisite, beautiful moment, might never happen again, because fate and the plans of others could rip it away from us both.

But before I could catch that thought and worry on it, he began to move, and everything else but this man and the pleasure rising between us disappeared. With his hands on my hips and mine on his shoulders, we moved as one, slowly at first but with ever increasing urgency, until my body shook with the force of it and all I wanted, all I could think about, was release. His, mine, ours.

When it came, it was explosive, wrenching a cry from my lips as his body went rigid against mine and his seed exploded into me.

It took forever to come down from the dizzying heights of completion. When I could finally breathe with something close to normality, I closed my eyes and rested my forehead against his. But for a long time, neither of us moved any further. Then his hand slid around the back of my neck, holding me still as he raised my face and kissed me long and slow. Heat and desire that have been well and truly sated, stirred, and deep inside, his cock twitched, suggesting it wouldn't take long—or all that much encouragement—for him to become erect again.

And I was perfectly okay with that.

"I guess I should have asked this before I pulled you into this bath," he murmured, his lips moving ever so slowly down my neck. "But are you protected against pregnancy?"

I laughed. "Indeed I am. And it's probably just as well, given the fullness of the load I just received."

"In my defense, it has been a while."

"That's not what the rumors would have us believe."

"Rumors cannot always be believed."

"So I'm not to believe all those statements about your legendary stamina? Your ability to rise to the occasion again with very little rest?"

The fact he was already half erect inside me again did confirm the latter, but I decided not to mention that.

He grinned. "I'm more than happy to prove both statements, but I suggest we do so out of this bath. Pruned skin is not exactly a good look, at least on me."

I laughed, caught his cheeks between my hands and kissed him, then lifted myself from his cock and stepped out of the bath. He followed me out and, once I'd shed the dripping gown, swept me up in his arms and carried me over to the bed, where he proceeded to show me just how long and hard a Zephrine prince could go.

I woke to the heat of Damon's body pressed against mine, the warmth of his breath teasing my neck, and his hand draped loosely across my waist. For several minutes, I did nothing more than lie there, enjoying the closeness, knowing full well it could be some time before another moment of peace such as this happened again.

Last night had been... well, a revelation. I'd always enjoyed sex, but I'd also always been very wary of letting all my guards down and losing myself in the moment and the man. Thanks to our marriage and the irrevocable nature of it, there had been no such worries with *this* man, and the end result had been mind-blowing. I'd never felt such a deep connection with another before, and while that might in part be because I'd always held back, I very much suspected it went deeper than that. And *that* was both scary and exhilarating. While the promise of a bright and perhaps even loving relationship had become a tantalizing possibility, I was well aware that the secrets both he and his father were hiding could yet destroy the fragile framework we'd started to build. While I really hadn't inherited

Mom's seeress abilities, per se, they sometimes bled through to my instincts, and they were definitely twitchy about the information they were withholding and what it could do to *us*.

I knew I'd have to confront him about my—and Mom's—suspicions, but I also couldn't help the desire to push that moment away for as long as possible.

But now was not the time to be gnawing over personal problems. I had a mission to complete, and I needed to get moving if I wanted to arrive at the aerie just after dawn.

Slowly, carefully, I slid from under Damon's arm and out of the bed. I'd forgotten to tell him about my mission last night and I really wasn't up to a discussion about it this morning. I was a soldier, and until I left Esan's dark and glorious halls for those of Zephrine, I still had a job to do.

He didn't stir, not then, not when I ran a bath, and not when I dressed. But that was hardly surprising. Maree's potion could only stave off the utter exhaustion caused by his blood magic for so long, and the man's monumental effort in bath and bed would probably have shortened its "working life."

I strapped on my sword, then walked back to the bed, leaning across to drop a kiss on his bare shoulder. He stirred briefly, murmuring something I couldn't quite catch, his hand sweeping the blankets as if searching for me. I placed mine over his briefly, stilling the movement, then I forced myself to leave him be when I wanted nothing more than to climb back in beside him. After gathering the rest of my weapons and Mom's short bow and map, I left.

The corridors were shadowed and quiet, the candles flickering in the wall sconces doing little to chase away the pre-dawn darkness. By the time I padded down the stairs, the guards had the front doors open. I nodded a greeting to them, then ran down the steps and over to the stables.

Mik must have heard me opening the side door, because he appeared on the upper landing that ran down the middle of the stable block, hastily pulling on his overshirt. While he and all our other stable hands had their own living accommodation down in the common quarter, they often used the loft compartments upstairs rather than head home between shorter shifts.

"Is there a problem, Miss Bryn?"

"No, Mik. I'm just here to grab a couple of things."

"You sure you don't need a hand?"

"Yes, but thanks."

As he nodded and disappeared, I grabbed a couple of carrots from the tub kept near the door and walked down to Desta's stall. She greeted me with a soft nicker and accepted the carrots in a regal manner. I smiled, rubbed her silky nose, and then headed down to the tack room. The smell of well-oiled leather hit me the minute I entered, and I breathed deep, sighing in pleasure as I walked through the racks of saddles until I found the section holding those designed for our largest coursers. I hadn't remembered to contact the saddlers, and one look confirmed there was very definitely nothing here that could, in any way, be adjusted to fit Kaia's back. The saddle trees just weren't wide enough. Breaking them was pointless—I might as well just ride her "bareback" given how uncomfortable broken saddles generally were for both rider and mount.

I continued on to the area holding all the tack. One breastplate was never going to get across Kaia's chest, and while I could certainly strap a few of them together, anchoring them would be a problem given there now wouldn't be a saddle. Attaching them directly to a girth also wasn't an option; aside from the positioning of her front legs and wings making that difficult, it would probably take a good number of them to get around her barrel. But maybe I could join a number together, sling them around her neck, and then fashion a simple U-shaped harness to anchor it—and me—to one of her spines. If I attached a couple of stirrups, that might help me maintain balance, especially given the wind turbulence I'd probably face. I had strong thighs—something Damon had discovered last night during one of our "lighter" moments—but riding a courser bareback would be vastly different to riding a drakkon.

Of course, if she turned upside down I'd probably still fall off, but at least if I was roped onto the girths, I'd just dangle from her neck rather than fall to my death.

Won't turn upside, she commented. *Uncomfortable way to fly.*

I grinned. *Good morning, Kaia. Have you been listening to my thoughts all night?*

No. You mate. Thoughts tedious.

I laughed and shoved girths, ropes, and some D-rings to connect everything into a rucksack, then lashed the short bow and quiver onto its back and headed out. After collecting Maree's promised packs of medicines, I headed for the gates. Mom, Kele, and two soldiers from my scout group—Sora and Jax, the former our wiry, middle-aged forward scout, the latter much younger, but possibly one of the best swordsmen I've ever seen—were waiting for me. Between Sora and Jax was a simple litter on which a freshly killed boar lay stretched.

"Is this a goodbye or good riddance greeting party?" I asked with a grin.

"I figured you'd forget to pack true necessities, like scribe pens and supplies for yourself, so I did them for you." Mom motioned toward the litter with her free hand. "I also included a meal for your drakkling."

"Gria was fed yesterday—"

Gria always hungry. Will eat.

"And she is also what in human terms would be called an adolescent," Mom continued, in obvious agreement with Kaia, though I wasn't entirely sure the two were currently connected. I certainly couldn't feel her presence along the mental lines. "Trust me, there is no filling man, woman, or beast during that growth period."

"I wasn't that bad—"

"I beg to differ." She handed the pack she was holding to Kele, then motioned her and the others to move out. Once they had, she returned her attention to me. "There's a climber's body harness in the pack. I thought it would be a useful means of attaching yourself to whatever rig you manage to construct for Kaia."

"I hadn't even thought of that."

"Didn't think you would, given your habit of scrambling over all sorts of mountainside with the barest of gear. I've also included additional webbing and bone straps, just in case one or both of you get hit." She caught my hand and pulled me into a fierce hug. "Please, be careful."

I hugged her back with my free arm. "I will."

"You've the map?"

I nodded. "Where's Father?"

"Sleeping. He was supervising the harbor's clearing most of the night." Her smile creased the corners of her eyes but couldn't erase the sadness and the fear that cloaked her. "I was under orders to wake him before you left, but the man is not infallible no matter what he thinks, and he does need to sleep sometimes."

"He'll be mighty annoyed."

"It wouldn't be the first time, and it's not like you won't be coming home to us." Her gaze met mine steadily. "No risks."

"No risks," I agreed, then stepped back. After a slight hesitation, I gave her a nod and walked away.

The weight of her gaze followed me through the gates and into the courtyard beyond.

Because she knew, like I knew, that the mere action of flying Kaia out to Jakarra was perhaps the biggest risk of all, and even if I did survive that, there was no guarantee I would survive whatever might wait on the island.

I caught up with Kele and the team. After I'd tied two of the three packs I was carrying onto the litter, we moved on, making good time up the mountain. Maneuvering the litter through some of the narrower tubes was sometimes tricky, but we did eventually reach the aerie with the boar and the packs in one piece.

The barrier shimmered as we approached, sending brief waves of red and gold running across its surface before fading into invisibility again. The drakkons were little more than larger shadows against the soft red glow of heat coming from the sands of the hatching caves.

"Wow," Sora murmured softly, her gaze on Kaia's dark outline. "They are huge."

"That they are." I took the back end of the litter from Jax, then motioned Kele to the front end. "Sora, you and Jax will have to wait out here."

"Why can't we go in?" Jax asked.

"Aside from the fact the entrance is magically barred and not tuned to either of you," Kele said, before I could answer, "we've spent hundreds of years decimating their numbers, and they're a little annoyed by the whole situation. They're likely to eat strangers, and to be honest, I can't say I blame them."

Jax grunted. "Shame, but at least I can see them from here."

"You can," I said, "but neither of you are to mention their presence here, and that is an order."

Túxn only knew, the last thing we needed was a stream of curious onlookers scrambling through the tunnels to catch a glimpse of them.

As Kele and I went through the barrier, the magic flared to life once again, briefly slowing our steps. Its sharp needles raced across my skin, pinpricks that seemed designed to taste who we were before letting us fully go through. It wasn't unpleasant, more uncomfortable.

A small price to pay to keep the drakkons safe.

Gria remained where we'd left her last night, curled up into an overly large ball. She didn't move once we entered the cavern proper, but Kaia's head snaked around. Her dark eyes held a bloody glow in the reddish light coming from the sands. *Wind strong. Wings healed. Good day to fly.*

It could take me a while to get used to being on your back, Kaia.

You ride runner. Won't fall.

She obviously had more confidence in my balancing skills than I did. We removed the packs, rolled the boar off the litter close to Gria, though the drakkling didn't wake, then Kele gave me the pack she was carrying.

"I expect a full report of what it's like to be aloft on a drakkon," she said. "No details to be spared."

I laughed and gave her a hug. "And I expect a jug of mead to be ready and waiting for me when I get back, as per usual."

She grinned. "I expect your man might have other ideas on that front."

"Nothing gets in the way of our downtime, not even a well-endowed man." Nothing other than the upcoming move to Zephrine, and that was at least a few days off yet. "And we have a tradition that must be followed."

"Indeed." She stepped back, saluted, then grabbed the rolled-up litter and retreated. I waited until the three of them had gone, then picked up the pack and walked over to Kaia.

What carry?

"Two packs are supplies I might need for the island. The third and fourth has supplies for me, and the ropes and girths I need to fashion a means of tying me onto you, so I don't fall to my death if we suddenly part company."

Best not part, she said. *What wood on back?*

"A short bow with arrows. We think it might penetrate winged ones' armor and kill them."

Kill birds too?

"Maybe."

We hunt?

"No, because we haven't enough arrows at the moment."

Get enough.

"We're working on it."

Work faster.

I laughed. "Are you always this bossy?"

Am queen.

I laughed again, emptied the pack containing the girths and what-not, then pulled out the climbing harness from the smaller one Mom had given me. Kaia watched in fascination as I sorted through everything and then joined all the girths together. After warning her what I was about to do, I asked her to hunker down, tossed one end of my girth rope through the valley between the last two spines at the base of her neck, then caught the two ends and joined them using another D-ring, creating a complete ring.

I stepped back and glanced up at her. "Is that okay? Not too tight?"

She moved her neck around. *Is good.*

"Now I need to work on the bit that'll keep me on." I hesitated. "I need to get up to your neck. Could you..."

Before I could finish, she stretched out her front leg, providing a scaly ramp for me to climb up. I grabbed everything I needed, then scrambled past her claws, up her legs, and across her shoulder, gripping the decidedly wicked-looking spur jutting out from the wing's thumb to steady myself as I moved over to her neck. Even though she was hunkered down, it was a scarily long way back to the ground.

Her neck spines close to her wings were smaller—in comparison to those further up her neck and behind her wings, anyway—which meant my neck and shoulders would be visible above them. Probably a good thing if I had to use Mom's short bow. They were also surprisingly rough, even though they looked smooth from a distance. I wondered if it was weather or just a natural occurrence.

Weather came her reply. *Soft when young. Hardens as age.*

Huh. I rose and, holding fast to the last spine, slid past it until I reached the gap. I tied one end of the rope to the girth, looped it around the final spine, then tied on the other end. After slicing away the excess rope, I slipped back and tested out the rig. The base of her spine was shaped rather like a courser's withers, but longer, which meant I was pressed against it more than her neck. Which in many ways made gripping easier, simply because my legs weren't as wide apart as they would have been had I been on the main part of her neck. I strapped the stirrups onto the rope, lashing them together so they didn't go sliding too far apart, then added a couple of D-rings to tie the climber's harness and the backpacks on to. With that all done, I clambered down her leg again.

"How's that all feel?"

Barely feel. Ready now?

I nodded. "Just got to climb into the harness and get the packs up there."

Hurry. Wind calls.

The climbing harness was one of the older styles—V-shaped front and back, with wide, comfortable shoulder straps that narrowed down to the waist belt they were attached to. The leg loops hung from this, and at the front was a thick double D-ring designed to lock the rope into place if there was a fall. There were also a couple of extra loops on the side of the belt to attach other gear.

I climbed into it, adjusted the legs a little, then grabbed the packs and climbed back up to Kaia's neck. Once seated, I attached myself to one D-ring and two of the packs to the others. The third—the one containing supplies for me and the additional webbing and bone straps—I squashed between my body and her spine before clipping it onto my harness. One of the few problems of bareback riding was an unexpected stop sending you crashing forward and, well, let's just say that hitting the withers with any sort of force was a painful experience for a man or a woman. That was just as likely to be true with a drakkon's spine.

I took a deep breath and released it slowly. It did nothing to ease the sudden spike in my heart rate. I was looking forward to this... had been dreaming of a moment like this all my life, even if I'd never thought it would happen. But now it was and, well, the reality was damn scary.

I not let fall, came Kaia's thought. *We go?*

Let's.

Excitement pulsed through her thoughts. Excitement, and a deep desire to rend and tear. She wanted revenge. *Needed* revenge. It was the only reason she was doing any of this.

She moved with surprising grace and speed toward the exit tunnel, her body rolling from side to side. I gripped her spine and flowed with the movement, even though it was very different to that of a courser. The skies were dark, the clouds heavy and barely lit by the rising light of dawn, and the air that whipped around us was

OF STEEL & SCALE   205

sharp with the scent of an oncoming storm, making me glad I'd decided to wear my thick waterproof leathers as well as a couple of layers of silk undergarments.

We reached the landing ledge. Kaia paused and raised her head, her nostrils flaring as she drew in the wind. *Where we go?*

I imagined the map in my mind, plotting out a course that would have us heading south, following the mountain range rather than cutting more directly across the ocean from Esan. It was far longer, but likely to be safer if we were at all wrong about the riders' ability to fly during the day.

Easy, she said.

I hoped she was right.

Hoped my theory that coming in from an unexpected direction would counter the possibly of whatever sentinels the gilded ones had out spotting us.

Kaia rose on her haunches. I gripped the rope, holding on tight with my thighs as she spread her wings wide and bellowed. It was long and loud, and echoed across the still peaks—the battle cry of a drakkon going to war. Then, without warning, she launched off the ledge.

Not up. Down.

Straight down the mountainside.

I clenched my teeth against the scream that tore up my throat as I was thrown back sharply by the sheer force of the wind, and tightened my grip on the front spine, using the pits on its weathered surface to wedge my fingers into and hold on. My heart felt like it was lodged in my throat, the wind tore at my cheeks and my plait, and the foothills loomed way too fast for comfort. The desire to close my eyes and pray was almost all consuming, but the need not to miss any little moment of this once-in-a-lifetime event was stronger still.

Just as it seemed we were about to crash, Kaia flicked her outstretched wings and soared upward with enough force to tear my fingers from her spine pits. The harness rope snapped tight, preventing me from sliding between her wings.

You still on. Harness work came Kaia's thought.

And if it hadn't? I asked wryly.

You dead or in claws.

I couldn't help but laugh. I guess diving headfirst off a cliff had certainly been one way to test the harness. *Perhaps next time you could warn me.*

Next time you expect.

I would. She continued to rise, and the mountains fell away, leaving us flying through the chilly, open space between the peaks and the thickly layered clouds. Though the sweep of her wings was slow and steady, we moved with surprising speed. The air was a whip that tore at clothes, hair, and skin, and the creeping chill across my cheeks forced me to pull up the neck of an undershirt to cover them, then tug down the coat's hood in an effort to avoid frostbite. I could use my inner flame, of course, but I was wary of doing so simply because we had no idea what might lie in wait for us on Jakarra.

The sun rose, but the day got gloomier. By the time we neared the end of our continent, it had started to rain. I kept my head down and finally raised the inner fires enough to battle the chill beginning to creep through me. Far below us, the sea was a sheer expanse of blue that just seemed to go on forever. I'd seen enough maps—and been on enough boats—to understand how vast our oceans were, but somehow they seemed even more expansive when viewed from on high.

As the day stretched on and the strength of the wind increased, Kaia dipped and soared, playing on the currents while allowing me to become more comfortable with her movements. My grin might be hidden by my undergarments, but it was so damn fierce my cheeks were aching with its force.

By the time the sun dipped toward the haze of late afternoon, the distant shadows of ragged peaks became visible through the silvery curtain of rain.

Jakarra.

Black, forbidding, and possibly forever broken.

I shivered and shoved the thought away. While there was life, there was hope, and I refused to accept the possibility that the gilded riders had erased Jakarra as thoroughly as they had Eastmead. The Jakarrans might be fishermen at heart, but they were also fiercely skilled bowmen. If anyone could survive the onslaught of the gilded ones, it would be my mother's people.

Let's check the old aerie first, I said, *and make sure it's safe for you to shelter in.*

No want shelter. Attack.

We can't attack until we know what we're facing.

Should fly over. See.

I hesitated. *Only if you keep high.*

You no see.

You can tell me what you see. But let's check the aerie first.

She grumbled softly but nevertheless dipped her wings and did a slow curving turn toward the southern end of the U-shaped range dominating the western end of the island. These mountains might be a smaller echo of the Black Glass Mountain range, but they were just as fierce and bleak, especially in the driving rain.

Kaia swooped over a peak, then banked and flew along the ragged, shadow-filled, barren-looking leeward side. As we neared the junction of what was the range's trunk and arm, a gaping maw became visible through the gloom. The old aerie. This one had no landing stone jutting out from the entrance, though ragged shafts of stone suggested it had once been there.

We should go in and check it's safe, I said.

If find foe, you flame? I eat?

I thought humans were too gristly?

Are. She banked and swooped toward the entrance. *Birds look fat and crunchy.*

That will be the metal wings.

Belly not covered. Looks tender.

Are you hungry or something? Food seems to be on your mind.

Am good. Have hunted.

But like Gria, you'll never say no to a meal.

She rumbled in response. I suspected it was amusement. As the huge mouth of the cavern drew closer, Kaia tucked her wings close to her body and swooped on. The wind and the rain dropped away as the darkness fell around us. She shifted her flight position, moving her rear legs forward, and gently landed. I wiped the rain from my face then raised a hand and created a small ball of flame, sending it tumbling into the darkness ahead. Between us and the entrance into the main breeding ground lay a surprising amount of rubble, and none of it appeared to have come from the walls.

I scanned the roofline and spotted jagged teeth of rock—rock that looked more like the floor's redder earth than the black of the walls. I frowned and, as my ball spun into the main cavern, flicked my fingers wider to increase its intensity.

The light played across the black stone walls and highlighted the layers of bleached, broken, and heavily chewed bones scattered all about.

These weren't ordinary bones, however.

They were the remains of all those who had once called this place home.

Drakkons.

This place death, Kaia said.

It was, and not just because of the bones. There was only one way in and out of this cavern, and that was probably the reason so many drakkons had been killed here. Drakkons had teeth and claws, but neither were any good against a foe capable of commanding earth and quickly cutting off the only exit.

No like, she added.

I didn't either. I might not have seeress abilities, but there were ghosts in this place, and they whispered of pain, confusion, and the agony of a slow, starving death.

Tears stung my eyes, but I blinked them away. There was nothing I could do about the past, but I sure as hell could change the future to ensure nothing like this ever happened again.

I drew in a deeper breath, then said, *You can't stay here. It's too dangerous. You'll have to find a roost on the windward side of the mountain. At least there you'll be able to see anyone approach and have time to escape.*

Another rumble. Escape wasn't exactly in her plans. Not if she thought she had any chance of bringing one of the bastards down.

We go?

Yes.

She turned and lumbered back to the entrance. At its edge, she hunkered down and then launched skyward, her wings pumping hard as she fought to gain height against the wind and the rain. The various landmarks far below us were all but indistinguishable, though I heard the roar of the Crystal River Falls—even above the fury of the storm—as we swept through the middle of the island. The only landmark that was truly visible was the brooding darkness of the blackwood forests that clung to the sides of the steep ravine sweeping from the toes of the Helvede Range to the first of the crevices that half ringed Illistin.

I couldn't see Illistin itself.

Couldn't see the port beyond it.

I closed my eyes, hoping it was nothing more than the rain and the fog, but deep in my heart I knew the truth. Illistin had been destroyed just as thoroughly as Eastmead had.

But why?

What in Vahree's name did such destruction gain them?

Even the Mareritt didn't go to such extremes, and they were a warrior race with an unshakeable belief in their own superiority.

Can you see anything, Kaia?

Death. She paused. *Gilded ones here.*

What? Where?

Deepen link. See.

I closed my eyes and reached deeper, strengthening the connection between us without going as deep or as full as I had before. When I opened my eyes, my vision was a weird mix of hers and mine. It was a somewhat nauseating sensation, so I quickly closed them again and just concentrated on what she was seeing. On the ground far below, there were two lines of metal tents—twelve in all —sitting atop the ridge just outside the main town. They were widely spaced, and each one had a gilded bird tethered outside of it. They were all hooded, and there didn't appear to be any sort of sentries standing about. Perhaps they didn't need them. Perhaps the senses of the birds were sharp enough to alert their riders of any approach.

That thought had barely crossed my mind when one of the birds looked up and squawked.

Rise, I urged Kaia.

With a quick flick of her wings, she did so, and the ground receded, the bird becoming little more than a golden glimmer in the gloom of the day. It was unlikely the riders would be able to see us, but we had no idea if the bird who'd spotted us was one of those with a band, and whether or not it allowed the bird to communicate with its rider in the same manner as Kaia and I were.

The glimmers remained on the ground. I hoped that meant we were right, and they *couldn't* fly during the day.

I broke our deeper connection, and we swung around, flying back toward the larger arm of the Helvede Range. There was no evidence the gilded riders had set up camp in the forests hugging the feet of the range, and no winged sentries further up. Which didn't mean they weren't there. If they were capable of magic strong enough to destroy a port, then they were certainly capable of creating earth shelters that looked no different to the mountainside around them.

We followed the long arm, rising higher as the mountainside did, discovering peaks still littered with snow. No wonder it was utterly freezing. I ramped up the inner fires a bit more and made a mental note to include gloves next time—*if* there was a next time. We soared over the final ragged mountaintop and then swept down the other side. My grin appeared again, even if the speed at which we were dropping was scary. I directed her to the ledge Mom had pointed out, and while the wind had certainly swept away most of the snow, thick drifts survived in the shadows.

Kaia banked, landing with surprising grace. I unclipped from the spine rope, grabbed the three packs, and then slithered down her thoughtfully extended leg.

Where entrance? she said.

I waved a hand toward the peak. "About an hour up that way."

You no reach by dark.

"No. And probably won't return until after sunrise tomorrow."

I hunt over water, then roost night.

I raised my eyebrows. "You eat fish?"

What fish?

I sent her an image.

Water beasts sweet but not big.

Then you're not hunting the right ones. Long fins can be as big as a male drakkon.

I look. She lowered her head for a ridge scratch and rumbled happily when I complied. *I go. Call when need.*

I stepped back, out of the way. She hunkered down, then launched into the air, her wings pumping, sending whirlwinds of air scurrying around me. Once she was gone, I squatted against a rock to shield from the actual wind, then tugged the scribe pen from my pack and sent my parents a report.

Half cleared partial access from port came the response. *Will send clippers tomorrow to west side of island.*

Clippers were the only ships we had capable of getting here within the limit of daylight. *No evidence of sentries on this side,* I sent back. *Seas clear of foreign ships between here and Eastmead.*

Good. Stay wary. Report when able.

Will do. Out.

I tucked the scribe pen and tablet away, took a long drink of water and a quick pee, then tugged out a slab of journey bread, munching on it as I scanned the area. It struck me as odd that there were no seabirds here. This part of the island was as harsh and as barren as the Black Glass Mountains, but birdlife thrived across its jagged sea cliffs. There was no reason that shouldn't be happening here.

Unless, of course, the gilded birds had frightened them all away.

By the time I'd finished the bread, the faint blush of dusk was staining the undersides of the clouds. I needed to hurry before night hit and using any sort of light became impossible thanks to the risk of it attracting the attention of the riders. I brushed the crumbs from my fingers, then shoved my arms through the smaller pack's arm loops and strapped it on my front. If nothing else, it would provide a little extra coverage if I slipped and fell on my face. Once I'd clipped the other two packs onto the harness—one each side—I threw a fire sphere into the air.

With its warm light chasing away the worst of the evening gloom already descending on the mountaintop, I began the long, tedious climb upward. The rain had made an already treacherous path more so, and I slipped, landing heavily on my knees, more than once. I was well used to "clambering all over mountainsides," as Mom had put it, but this was a whole new level of dangerousness.

Doing so in utter darkness for the last third only increased the danger and the terror.

By the time I reached the southern entrance into the deeper caverns, I was dripping with sweat and more than a little achy. I was also as tired as hell, but some of that was definitely my own fault. I should have slept last night rather than playing around with my husband.

I did not, in any way, regret playing around with my husband.

I rested my head against one side of the key-like entrance and briefly closed my eyes, half wondering what he was doing. Probably preparing for our eventual trip home, though a few of the things he'd said last night had me thinking he was no more looking forward to it than me. I couldn't help but wonder if that was due to his acerbic relationship with his father or something else.

There was just so much I didn't know about the man and his family.

So much I didn't know about general, day-to-day life in Zephrine. All I knew was that, for me, it would be very different. I wouldn't be a soldier. I would be the wife of the heir.

What in the wind's name was I going to do with my days?

I shoved the worry away and dragged the water bottle from the pack, taking a long drink. There wasn't much left, so I had to conserve it in case it took me longer than expected to reach the main arms into the refuge caverns. After I grabbed another slab of journey bread, I tugged a light tube free and then continued on.

Though these tunnels were far easier to traverse than those above Esan, I was very glad to have Mom's map to guide me, because the place was a maze. By the time I reached the closest of the three tunnels that led directly into the refuge tunnel, I was shaking with weariness. I stopped short of the entrance and raised the light tube, letting its light caress the stony walls ahead. I couldn't see any guards, but instinct nevertheless said they were there.

"Jakarran sentry, this is Captain Bryn Silva from the Esan fortress. I'm here to gain information in regard to the island's position and needs. I need to speak to whomever is in charge as a matter of urgency."

There was a long moment of silence, then, "Drop your weapons and packs, and raise your hands."

The voice was male and curt.

"We're wasting time, soldier—"

"Do it, or I'll shoot first and ask questions later."

I made a low sound in the back of my throat but in truth couldn't fault the soldier's caution. I stripped off my packs, sword, and bow, placing them and the light tube on the ground in front of me before stepping back and raising my hands.

After another long stretch of silence, a figure stepped out from what was obviously a sentry post cut into the side wall of the tunnel. I suspected there might be another on the right side.

His sword remained at his side, but his bow was nocked, the arrow aimed straight at my heart.

"Ursek," the soldier continued. "Grab her things."

So, I'd been right. There *was* someone else here. As another man stepped out of the shadows on the left, there was a brief flash of movement on the right. There were at least three people here, and I rather suspected there would be more. It did make more sense to have at least four, if not six, people on duty at each of the tunnels, given the obvious strength of the foe. I wouldn't even be surprised if there was an earth witch here somewhere—if any had survived the slaughter, that is.

"Tell me, soldier, is Garran Silva still alive?" I asked.

Neither of them replied. The shorter of the two men moved forward to collect my things, hesitating briefly when he saw the bow. "Blackwood bow," he said. "Jakarran crafted."

"Could have gotten it from the spoils," the other man growled.

"It was a gift from my mother, who was a bow master here. As I said, I'm Captain Bryn Silva. Garran is my cousin and my father's heir. I need to speak to him or whoever is in charge, so could you two please hurry yourselves up. Time is ticking."

The shorter man cast an uncertain look at his companion, who simply shrugged and said, "We have orders. We will obey them. Now move, Captain, down that way."

He stepped back and motioned with his head toward the tunnel. I waited until the shorter man had gathered my things and then followed several steps behind him. There were, I noted with a quick look to the right, at least two other people here. Which was good—at least this sentry point would not be left unmanned while these two escorted me down.

The taller man remained a few yards behind me, and while I couldn't see it, I had no doubt the arrow remained nocked and aimed. I could almost feel the itch of its tip pressing against my spine.

We continued on for another ten minutes, then the air began to warm, and the gentle wash of conversation and living grew louder. We reached a plateau guarded by another two men but were quickly cleared and walked on to a wide platform. A large cavern stretched out before us, high and wide and teeming with people. Illistin might have been destroyed, but a good percentage of her inhabitants appeared to have survived.

Now I just had to find out if Garran and his family had.

The cavern had two distinct sections. The floor below was a city of tents and temporary structures that appeared to be bunkhouses, while the wide platform on which we stood ringed the midpoint of the cavern and had multiple hollowed out caves that appeared to be designated medical, military, and organizational areas.

We walked around to the left, moving quickly past the various caves, curiosity and gazes chasing our steps. I ignored them as best I could, my gaze on the large cavern we were approaching. It was obviously the makeshift war room, as there were a ton of maps strewn across multiple tables, as well as troop placement and topography boards. There were a good dozen people gathered around one of the latter, but I didn't immediately recognize any of them. I hoped that meant Garran was either resting or at the back of the cave, but I had bad, *bad* feeling it did not.

Once we were close enough to the entrance, I was ordered to stop and wait. The first guard went inside while the second continued to watch me closely, though he had at least lowered his bow. I crossed my arms and scanned the area below again. There were kids running around an obviously hastily set up play area, their bright laughter piercing the gloom that curtained the rest of the cave. Most of the folk down there were either side of the spectrum—younger or older. There didn't seem to be many down there of fighting age. Which probably meant they'd been drafted in as soldiers or as support personnel.

They could also be dead, I supposed, but surely not even the winged riders could—or even would—waste time being that precise with their kills.

"What?" a sharp voice said from the depths of the cave ahead, drawing my attention back. "Show me."

I didn't immediately recognize the voice, but the man who

followed my guard out of the shadowed interior of the cave was tall, with short, steel-gray hair, reddish skin, and blue eyes.

He also wasn't a stranger, though I hadn't seen him much over the course of the last five years other than at a few official engagements.

This was Katter Reed—Garran's uncle—and if he was in control, then Garran, his family, and his parents were either safe on another island or dead.

"Administrator Reed—"

"There's no need for formality here, Bryn," he cut in, his gaze sweeping my length then moving past, obviously looking for the rest of my detachment. Surprise, disappointment, and perhaps even a touch of anger swept through his expression before he got it under control. "You came alone?"

"I did—"

"Then how in Vahree's name did you get here? And why alone?"

"I came on drakkon back and—"

"You *what?*" His voice and expression were both incredulous.

Behind him, a soft wave of disbelief filled the air then fell silent again.

I couldn't say I blamed any of them. I still found it hard to believe myself, and I'd been astride her back. "Long story, but we've gained the help of a queen because our foes killed one of her drakklings."

"But how—" He stopped, obviously remembering what I was, and shook his head. "Strange times indeed. Tell me, why send you rather than ships or aid? What's happened?"

"Cutters were sent the night we received the first reports of the attack. It was thought their speed and maneuverability would allow them to escape the notice of the winged riders; we were wrong. The harbor was then attacked and blocked by their magic."

Katter scraped a hand across his worn, bristly features. "This just gets better and better, doesn't it?"

"Well, there is *some* good news—I scribed Esan before I came into the tunnel system here and got an update. The earth witches have managed to partially clear the harbor, but the remaining ships can't be sent out until first light. It appears—at least to date—that their birds are unable to fly during the day." I paused, my gaze once again searching the shadows and the unfamiliar faces. "Where's Garran?"

Grief briefly twisted his expression, and my heart clenched.

"Missing, presumed dead, along with all those who defended the town while the rest of us evacuated."

"And his family? His parents?" I whispered, blinking desperately against the tears that stung my eyes. While it was rare these days for Garran and me to meet outside official engagements or family get-togethers, as kids and teenagers we spent long months together; he in Esan over summer learning the trade of kingship, and me the winter here, learning bow craft from Mom's teachers and the art of hunting and tracking from Elric, Garran's dad, who hailed from one of the smaller islands.

"Elric was with his son, and we are unsure as to Glenda's where-abouts, but we are still in the process of registering everyone who made it up here."

For Mom's sake, I really hoped her sister was here somewhere rather than missing or dead. She'd always been closer to Glenda than her other siblings. "And Hanna?"

He smiled. "Here with their son."

"Their *son*?"

"She went into labor on the way up here, but the boy was deliv-ered safely, and she's okay." He glanced at my shorter guard. "Ursek, please return the captain's packs and weapons to her, then you and Oscar head back to your post."

The short man did so, then stepped back and saluted. As the two men left, I handed the two larger packs to Katter. "Medical supplies —nowhere near enough, I know, but all I could carry."

"And certainly better than nothing." He glanced around and motioned to one of the men. "Get these across to medical. Captain, follow me."

He spun and walked back into the cave, stopping at a table

holding the topography map. "We sent scouts out this morning to get some idea where the enemy lines are, but as yet they have not returned. I don't suppose you saw anything from your drakkon's back?"

Another buzz of soft incredulousness went through the room, but quickly fell away.

"Their force is gathered here." I pointed to the area above Illistin. "We saw twelve gilded birds and riders positioned there, but given the destruction of the port and the town, there has to be at least a number of blood witches amongst their number."

"Why do you believe they are capable of blood magic?" the stony-faced gentleman standing opposite me said. "We saw no evidence of it."

"Nor did our earth witches until it was entirely too late, and there's only the one stationed in Jakarra, isn't there?"

"Aye," a second, much younger man said. He had brown hair and eyes, and a rather "earthy" air that said he was the witch in question. "But there was no blood magic used here to raise the earth or destroy the pier and the boats. It wasn't necessary, not for the latter at least. They simply sank the lot with what appeared to be acidic manure bombs."

"Yeah, we've come across those things. Our earth witches are working on a means of strengthening stone and wood against it." I glanced at Katter again. "Why haven't you scribed for help? I know the pens don't work this deep underground, but surely you could have sent a team—"

"We've no pens," he cut in grimly. "This cavern was designed as a temporary refuge against tropical storms and tsunamis. We have enough essentials—food, water, and medical supplies—to last us a few weeks if necessary, but we never imagined we'd come under physical attack, and never thought to include weapons or scribes in the stores."

I was guessing they would from now on, when it was all too late. Hindsight was a wonderful thing.

"Then I'll leave mine once I make my final report." I glanced down at the map again. "What little remains of Illistin burns. I saw no movement in the town nor any sign of bodies. The paths up here appeared empty, but that does not mean—"

I stopped as a siren rang out—two short blasts then one long one.

My pulse rate stuttered briefly, then leapt into overdrive.

The cavern was under attack.

10

I STRAIGHTENED ABRUPTLY. "How many people have you got at the entrance?"

"Ten." He glanced at the earth mage. "Rudy, get down there and raise a barrier."

"I'll go with—"

"No, in Vahree's name, you won't." Katter's gaze snapped back to me. "There's been enough royal blood shed on this soil already. I'll not risk—"

"You can't *not* risk it," I cut in. "I'm more than likely the best-trained soldier you have right now, and I'm a fire witch besides."

He sucked in a breath, displeasure flickering through his bright eyes. But he knew well enough I could have easily pulled rank and overridden him. Not as a soldier—I was a captain, not a commander—but as a princess. I might not be my father's heir, but my position still outranked his.

"Fine," he snapped. "Follow Rudy."

I dropped my pack, bow, and quiver onto the ground next to the table, then strapped on my sword and knife as I ran out after Rudy. The siren cut out suddenly, and the brief, deep silence was eerie. Then the sound of footsteps and voices rose again as those on the ground level were ushered up a level and into the deeper tunnels.

We ran down sweeping stone steps, then into a wide, unnaturally smooth tunnel lit by regularly placed light tubes. The sound of screaming echoed from up ahead, which definitely wasn't a good sign, given the voices held a Jakarran accent rather than the guttural intonations of the riders. But even worse was the ground's trembling, which became more and more evident the closer we got to the entrance cavern. Dust was shimmering down from the tunnel's roofline and that was an even worse sign.

Because if this area was about to be hit by a quake, the tremors wouldn't have been confined to just this part of the tunnel.

This was the work of mages, not nature.

"Rudy—"

"I feel it."

"Can you stop it?"

"Maybe." The gaze he cast over his shoulder was determined. "It will of course depend on just how many of them there are."

"Then your best bet is to thin out their ranks." I drew my sword, its blade bright in the semi- shadowed tunnel. "Stop here and feel for their weight on the ground—it'll be different to that of the soldiers attacking us. When you find them, open a massive chasm underneath them and, once they've dropped, backfill it. If they survive the fall, they'll be too busy saving their own lives to worry about us."

It wasn't an original idea—we'd employed it many times over the decades after our mages had made the discovery about the weight differences. It had stopped the Mareritt for a good while, but in recent times, their mages had simply taken to climbing trees before spelling and hiding their presence that way. Mareritt were many things, but they weren't dumb.

"Nasty," Rudy said. "I like it."

As he dropped and pressed his hands against the stone, I ran on, sweeping around the tunnel's curve. I came out into a small but natural vestibule and utter chaos.

Five guards were on the ground, writhing and screaming as their flesh bubbled and steamed. The stench of their burning flesh filled the air, though it was almost overwhelmed by the faintly sweet but musty scent of the liquid dung the riders used. Two men and a woman were hunkered behind the semicircular barrier that surrounded the jagged, angular entrance, alternately rising and firing arrows into the entrance tunnel. It was hard to say if the arrows were effective or not, as the tunnel's shadows hid our foe, but two of the three were using standard metal arrowheads. The final two guards stood either side of the entrance, their swords sheathed but bows notched and ready. Both their arrowheads were Ithican glass. As I belted toward the barrier, the guard on the left of the entrance nodded at the other, who quickly stepped sideways, aimed his bow, and unleashed his arrow in one smooth movement, and then retreated. A stream of brown liquid chased after him, splashing across the area between the entrance and the barrier, melting the rock, and deepening the crevices that already crisscrossed the area. Gold glinted briefly in the deep of the entrance's tunnel, moving with speed toward the small chamber rather than away. I called to my fire but before I could unleash it, two gold-armored warriors burst from the tunnel, one with an arrow still sticking out of his shoulder, both of them swinging wickedly barbed metal clubs that were at least four feet in length and a good fist wide. One of the guards immediately went down, his gut torn open by the club. The second was quicker, ducking and scrambling away; the club aimed at his head smashed into the wall behind him instead, sending thick shards of rock slicing through the air.

The guards behind the barrier were notching and unleashing arrows in a steady stream but none of them got through the riders' armor or helmets. The two of them roared, raised their thick clubs above their heads, and charged, one at the barrier, the other at the guard who'd escaped. As he stood his ground and notched another Ithican arrow, I slid to a stop and unleashed my fire, lassoing it around the two warriors and pulling them tightly together.

They roared in fury, the harsh sound echoing. As one tore at the leash with the wicked points of metal littering his club's length, the other batted away the Ithican arrows aimed his way. I fed more strength into the fire, increasing its intensity, until it was sheet of sheer flame that burned white hot around them. Their clubs melted first, then their golden armor began to ooze, gradually at first, then becoming thin, glittering streams that ran down their bodies onto the floor. They writhed and screamed, the sound a guttural echo of the men and women who lay scattered on the floor around me. Then their armor was gone, and only flesh and bone remained. They were ashed in seconds.

As their dust fell lightly to the floor, I flicked the thick, fiery leash deeper into the tunnel. Heard another scream, then the harsh sound of boots on stone, retreating fast.

For the moment, we were safe. I took a deep breath and called back my flames. It was only then that I realized the ground tremors had stopped. I glanced up at the ceiling. There were a few minor cracks closer to the entrance, but dust no longer fell.

The three soldiers hunkered behind the barrier rose and turned. I recognized the one armed with the Ithican glass arrows. His name was Tayn, and he was tall and thin, with a scar across his right cheek, the result of an arrow coming a little too close for comfort during a stupid hunting game he and Garran had been playing as teenagers. I hadn't been a part of that one, though I'd certainly witnessed the fury that had descended on Garran for taking such a stupid risk.

It had never stopped him from taking risks, though, simply because caution was not part of his nature. It was probably why he was now missing—though as heir he should have retreated, it wasn't in his nature to do so, just as it wasn't in my father's or even mine.

The injured had stopped screaming and writhing, but the silence remained heavy with their pain, and the scent of their agony and burning flesh still rode the air. I hoped the shock of their wounds had simply pushed them into unconsciousness rather than death, but I feared Vahree might have already claimed at least some of their souls.

Tayn ordered the woman standing next to him to go fetch the medics, sent another soldier to check on the injured and do what he could do to help, and the surviving entrance archer back to his post before finally turning his attention to me. "Bryn, I mean, Captain Silva, that was a well-timed intervention."

"Not timed well enough, I'm afraid, and there's no need for formalities right now, Tayn."

He half smiled, then glanced past me. "You're alone?"

His surprise was barely evident but understandable, given the situation and who I was—meaning the captain of a twelve-strong scouting squad rather than a princess.

"I just came here to get an update, as you've no working scribes and they damaged our harbor."

He frowned. "How did you get here, then?"

"Long story." I glanced around as footsteps approached. It was Rudy, looking drawn and yet triumphant. "I take it the chasm idea was a success?"

"Indeed. There were three of them out there—there was no way I could have held or repaired the earth against the combined might of whatever spell they were concocting."

Three blood witches dead was a good win for us, but I couldn't help but wonder how many more they had tucked safely away.

"When you were feeling for the mages, did you get any idea how many others were out there?"

Kaia and I had only seen a dozen birds, but that didn't mean there weren't also "regular" soldiers here on the island, well hidden from even a drakkon's keen sight. Maybe it was nothing more than wishful thinking, but surely a force of twelve, however deadly their weapons, couldn't so totally erase a town as large as Illistin, though I guess it *was* possible some of their numbers had already left for Esan. The Black Glass Mountains were vast, and an armed force could hide up there for years without us ever spotting them.

Not that I thought we had years. Hell, I doubted we even had months.

Rudy hesitated. "There were at least five close to the entrance and an odd weight on a ledge halfway up the mountain that's obviously a sentry point. I couldn't feel anyone farther down the slope, but it does get harder to differentiate between the weight of trees and stone from that of man the further away we get. It's possible they are in the forest, just standing beyond my ability to sense them."

I glanced at Tayn. "I might head down the tunnel to investigate—"

"*We'll* head down the tunnel to investigate," Tayn cut in. "Forgive me, Captain, but I'm more familiar with the area than you."

I half smiled. "Fine, but I will lead the way if you don't mind. My flames are a little more effective at wholesale destruction than your Ithican arrow."

"Or even your sword." He smiled and motioned me forward. "We discovered the hard way that those bastards have a long reach despite their short stature."

I glanced at him sharply. "Do you mean the riders? Or have they a ground force here?"

The men who'd attacked us here were certainly wearing the armor, but that didn't mean they were riders rather than regular soldiers.

"The riders, though they may well have a ground force here by now."

I frowned. "How, though? They destroyed the harbor, and those birds are not drakkon-sized and wouldn't be able to lift more than a couple of men."

"There's plenty of areas beyond the main harbor where a longship could be run aground easily enough."

Such an action would make military sense, especially if you wanted to ensure your foe were kept unaware of the true size of your force. "Were you with Garran when the attack went down?"

He shook his head. "After your father sent word of Eastmead's destruction and a warning to be alert for a possible attack, we enacted emergency procedures, getting everyone ready to move at short notice. I was in charge of covering the retreat, Riana's crew were on the watchtower, and Garran the harbor guard. The latter was hit first. No boats survived, but I can't say how Garran and his team fared. From the little I saw, the raiders seemed determined that none of us escape. They certainly weren't taking prisoners."

"That was their tactic at Eastmead, too."

I slowed my pace as we entered the tunnel, my grip tightening on my sword and flames flickering around the fingers of my free hand. Like the antechamber, the tunnel's stone was rough and uneven, and just wide enough to walk through single file, while its walls tapered to the right and up to a point. Anyone over six foot would have a painful journey if they weren't mindful of their head.

"How in Vahree's name did you get an entire town through here with any sort of speed?" I asked, fighting the urge to duck. Though I wasn't quite six foot in height, the ceiling still felt uncomfortably close.

"We tend to be shorter around these parts, remember, and we're well versed in emergency evacuations."

No doubt, given how often tropical storms hit with little notice. Unlike most islands, there was no weather mage living on Jakarra— the old woman who'd held the position for nigh on a century had died a good ten years ago, and the island hadn't had much luck luring a new one here.

We came across the first body around twenty feet in. He was face down on the ground, the glass point of an arrowhead sticking out the back of his helmeted head. Few men could survive a wound like that, but I nevertheless flicked fire at his helmet. A sword point could be ignored—I knew that from experience—but having your flesh lit or, in this case, your armor melting around your face? I doubted there was a man or woman alive who'd ignore that, no matter how stoic they were or what continent they were from.

He didn't move. We stepped over him and walked on. The tunnel curved gently to the left, then opened out a fraction as we neared the entrance. Like the rest of the tunnel, it had a decided lean. It also had a "wing"—basically, a piece of rock that jutted out at an angle from the left, preventing anyone who might be below from seeing us. It had no top, however, so any rider flying past would spot us standing there.

I motioned Tayn to stop, then edged forward carefully and looked up. The skies were dark, without stars or moon, and the air crisp and still. The mountain rose above us, dark and brooding, but there was no sign of the sentry Rudy had mentioned. Hopefully that meant he wouldn't see me. I moved to the end of the long outcrop and carefully peered around the end.

The first thing I noticed was the naked body lying halfway down the rough, debris-filled slope between us and the forest.

His skin was pale but heavily inked, though from where I stood, it was hard to make out what the images depicted. His wrists, neck, and his stomach had been sliced open, his entrails fat snakes that littered the ground around him. This was obviously the blood sacrifice, and I couldn't help but wonder if he'd been a Jakarran defender or one of their own. As a general rule, inking had never been popular on the mainland, but it was amongst island fisherfolk; many liked to keep visual reminders of friends, conquests, and fishing triumphs to help them get through the often-long trips to find decent catches. Or so Garran had once told me.

Túxn, please don't let him be dead.

I pushed away the grief that rose with the thought and studied the forests halfway down the slope. They were shadowed and dark, almost indistinguishable from the night itself. There were no campfires or anything else to indicate a force of men hid within those trees. Few military camps, whether small or large, were silent, so it likely meant no one was down there.

Unless, of course, they were using some sort of magical shield to cover their noise.

I couldn't see Illistin from where we stood, but I could smell smoke, and there was a faint orange glow visible in the distance. She still burned.

Frustration stirred, as did anger. We had to find a way to stop these bastards before all of Arleeon met the same fate. Although right now, I'd settle for a means of protecting Esan against the riders, their birds' acidic shit, and their mages. Hopefully, Damon could get in contact with his Angolan kin, and between them work out a protection spell large enough to shield Esan.

But that would take time.

Time we didn't have.

Was that intuition, or simple fear? I suspected it might be a bit of both.

"Anything?" Tayn asked.

"No immediate indication they're in the forest. Doesn't mean they're not there, of course."

He stepped up beside me and peered out. Horror immediately flooded his expression.

"In Vahree's name," he whispered, "is that a warning? Or something else?"

"It's a sacrifice." My voice was grim. "Their mages were using his blood to raise their magic. If you look closely enough, you can see the disturbed stone just beyond him—that's where Rudy opened his chasm and buried the bastards."

"And thank Vahree he did. If this is what they intend to do to all—"

"None of those in Eastmead met this fate." At least, none of the ones I'd seen had, anyway. I guess it was possible the bottom layer of bodies might have been sacrificed in this manner, but something within doubted it. Eastmead had been utterly destroyed, but it was the destruction that came with a white-hot fire rather than the earth rising up. Of course, it was also very possible the intensity of the flames *had* been a result of magic. "Did you know him?"

"His face doesn't look familiar, but his inkings are reminiscent of ones done on Halcraft."

Which was the second smallest island in the Jakarran cluster. If this man was from there, then that island and the three others might have already been decimated, though we'd had no word from them and there was no indication so far that was the case.

While it did make strategic sense to attack the largest island first, it was unlikely they'd have left the other four untouched.

I scanned the long expanse of slope then said, somewhat grimly, "What we need is a means of stopping any more of those riders or soldiers getting into this tunnel."

"What about a trapping pit?" Tayn said. "With the weight of their armor, they shouldn't be able to jump very far, so a deep pit around the entrance that also takes in the first couple of yards of the tunnel should more than do."

I hesitated and glanced down. "The stone here is straight lava stone. It's notoriously hard to excavate, especially for one man."

"Then we just—" He stopped abruptly, cocking his head sideways. "What is that sound?"

I frowned and, after a few seconds, caught the creak of leather accompanied by the soft sighing of wind. The former very much reminded me of the noise you sometimes got with new saddles when the panel leather rubbed against the back of the flaps, or when there was a problem with the tree or head plate. Given there were no coursers on this island, let alone halfway up a steep mountain, there could be only one source.

"Back, get back," I whispered and followed him quickly into the mouth of the cave.

The sighing sharpened and, a heartbeat later, gold glimmered as a bird and its rider swept over our heads and swooped toward the forest. Deeper in the trees, light flashed, two quick pulses that briefly lit the night.

We might not be able to see them, but there were definitely men down in those trees.

"We'll need to work on our defenses tonight, I'm thinking," Tayn said grimly.

"Yes, and don't just rely on the pit. Maybe something simple like greasing the ground would at least slow them down."

He nodded. "I'm not sure what we've got, but we'll work on it." His gaze shot to mine. "It would help, though, if Esan came to our aid."

"They will. Are."

He studied me for a moment, then spun and led the way back through the tunnel into the antechamber. There were twenty or so people crowding the small space now, most of them healers and stretcher-bearers taking care of the injured and the dead.

"I'll go report to Katter. Good luck with everything, Tayn, and keep safe."

He smiled and lightly saluted. "You too, Captain. You too."

I nodded, wove through the crowd, then increased my pace once I reached the larger tunnel. Katter glanced up from whatever he was reading as I entered the temporary war room. "Thank you for your assistance down there."

Obviously, the woman who'd been sent to call out the medics had also reported to Katter.

"Welcome." I hesitated. "I need to rest up before I head back out —is there somewhere I can bunk down for a few hours? And if you can write up a list of everything you need, I'll scribe it once I'm back in range."

He nodded and glanced at the woman to his right. "Layla, escort the captain over to the officers' quarters."

As he got back to reading the missive, the woman said, "This way."

I collected my pack, bow, and quiver, then followed her out. The officers' quarters lay across the other side of this level and were basically a deep tunnel holding a series of narrow stone chambers that could be curtained off. Each contained little more than a bed and a storage shelf.

Layla led me past the first ten—at least four of which were empty —then swept aside the curtain and motioned toward the bed. "The noise from the lower chamber should be less noticeable here. The privies are down the far end, and there's a washroom there as well, if you want a quick clean-up. Fresh towels and soapweed are kept on the open shelving there."

"Thanks. Can you ask someone to wake me up in four hours?"

"Will do, Captain. Sleep well."

She turned and immediately left. I dropped everything onto the bed, then went down to make use of the facilities and clean up a little. After stripping off my boots and jacket, I lay down and closed my eyes. It seemed I'd barely fallen asleep when there was someone beyond the curtain calling my name.

"Yes?" I said, struggling into a sitting position. My eyes felt heavy, and there was a deep ache in the back of my head, which was due to either doing too much on too little sleep, or my courses coming in. While all female soldiers took a specially designed potion to prevent both pregnancy *and* the inconvenience of actually bleeding every month, that never stopped us getting all the usual symptoms. Mine was generally headaches, crankiness, and an overwhelming urge to eat sweet things.

"You asked to be woken in four hours, Captain."

"Yes, indeed, thanks."

"Administrator Reed wishes to know if you would like something to eat before you leave."

"Trail bread and a flask of water will do just fine. Thanks."

"He waits for you in the war room, Captain."

"Tell him I'll be there shortly."

"Aye," the soldier said, and then left, his boots echoing on the stone.

I lightly scrubbed my hands down my face, then pulled on my boots and staggered more than walked down to use the facilities and splash my face with cold water in an effort to get some wakefulness happening.

After tugging on my coat, I dug the pain herbs out of my pack and took them, then strapped on my sword and knife, and slung the bow and quiver across my back. After clipping the backpack to my belt, I headed out. The pack bumped against my thigh with every step, but at least it left my hands free—a good thing, given I'd be climbing rather than descending through the mountain tunnels this time.

Katter was almost in the same position as he'd been when I'd left a few hours ago.

I greeted him, then said softly, "You should get some rest, Katter. You're no good to anyone if you drop from exhaustion."

He smiled and scrubbed a hand through his hair. "I will once dawn wakes and things calm down at the entrance."

"There's been another attack?"

He grimaced. "Let's call it a prelim skirmish. No riders this time, and they weren't wearing the golden armor, so we had no problems driving them back. Good suggestion about the grease, by the way. It helped."

I nodded. "Has Rudy managed to set up the trapping pit?"

"He had to grab some rest first, but he's working on it now." He hesitated. "Jay and Riyale will accompany you back to the exit, and secure the scribe tablet once you make the report. We'll set up another sentry point there, just to be safe."

I nodded again. "It's unlikely any reinforcements and supplies we can get here will be able to use that entrance. It's too high up the mountain and would take too long for those on foot to reach."

"Indeed, but it is the perfect place to scribe. We'll also be able to see incoming ships from that vantage point and arrange an easier— and likely safer—docking area."

If the weather hadn't closed in around the peaks, that was. I accepted the ration pack he gave me, then formally saluted. "Please send my regards to Hanna, and tell her I'll see her in happier times."

"I will."

"Thank you, Administrator." I hesitated. "Perhaps we can share a fine jug or two of mead once this is all over?"

"I look forward to it, Captain." He lightly returned my salute, and once again got back to his missives.

I glanced at my escort, then turned and headed out. We made good time out of the main cavern and moved quickly through the closer tunnels before slowing when we reached the one that looped up to the upper ledge. The light from the tubes danced across the dark stone, lending it a bluish-purple glow that was almost pretty. I ate some of my rations along the way and sipped at the water, but really didn't feel any better. The headache remained, and it was bad enough that I wished I'd brought more pain relief along with me.

It was hard to know the precise time we finally reached the key-shaped tunnel exit, because clouds hugged the mountain close and there was nothing but a deep blanket of damp gray as far as the eye could see.

It wouldn't disrupt the scribe's ability to make contact, and it would certainly offer good protection as I scrambled down the mountain to meet Kaia, but it would make that descent damnably unpleasant.

I tugged the tablet and pen from the pack and squatted against the wall while I sent a quick rundown of the situation, then asked if the boats had left yet.

Will two hours after dawn has risen.

I frowned and sent back, *What time is it now? And why wait so long?*

The sun rises in an hour. We wait because the riders have been sighted a few hours after dawn and before sunset.

Which suggested that it was really only the middle of the day, when the sun was at its strongest, that they were restricted—and *that* was not good news. *Has there been another attack?*

No, but several outposts along the Blue Steel range have reported sightings. They appear to be scouting beyond Esan.

Planning their conquest over the rest of Arleeon if they succeed in overrunning us, no doubt.

Yes. The tiny ink blot that was the quill he was holding pulsed gently for several seconds. *What of Garran's family? His parents?*

I hesitated. This really wasn't a question I wanted to answer, especially when we had no confirmation as to their fate. But I was a captain, and this was not the first time I'd had to be the bearer of bad news.

Hanna and their son are alive. No reports yet on those who remained to defend the city. Glenda is currently unaccounted for, but they haven't yet registered all the survivors. She may be here but helping with the wounded. Which was highly unlikely, given if that were true, Katter would have known. *I'm leaving the tablet with Katter's men. They have a list of supplies they need ASAP, if you've time to add them to the boats.*

We have. The ink blot pulsed for a second or two. *Stay wary.*

Hoping to be home by dusk.

If you're not back by then, we'll send out a search party.

That would be pointless, given I could be anywhere between here and home, and the tracking stone's range is not that good.

You taking the same route?

Yes—it's safer than flying direct, especially with the riders being active beyond dawn.

Then at least this time, your mother will have a good idea where to send the gray hawks.

It would probably take the hawks far too long to find us, given the sheer scale of the search area, but they'd certainly offer a better chance than simply relying on the tracking stones.

Handing you over to Katter's people now. See you soon.

You will.

I smiled and passed the tablet over to Jay. "They're waiting for the list."

"Thank you, Captain. Safe journey down the mountain." He briefly scanned the blanket of gray. "It's not going to be pleasant in this weather."

"At least it isn't raining yet."

I rose and, after a nod to them both, started the long hike down to the ledge. With the thick damp clouds clinging to every surface, it was every bit as treacherous as I feared. I slipped more than once, and though quick reflexes saved me from multiple tumbles, I nevertheless gained multiple scratches. My jacket was thick, but even leather could tear if sliced with a sharp enough knife—and many of the rocks littering this slope were honed by wind and weather to a point any smith would be proud of. I was close to the ledge and bleeding from a half dozen wounds scattered across my hands and shins when I finally reached for Kaia.

You awake?

Bored.

I couldn't help but smile at the tartness of her reply. *Did you hunt?*

Hunger remains.

Being aboard a very hungry drakkon probably wasn't a great idea. *Once we reach the mainland, we can take a break so you can hunt.*

Longhorn? We fly near.

Sure.

Satisfaction rumbled through our link. I smiled and continued on warily, sliding down the final few feet to the platform. The world remained a sea of gray, but I could hear the distant sigh of air and feel Kaia's ever-increasing closeness. I quickly treated the worst of my wounds, then dragged the harness out of my pack and climbed into it. Once that was done, I slung the quiver and bow over my back and attached the pack.

As the wind of Kaia's approach grew stronger, I stepped back, not only to give her more room but to avoid being accidentally squashed. She appeared out of the gloom, her scales gleaming with golden fire, and wings banked as she braked. I couldn't help but smile. I would never—*ever*—get over the beauty and the elegance of our drakkons.

She landed lightly, then snaked her head around for a scratch. Once I'd complied, I scrambled up her extended leg and clipped on the spine rope. She crouched and then leapt skyward, her wings pumping hard as she climbed slowly but steadily.

The tumultuous stream of icy air blasting my face and fingers soon had me shivering, and I once again tugged the long collar of an undershirt up and pushed enough heat through to my extremities to keep frostbite at bay. The jacket and layers were doing enough to keep the chill away from the rest of me, even if I wasn't toasty warm, so I resisted raising the inner fires any further. We remained in enemy territory, and my headache and overall weariness meant my reserves weren't what they could and should have been.

We'll need to fly faster once we're clear of this fog, Kaia. The winged ones have been sighted flying in the hours after sunrise.

Will. Not cloudy over water, so see if near.

It wasn't seeing them I was worried about. It was outrunning both the birds and whatever weapons their riders might be carrying.

Am faster.

I hoped she was right but feared we just didn't know enough about them to be certain of anything. Besides, they were now aware of the drakkons' presence in Arleeon, so it was very possible they'd develop a weapon to neutralize them.

We soon cleared the mountains, and Kaia increased her speed. As the low-lying fog began to dissipate, the day brightened, the last flags of morning color lending the heavy clouds dotting the sky a pastel hue. The seas far below were white capped and wild, and its blue emptiness stretched on for as far as the eye could see. It wasn't like our boats would be anywhere close to Jakarra yet, even if they had risked leaving earlier, but that didn't stop me continually checking for them. If our ships didn't make it this time, the survivors would be in big trouble.

As one hour became two, and the distant, shadowy mountains that lined Arleeon's shores finally came into view, I began to relax.

I should have known better than to tempt Túxn like that.

Kaia's head snapped around and she bellowed, the sound echoing harshly across the roar of the wind. I turned, gaze scanning the shroud of clouds behind us. And there, in the distance, was the subtle glint of gold. Not one, not two, but three riders.

Vahree help us...

Fly hard, I said urgently.

Fight, she snapped. *Better.*

We can't beat three, Kaia.

You have fire. I have teeth and claws.

And they have spears and liquid shit that burns.

What shit?

I sent her images of both courser and bird manure.

Kak no burn, she replied.

This one does. I sent more images, this time of the damage it had done to the men and women defending the cavern's entrance.

I not soft human.

This liquid cuts through stone, Kaia, so it will certainly ash drakkon scale.

Fury burned through her thoughts, but she nevertheless increased her speed, her wings pumping so fast they were almost a blur. The riders neither drew nearer nor fell away. It was almost as if they were herding us...

I swore, untied the long viewer from the side of my pack, then lifted it to my eye, twisting the focus ring around until the shoreline became clear.

And once again saw the distant glint of gold.

Riders. Two of them of this time, coming straight at us.

We fight, Kaia said. *No choice.*

No, we didn't. Not now.

We need to punch through the two ahead and keep on flying.

I rise into cloud then dive behind. You flame. Stay on.

I half-laughed. *That's certainly the plan.*

Her amusement rumbled through me, but it was mixed now with excitement and the bloody need to rent and tear. The queen was eager to begin her quest for revenge.

I wished I could say I was totally behind that emotion, but in truth, all I felt was fear. There were just too many unknowns for me to be entirely comfortable battling these people and their birds. But as my father often said, fear was a means of keeping focus as long as you didn't let it gain control over your actions.

I drew in a deeper breath and released it slowly, imagining all the emotion, the fear, and the uncertainty flowing out of my body—something all raw recruits were taught, and a lesson considered almost as vital as sword and bow craft. Then I shifted my feet a little deeper into the stirrups and double-checked all the knots and clips holding me onto Kaia.

With that done, all I could do was watch and wait.

The riders behind us had spread out and drawn closer, no doubt anticipating us diving either left or right in an attempt to flee once the riders ahead came into plain sight. They didn't, not for what seemed like forever. The sun was riding higher in the sky now, making me wonder how much longer the riders could keep their birds aloft—if, that is, we'd been right about their restrictions.

We were about to find out the hard way.

The birds directly ahead shone like golden stars against the gray of the clouds. Kaia flew on at speed, her mind focused and ready. I'd seen many drakkons hunt over the years, but this was different.

This really was Kaia going to war.

As the birds drew closer, the riders became visible. One was holding a spear at the ready, the other a larger version of the metal tubes we'd discovered near The Beak.

You need to be upwind when you attack, I said. *That metal tube is what sprays the kak.*

Will. Her tone suggested any idiot would know that.

A smile tugged at my lips again, but quickly faded as I glanced behind us. The three riders had now formed a half circle, the two on the ends higher than the one in the middle. Fire burned around my fingertips, but I clenched them hard, resisting the urge to unleash. They were too far away for either flame or arrows to be effective; better to save both until a kill was a true possibility.

But Vahree only knew it was hard to sit here and do nothing except watch possible death fly ever closer.

The birds ahead were close enough now that I could see the wicked point on their beaks and the talons that protruded from the fluff of their underbellies. They were long, sharp, and deadly looking. Almost as deadly as the long spear one rider held.

Hold, Kaia warned, and then swept up vertically, climbing hard and fast into the clouds.

I gripped tight with my thighs, one hand on the rope, the other burning with so much heat my fingers were almost incandescent. Then, with surprising agility for a creature so large, Kaia belly rolled and dropped back down the way she'd came. It all happened so quickly I barely even lifted from her back. We came out of the clouds hard and fast, dropping underneath and *behind* the riders. As Kaia rolled onto her side and raked her murderous claws along one bird's soft underbelly, I unleashed my flames, spearing them toward the rider's helmet and weapon. As the metal melted around his face, he screamed, a harsh sound echoed by his mount. It lashed out with its long legs, its dagger claws scoring the sky where Kaia had been only seconds before. As she continued to bank away, she flicked her long tail, smacking the end across the bird's head and neck. There was an audible snap as it was sent tumbling through the air.

It was then I saw the stream of brown arcing toward us. Horror dawned. *Kaia!*

See.

She flicked her wings and rose so sharply that I slipped back before the rope snapped tight, bringing me to an abrupt halt. The dark spray splashed across the end of her tail instead of her body and she bellowed again in fury and pain. I twisted around and threw flames at the bird and its rider, though there wasn't a whole lot of heat behind it. They fell away from the stream, the flames doing little more than scorching tail feathers before fizzing out.

Kaia body rolled again and came up under the bird. The rider twisted around and aimed his weapon, but before he could hit the trigger, Kaia's teeth ripped into the bird's unprotected underbelly and tore it apart. As feathers, blood, and gore spilled all around us, the bird screamed, and dropped away. Kaia raised her head and swallowed the thick chunk of flesh and muscle she'd torn from the bird, then bellowed her triumph.

It was a sound that turned to pain. A heartbeat later, we also began to lose height.

Kaia?

Wing.

I quickly scanned the right wing, and then left. The latter was in tatters, the membrane destroyed by a thin, sweeping arc between three of the wing's phalanges.

I looked down and saw the rider raise his weapon in triumph even as he fell to his death.

Drop to the sea, I said urgently. *The salt will sting but the water will stop the liquid from destroying any more of your wing.*

Others catch.

They'll catch us sooner if you don't stop that acid eating the rest of your wing. You must soak it for ten minutes, at least.

A deep, unhappy sounding rumble vibrated through her, but she nevertheless dropped sharply and swept down toward the waves. I twisted around; the remaining three riders weren't yet within firing range but the distance between us was ever decreasing, and the land remained a very long way away.

We would get there. Somehow.

I would not let these bastards win. Would not let them deprive Gria of her mother when they'd already taken her brother.

Kaia banked sideways and skimmed the choppy ocean, dragging both her battered wing and her tail through the waves, forcing me to grip tightly with legs and hands or risk tumbling from her back. I have no idea how she was managing to stay aloft in the position, and I didn't dare think about it too hard because I just might jinx things.

Her pain flooded our link, dragging tears to my eyes, but she kept her wing and tail in the water. A flume rose behind us, the spray glittering in the ever-increasing brightness of the day.

The riders drew ever closer. In Vahree's name, how were they still aloft? We were well past sunrise now, so why didn't these bastards just leave?

Had we really been *that* wrong about their capabilities? It was possible, I guess, but something within me just didn't believe it.

We flew on in that impossible position for what seemed like ages but was probably little more than ten minutes or so before Kaia right herself and flew on. She remained low, the broken bits of her wing flapping like sheets in the wind. Pain continued to rumble through our connection, but so too did determination. She had no intention of dying today, either.

We flew on, but with a large chunk of her wing's membrane torn, Kaia's speed was dropping, and the birds were now within fighting range.

The one to our right made the first move, arrowing in hard and fast. He raised a long spear and drew his arm back, the black arrowhead gleaming with deadly intent against the blue sky.

I called to my fire and flung it toward him. Pain erupted through my brain, but I narrowed my gaze and blinked away the tears, watching the progress of my fireball. His bird banked away at the last minute and my fireball tumbled past them both. But as the bird resumed its original path and its rider raised his weapon again, I looped the fireball back around and arrowed it straight at the two of them. A heartbeat before it hit, I flicked my fingers wide, increasing the intensity of my weapon and wrapping the two of them in white-hot flame.

They went up in a whoosh, their agony barely given voice before the flames consumed them.

As they became little more than molten metal and ash, what sounded like a battle cry rose from the remaining two. They were giving chase, not giving up.

I swore and studied the distant shoreline. If we could get there, if we could find somewhere to shelter, we might have a chance of surviving....

Kaia tried to increase her speed, but the damage to her left wing

—and the stress she was putting it under—not only meant more of the membrane was tearing, but also that her thrust was reduced. She was relying more and more on her right wing and that, in turn, meant we were slowly moving to the right.

I called to my fire, but pain seized my brain, and the mote in my eye burst. Blood trickled over my eyelashes, but I ignored it, forced flames to my fingers, and cast it toward the nearest rider. It banked away, and I flicked my fire after him, forcing him further away before the distance became too great between us and the flames faded.

The other one continued to follow us, neither coming any closer nor falling away. Waiting, I suspected, for Kaia's wing to fully fail.

The headlands grew closer, the sun brighter as it rose toward midmorning. The waves grew larger and more numerous as we raced toward the dark sands that designated home but not safety.

My gaze rose and, after a second, I recognized where exactly we were. I'd been to this area a long time ago. Had saved a young female drakkon here once....

The thought had barely crossed my mind when Kaia bellowed, a long and haunting sound that resonated with unusual strength. It was a cry that washed across the waves below us, swept over the shoreline, and rose to echo amongst the peaks.

If it was a call for help, there was no response.

She bellowed again, this time with more force.

For several heartbeats, the only answer was the distant cry of kayin.

Then a red drakkon rose over the top of the mountains, her scales dripping like blood in the brightness of the day. Another drakkon rose behind her, also red, but smaller.

Three against two were far better odds....

It was at that very point when the brown liquid tore through Kaia's right wing.

11

AS KAIA'S WING CRUMPLED, I turned and flung fire at the closest rider. His mount twisted away, and my flames singed its tail feathers, melting their tips but doing little else. They simply didn't have enough heat—*I* simply didn't have enough heat left.

As white-hot lances of agony cut through my brain and blood flooded over my lashes, I dragged my bow from across my back, then pulled two arrows free. One I held in my teeth, the other I notched and drew back. I sighted on the nearest bird, unleashed, and then notched the next arrow. As the bird banked away, I quickly calculated its path and our fall trajectory, then released. The arrow flew straight and true, sinking deep into the joint between the bird's wing and body. It wasn't the killing shot it would have been with a much smaller bird, but it was nevertheless one that would make its ability to fly more difficult.

The incoming drakkons bellowed, and the rider of the bird I'd injured made a motion to his companion, and the two retreated toward the island.

I sucked in a breath, relieved. One problem down, another to go.

I slung my bow back across my shoulders and returned my attention to the dark sands that were approaching with alarming speed. We were definitely going to crash, and if I remained on Kaia, I'd more than likely die, crushed by her weight if she stumbled and fell.

Jumping wasn't exactly a great option either but...

I hastily unclipped the harness and backpack, then slipped my feet from the stirrups and shifted my weight, rising on her back enough that my feet were now underneath me. I gripped the rope around her spine to steady myself, but it was a precarious, dangerous position given how violently she now lurched as she battled to slow her speed and keep some semblance of control. At the last possible moment, she lifted herself up and shoved her legs forward. Her talons hit the dark sand first, but we were going too fast, and she began to tumble. I threw the backpack down, then leapt clear as her whole body went up and over me. I fell for what seemed an eternally long time, only to have the sand sweep up to me with surprising rapidness. I hit, somehow managing to keep my knees slightly bent against the shock of landing, but my left foot ended up in some sort of depression and pain tore up my leg. I gritted my teeth against the scream that rolled up my throat and followed the momentum of the fall, pushing forward into a roll in a desperate effort to absorb more of the impact and prevent bones from breaking.

I landed hard enough on my back to be winded, and for several seconds, did nothing more than stare up at the blue sky, echoes of shock and pain reverberating through me. I was alive... but was Kaia?

I scrambled upright and swung around. The dark sand was deeply trenched and led into the trees and a trail of destruction. I swore and ran; my ankle protested violently against the movement and the pain that burned up my leg was so fierce I felt like I was going to be sick. I sucked in the sharp, salty air and did my best to ignore it, stumbling on up the beach and into the trees.

The destruction ran deep. But then, she was a big drakkon.

Kaia? Are you okay? Are you hurt from the crash?

There was a long pause, and my heart hammered in fear. She couldn't be dead. Vahree surely wouldn't be so cruel....

Here came her sharp, somewhat annoyed reply. *Wing broke.*

Can you move?

Stuck.

I slowed but continued to follow her path of destruction into the deeper shadows of the forest. *And the acid?*

Burns.

Then you need to get back into the ocean and soak it.

Will when not stuck.

That comment definitely held more than an edge of bite to it, and relief slipped through me. If she could snap back, then she wasn't any more seriously hurt than she had been before crash-landing.

I clambered over the trunk of a fallen tree, ran around its thick crown, and followed the crack of wood and heavy grunting till I found her. She was partially upright, her body lodged between two trees, but it was the long stream of membrane from her left wing that had wrapped around the trunk of a third tree that appeared to be anchoring her in place. The position of her body in the trees meant she couldn't twist around and free herself, and if she simply tore it completely away, she might never fly again. Phalanges and membrane could be repaired and healed, but I doubted it was possible for the latter to be torn free then successfully reattached.

Help, she said.

Trying, I replied, in the same tart tone she used earlier.

A rumble of amusement ran through our link. At least she saw the humor in the situation.

I stepped over the raw end of her tail, limped across to the tree, then walked around it until I found the end of the membrane. Carefully, trying not to tear it any further, I picked it up and began to unwrap it. It was a large piece, and it was damnably awkward to free it from the tree without causing any further damage, but I eventually succeeded. Once she was free, she tucked her wings in as much as she could, then backed out of the trees. There were gouges along the side I could see, and one of her back spines had been broken, but wings aside, she appeared unhurt.

From high above us came a deep bellow. Kaia raised her head and answered, and a heartbeat later, the two drakkons we'd seen earlier landed on the beach, the larger of the two peering curiously into the chaotic gap in the trees. The smaller drakkon, a male at full maturity from the look of it, kept to one side, his thoughts filled with wary interest.

The female shifted her weight a fraction, drawing my gaze again, and it was then I spotted the lightning-like slash of gold across her chest. It was the red drakkon who'd debated the merits of eating humans with me while I'd healed her.

Know you, she said.

Yes.

No eat.

Well, good, I thought, amused, though I wasn't entirely sure if she meant she wouldn't eat me now or that she hadn't eaten humans since our discussion.

Is kin, Kaia rumbled. *You hurt, I kill.*

The younger female lowered her head, as if in acknowledgment and deference. *What kin?*

Kaia explained what it meant as she moved out of the forest, her broken right wing dragging on the ground and clearly still bubbling. The acid hadn't initially taken out as much of the membrane on the right as on the left, but if she didn't neutralize it, it soon would.

And until she did neutralize it, it was pointless for me to try to fix it.

The two younger drakkons moved apart to give her room, and she walked into the ocean, stopping when it was at her chest and spreading her wings out as best she could. The waves crashed over them, and pain rumbled through our link once again.

Can heal broke wing? she asked.

Possibly, depending on how bad the break is and whether I have enough strapping with me.

Where more strapping? Esan?

Yes.

Rua carry there.

Rua made a squawk that very much echoed her mental *What?*

Kaia's head snapped around, her teeth bared, and our mental link was briefly cut as she and the younger drakkon conversed. The young drakkon lowered her head again. This time it was very definitely deferential.

I am the queen, Kaia had once told me. *They will obey.*

This was evidence that she had not been kidding.

Even if I can repair enough of your wing to fly, you shouldn't fly straight away. You need to give the straps time to set.

Gria flew.

The damage to her wing wasn't as great. What we need is to find somewhere more sheltered—are there any caves within walking distance along this shore?

Tarn look, Kaia ordered. *Rua hunt. Am hungry.*

The two younger drakkons bowed, then stepped back and took off. The sweep of their wings whipped the sand up around us, and I turned away from the stinging storm to protect my face.

It was then I spotted the distant shape on the horizon.

A ship.

Hope leapt briefly, then just as quickly departed. It couldn't be from Esan—we were too far south, for a start, and they'd have to be a long way off from the fastest route to Jakarra to even get here.

Unless some of the Jakarran boats had escaped, this was either a fisherman from Southport or the enemy... and I wasn't liking the chances of it being one of the first two options.

I looked around frantically for my pack and spotted it yards up the beach. I quickly limped over and, as I pulled the long viewer free, prayed for Túxn's luck to be with us.

It was, at least partially. The long viewer was intact, but the lens glass was cracked, and the image more than a little fuzzy. But it was sharp enough to make out the boat's deep belly, the line of open oar slats that lined its length, and the single mast that held red sails on which a crest had been inked—a long-clawed bird flying over crossed spears.

That was not a crest used by anyone within Arleeon or her islands, and as far as I was aware, none of our trading partners had crests like that.

This ship belonged to our foe. And if they had one ship here, they would have others, and that was certainly confirmation of my earlier fears—the riders *weren't* all we had to worry about.

We fight, Kaia said.

We can't. We have no weapons.

You have flame.

My flame is all but gone, and will take time to regenerate. I thrust a hand through my tangled hair in frustration, tearing bits free that floated away on the sharp breeze.

Rua and Tarn fight.

That ship might have acid weapons. We can't risk their lives, Kaia.

Many would.

I'm not many

No. Why I seek for help.

I couldn't help but smile. Who could have guessed that all those years of watching her hunt would lead to her not only trusting me, but also the formation of a bond that went beyond mere trust?

What do then? she continued.

"I don't know." I raised the long viewer again and saw the harpoon sitting high on the bow. "They're not hunting us. They're hunting for food."

Water beasts?

"Yes."

I dropped the long viewer onto my pack, limped into the waves, and thrust a hand under the water. We were a long way from that ship and whatever it was hunting, but I had no doubt desperation would add extra strength to the call.

After a few minutes, I felt the presence of a pod of long fins. I homed in on them and quickly realized they were unaware of the danger that lurked above them. I sent out a broad beam warning followed by a request for aid to sink that ship.

There was a long pause before a distant voice, *How?*

I deepened the connection and sent an image of the ship, envisaging five or six long fins leaping high out of the water and smashing onto the boat either side of the mast. Then I sent images of the boat breaking, the long fins swimming away, and the boat sinking.

Basically, I was teaching this pod how to sink our boats, and *this* boat was not as large or as sturdy as most of our fleet.

There was another long pause before she said, *You warn, we do. Thank you.*

She didn't reply, and I didn't withdraw, despite the fact the intensity of the connection was *not* helping my headache. I kept track of them as they dove deep, keeping well under until they were behind the boat. Six then split away from the main group and began the ascent. I spun and limped back for the long viewer, picking it up and quickly focusing it—just in time to see the six rounded black bodies surge high out of the water and, with perfect synchronicity, came down as one along the boat's entire length.

The boat—and the people—never stood a chance. The sheer weight of six long fins shattered the wooden structure even as it drove the boat under waves. I watched for the longest of times, but little more than broken bits of wood resurfaced.

For the moment, we were safe.

I sucked in a breath, then glanced around as the male returned. He landed neatly further up the beach and gave me the side eye. *Hollow five wing sweeps away. Hide all.*

Thank you, Tarn, I said.

He reared back on his hind legs and shook his head, as if trying to get rid of my reply. *Hear you?*

Yes, I said.

Why?

I hesitated. Kaia jumped in and said, *Is kin.*

Obviously, that was the only explanation needed, and the male seemed to accept it. *Guard from cliff.*

Kaia rumbled her approval and, as the male flew off, said, *They come to aerie?*

I rubbed my forehead against the increasing ferocity of the headache and switched to voice rather than internal conversation. "If you want."

Safer.

I half smiled. "And the male can guard Gria when you're not there?"

Plan. Also, cave larger.

"Does that mean you're going to relocate your grace there?"

Not yet.

Not until we'd dealt with these birds, she meant. And I couldn't say I blamed her.

Rua return, she added. *Has two longhorn.*

The latter was said with a thick rumble of approval. The younger female crested the mountain a few seconds later and swept down, one longhorn grasped in her rear talons and what looked to be a calf in her mouth. She banked her wings to slow, then dropped both her prizes on the sand within Kaia's reach.

Is good, Kaia said.

Rua looked pleased. She backed away but didn't land, her head swinging around to me. *You need?*

I'm good, but thank you.

She nodded and flew up to join the male on watch.

Pair, Kaia commented.

"Are they part of an aerie?"

No room. Forced out.

I glanced at her, surprised. "Does that happen often?"

When no room.

If a young breeding pair had been kicked out because the aerie was at capacity, that meant Esan's drakkons were more numerous than we'd thought. And that was definitely a good thing.

I limped over to grab my pack and pulled out the last of my rations. In all honesty, I wouldn't have minded a well-roasted kayin or even a capra to boost my energy reserves right now, but I didn't like raw meat and I couldn't risk creating a fire, even though it would be easy enough to make a firepit in these sands, and there certainly was enough broken wood within the forest to fuel it.

Once Kaia's wings had dried, she shifted position, digging herself a little deeper into the sand so that I could reach her wings more easily and check the full extent of the damage. Several phalanges on both wings had been broken, but they were an easy enough fix if I had enough straps. It was the right wing's broken radius bone and the large amount of torn membrane on the left wing that were the main problem. Without those two things fixed, she definitely wouldn't fly.

I took a deep breath and then said, "I need to realign the bones on your right wing. This will hurt."

Know. Do.

I hesitated, then got down to work, carefully positioning the bone, then wrapping half a dozen straps around the break to hold it in place. Then I retrieved some silk webbing and strung it between the phalanges on either side, attached the leathery membrane to it, then sealed it on. Broken patches remained, but at least the membrane had a framework to regrow on.

With that done, I moved over to the left wing and the larger swath of membrane that had been torn away from the area between her shoulder and elbow. I repaired the nearby phalange first, then strung the webbing between it and the remaining patches of membrane, sealing it in place before unraveling the large sheet of torn tissue and attaching it. I didn't have a whole lot of sealer or straps left after that, so repaired the worst of the tears, then spread antiseptic cream over her other wounds, particularly her raw tail. When I'd done as much as I could, I stepped back and wiped the sweat from my forehead.

"That's all I can do, Kaia."

She pushed out of the sand and warily closed her wings, and then opened them again and lightly fanned. *Is good. Can fly.*

"Not yet," I said hastily. "We need to give the straps a little more time to set, otherwise we risk them popping during flight."

Need leave before light fades. Not safe here.

I glanced up sharply and realized noon had come and gone. "We will, but in the meantime, we should find that hollow Tarn mentioned and get out of sight."

Not safe in hollow. Rather fly.

"And I'd rather you get back to Gria in one piece, thank you very much."

It was tersely said, and amusement ran through her thoughts. *You in heat?*

"No, I am *not*."

Sound like. Her amusement fell away. *Fly now. Safer. Bones heal fast.*

"Bones don't heal that fast, Kaia, especially when you're putting them under the stress of flight."

Our bones different.

I sucked in a breath and released it slowly, torn between the need to get out of here and the desire to keep her safe.

I good. We go. If wing fail, Rua and Tarn catch.

"How? You're almost double their size."

I trust you. You trust me.

"Fine," I grumbled. "We go."

She immediately shifted and extended her leg. I grabbed the pack, then clambered up, positioning myself behind her spine before attaching the harness. The minute I had, she bellowed, a sharp command aimed at the other drakkons, then hunkered down and launched into the air, her wings pumping hard, sending a storm of sand flying all around us. I closed my eyes, tugged my undershirt up over my mouth and nose to stop breathing in the muck, and waited, heart in mouth, for wings to tear and bones to break.

They didn't.

We remained aloft, though she kept low and close to the cliffs, using the uplift to soar more than fly. Tarn flew behind us, Rua to our right. She kept studying us and even without skimming her thoughts, it was pretty obvious she was curious.

Why allow on back? she asked eventually.

Safer for both, Kaia said. *She flame.*

Flame? Rua asked.

Kaia described how she and I had battled the riders and defeated them, and Rua grew thoughtful. *Share?*

My kin, Kaia snapped.

Where find kin?

I grinned. It was just too perfect an opportunity... and it was doubtful Kele would object to me nominating her as a possible drakkon rider. *There is another who can flame at our breeding grounds, but she cannot speak directly to minds like me.*

Kaia help talk?

Will, she said.

Rua looked pleased, and my smile grew. Wait until Kele found out....

We flew on, and after a couple of hours, when it became very obvious the straps and seals were not going to fail, Kaia rose and headed inland, following the spine of the Black Glass Mountains back to Esan.

Dusk's pink fingers were just beginning to claim the sky when I spotted the glint of gold. I swore, dragged the long viewer free, and focused the broken sight.

Riders, two of them, coming in fast from around the direction of the Throat, suggesting that at least one of them was the sentry I'd spotted earlier.

We fight came Kaia's unsurprising response.

We run, I said. *Not to the aerie, because we can't risk them finding out about it.*

Then fight.

No. Fly to Esan.

What good that?

Esan have spears that can bring the riders down, plus Kele and a few others can flame.

Rua and Tarn no like Esan.

But they trust you, and will obey you, right?

Yes.

Then we fly into Esan and land in that courtyard. There will be room for all three. As long as all the humans got out of the way.

Kaia grumbled unhappily—a sound echoed by the other two drakkons—then as one they swept around to the left and increased their speed, arrowing toward the dark blot of mountain that housed Esan.

It seemed an extraordinarily long way away.

Ten minutes later, Tarn trumpeted a sharp warning. I twisted around and saw another two birds appear on the horizon to our left, their wings a golden blur as they arrowed toward us.

Keep going, I urged all three.

Their speed didn't increase. They were already flying as fast as they could. Or rather, as fast as Kaia could given the condition of her wings.

We flew over the capras' valley and swung right around the range I'd clambered over half my life. We were close, so close, to Esan now....

But so too were the birds. I could see the glint of their riders' armor.

A sharp squawk had me looking up. A gray hawk circled high above us.

Veri.

Mom had sent her aloft. She would know we were coming in fast....

Hope surged. But too soon, far too soon.

Tarn bellowed, a sound filled with pain. I glanced around, saw the claw attached to his shoulders, its metal mouth digging deep into his flesh. It was attached to a long rope that was held by the closest rider, who banked hard and dragged Tarn down and away.

I swore and unleashed a long stream of fire, cindering the rope first, then flinging it on into the bird's sharp features. There wasn't enough heat left to burn metal wings, but its eyes weren't protected and a far easier target.

As the heat burned out its eye sockets and the bird screamed and fell away, Kaia dropped, positioning herself above Tarn, protecting the younger drakkon. We flew on, around the mountain. Esan came into view, her walls lined with people. Rua faltered, but Kaia bellowed a demand they follow and took the lead, sweeping down and around until we were flying directly at the fortress.

The drakkons banked abruptly, and something wicked looking flew past us, its long rope tail flapping in the breeze as it fell away.

Another spear.

I twisted around. There were three riders still behind us, and they didn't appear too put off by Esan's closeness.

I flung fire their way, but it was little more than a pale shadow of heat that didn't even reach the nearest bird. Agony surged, seizing my brain as the mote in my eye popped again. I blinked the blood away and concentrated on the upper wall, looking for familiar faces.

Saw Damon, blood pouring down raised arms.

He was raising a spell....

The drakkons banked again, and again a spear flew past. I twisted around, saw the nearest rider raise a long metal tube.

Vahree help us....

We swept over the first wall. Arrows flew, not at us, but at the riders that followed. The ballistas were swung into action, unleashing their bolts with deadly force, but the birds were smaller, more agile targets, and they merely flicked their wings, dancing through the storm of missiles with seeming ease.

The velocity of the wind abruptly increased, and overhead thunder rumbled. Lightning sliced down, into the nearest bird, cindering metal, feather, and flesh. Then magic surged, sharp and familiar, sweeping over the three drakkons and seeming to condense behind us. I twisted around. There was nothing to see, no sharp shimmer of air to give any indication a barrier might be present... until the birds smacked into something solid and stopped hard. Then the wind swung around them, grabbed the three, and smashed them down onto the walls. The soldiers standing there finished what wind and magic had started.

Kaia trumpeted hard, and as one, the three drakkons braked, stretched out their feet, and landed with surprising lightness in the middle of the cleared upper courtyard.

Home. We'd actually made it *home*.

The wave of relief that surged was so damn fierce, a sob escaped. I quickly swallowed the rest, detached the harness, then rose on Kaia's back, and shouted, "Everyone stay back. The drakkons won't attack, but they are skittish and afraid."

"You heard the captain," my father bellowed when there was no immediate response. "Move out of the way *now*."

As everyone crowding the edges of the courtyard retreated indoors, I twisted around. Mom was descending the stairs and coming toward us, but my father was standing on the wall next to Damon. His expression was amused and relieved. Damon's was... I wasn't sure what Damon's was, because I fell into his gaze and sort of got lost for several seconds.

A knowing smile stretched his lips. I sent him a mock scowl and returned my attention to the drakkons. "Kaia, can you extend your leg for me?"

She immediately did so, then glanced around as Mom drew near. *Heard you before.*

"Indeed, you have," Mom said, stopping beside me and giving me a brief but fierce hug. "But we have not been formally introduced. I am Marin Silva, Bryn's mother. It is a pleasure to meet you, Queen Kaia."

Kaia rumbled in appreciation and lowered her head for a scratch. Mom complied. "We need to help that young male of yours—can you tell him we mean him no harm, though removing the claw will hurt?"

She could have told him all that herself, but he'd believe it more coming from Kaia. She complied, and what followed was several long hours of Mom and me tending to the drakkons' wounds while they consumed a meal of fat boars we'd ordered killed and brought in for them. Rua and Tarn remained wary, and I suspected it was only Kaia's presence that kept them here, but they were nevertheless looking around with growing interest.

When it was all done, Kaia said, *We go now.*

I frowned. It was dark and very possible the riders would be active—if any remained in the area, that was. They surely didn't have an unlimited supply, and we'd taken out quite a few of them over the course of the long day. But the truth was, the drakkons really couldn't stay here. Aside from the fact their bulk filled the courtyard, there was no guarantee someone wouldn't try to get too close or make some move that spooked them into reacting. The situation was simply too new for everyone not to be cautious.

"Be careful," I said, removing her harness. "Tell me when you reach the aerie."

Will. She accepted another scratch, then, as Mom and I stepped back, rose on her haunches and bellowed long and loud. It was, in many ways, a declaration of acceptance.

This place was now her home, and she had no intention of losing it to man or winged monster.

As the sound echoed through the farthest reaches of the fortress, she launched into the air, her scales gleaming molten in the many lights lining the walls. The two younger drakkons followed suit, and a murmur of awe ran around the courtyard as the three of them disappeared into the darkness.

Footsteps approached. My father and Damon. Mom stepped in front of me and held out a hand, finger raised. "There will be no reporting this evening, Rion. Bryn is dead on her feet, and she needs—"

"Marin, I love you and all, but your habit of jumping in before I can even speak can be rather annoying."

Mom raised an eyebrow, amusement teasing her lips. "And is that not the true purpose of a wife?"

He rolled his eyes, stepped past me, and enveloped me in a fierce hug. "That was one hell of an entrance, Bryn. Where did you pick up—"

"Rion," Mom cut in. "Honestly, you cannot be trusted. Come, let us depart and leave the two newlyweds to their hellos."

My father made a grumbly sound that rather amusingly reminded me of Kaia's responses, then hooked Mom's arm through his and guided her away.

Leaving me staring at Damon.

"Nice to see you alive and well, wife," he said, amusement teasing the lips I ached to kiss.

"Good to be alive and well, husband," I replied evenly. "Thank you for that timely save up on the wall."

"I could hardly let them destroy you when I've barely even begun to play with you."

"I'm not sure I've the energy to play right now."

"Then I shall do all the work."

My pulse leapt at the thought. "There is another problem."

He raised that eyebrow, the movement languid and decidedly sexy. "And what might that be?"

"I desperately need a bath. I'm a mess and I stink."

His blue eyes slowly and very thoroughly scanned my length. It felt like he was caressing every single inch of me, and my skin burned in response.

"I'm afraid I would have to agree with that statement." He paused, and amusement crinkled the corners of his bright eyes. "I am, however, ridiculously turned on by both."

I laughed and threw myself into his waiting arms. He held me close and kissed me long and hard, with all the fervor and passion a woman could want.

Then, with a warm chuckle, he swept me up into his arms and carried me up the steps into the palace and then our bedroom, where I was bathed, fed, and then loved. And he did indeed do all the work.

It was the perfect way to end a day in which death had come far too close, far too often.

And yet, as sleep finally folded around the both of us, I couldn't help but think such happiness couldn't and wouldn't last.

Vahree was never one to let his prizes go so easily, and he would come hunting us all again far too soon.

ALSO BY KERI ARTHUR

Drakkon Kin Trilogy
Of Steel & Scale (Nov 2024)
Of Scale & Blood (May, 2025)
Of Blood & Fire (Sept, 2025)

Relic Hunters Series
Crown of Shadows (Feb 2022)
Sword of Darkness (Oct 2022)
Ring of Ruin (June 2023)
Shield of Fire (March 2024)
Horn of Winter (Jan 2025)

Lizzie Grace Series
Blood Kissed (May 2017)
Hell's Bell (Feb 2018)
Hunter Hunted (Aug 2018)
Demon's Dance (Feb 2019)
Wicked Wings (Oct 2019)
Deadly Vows (Jun 2020)
Magic Misled (Feb 2021)
Broken Bonds (Oct 2021)
Sorrows Song (June 2022)
Wraith's Revenge (Feb 2023)
Killer's Kiss (Oct 2023)
Shadow's End (July 2024)

The Witch King's Crown Trilogy
Blackbird Rising (Feb 2020)

Blackbird Broken (Oct 2020)

Blackbird Crowned (June 2021)

Kingdoms of Earth & Air
Unlit (May 2018)

Cursed (Nov 2018)

Burn (June 2019)

The Outcast series
City of Light (Jan 2016)

Winter Halo (Nov 2016)

The Black Tide (Dec 2017)

Souls of Fire series
Fireborn (July 2014)

Wicked Embers (July 2015)

Flameout (July 2016)

Ashes Reborn (Sept 2017)

Dark Angels series
Darkness Unbound (Sept 27th 2011)

Darkness Rising (Oct 26th 2011)

Darkness Devours (July 5th 2012)

Darkness Hunts (Nov 6th 2012)

Darkness Unmasked (June 4 2013)

Darkness Splintered (Nov 2013)

Darkness Falls (Dec 2014)

Riley Jenson Guardian Series
Full Moon Rising (Dec 2006)
Kissing Sin (Jan 2007)
Tempting Evil (Feb 2007)
Dangerous Games (March 2007)
Embraced by Darkness (July 2007)
The Darkest Kiss (April 2008)
Deadly Desire (March 2009)
Bound to Shadows (Oct 2009)
Moon Sworn (May 2010)

Myth and Magic series
Destiny Kills (Oct 2008)
Mercy Burns (March 2011)

Nikki & Micheal series
Dancing with the Devil (March 2001 / Aug 2013)
Hearts in Darkness Dec (2001/ Sept 2013)
Chasing the Shadows Nov (2002/Oct 2013)
Kiss the Night Goodbye (March 2004/Nov 2013)

Damask Circle series
Circle of Fire (Aug 2010 / Feb 2014)
Circle of Death (July 2002/March 2014)
Circle of Desire (July 2003/April 2014)

Ripple Creek series
Beneath a Rising Moon (June 2003/July 2012)

Beneath a Darkening Moon (Dec 2004/Oct 2012)

Spook Squad series

Memory Zero (June 2004/26 Aug 2014)

Generation 18 (Sept 2004/30 Sept 2014)

Penumbra (Nov 2005/29 Oct 2014)

Stand Alone Novels

Who Needs Enemies (E-book only, Sept 1 2013)

Novella

Lifemate Connections (March 2007)

Anthology Short Stories

The Mammoth Book of Vampire Romance (2008)

Wolfbane and Mistletoe--2008

Hotter than Hell--2008

ABOUT THE AUTHOR

Keri Arthur, the author of the New York Times bestselling **_Riley Jenson Guardian series_**, has written sixty novels–37 of them with traditional publishers Random House/Penguin/Piatkus—and is now fully self-published. She's won seven Australian Romance Readers Awards for Favourite Sci-Fi, Fantasy, or Futuristic Romance & the Romance Writers of Australia RBY Award for Speculative Fiction. Her Lizzie Grace series won ARRA's Fav Continuing Romance Series in 2022 and she has in the past won The Romantic Times Career Achievement Award for Urban Fantasy. When she's not at her computer writing the next book, she can be found somewhere in the Australian countryside taking photos.

for more information:
www.keriarthur.com
keriarthurauthor@gmail.com
Buy eBooks & Audiobooks directly from Keri & save:
www.payhip.com/KeriArthur

facebook.com/AuthorKeriArthur
x.com/kezarthur
instagram.com/kezarthur

Milton Keynes UK
Ingram Content Group UK Ltd.
UKHW030635191124
451300UK00005B/64